Havana Sunrise

A Chase Gordon Tropical Thriller

Douglas Pratt

MANTA PRESS

Havana Sunrise is a work of fiction. Any names, places, characters, and incidents are products of the author's imagination or are used fictitiously. Any resemblance to actual persons, either living or dead, events, or locales is entirely coincidental.

Copyright © 2023 by Douglas Pratt

Cover art by

Ryan Schwarz

The Cover Designer

www.thecoverdesigner.com

All rights reserved.

No portion of this book may be reproduced in any form without written permission from the publisher or author, except as permitted by U.S. copyright law.

For Ashlee
WIthout you none of these adventures could happen

1

Cotton filled my mouth. Not cotton so much as the gunk that occurred after wet toilet paper dried up in a clump and then flaked off. My chapped lips cracked, as if I was breathing through them for days. I ran my tongue over them, trying to moisten them, to no avail. I did not know how long I'd been asleep, or really when I went to sleep. It took little observation to see I woke up in a hotel room. I didn't even need to open my eyes. My body lay nestled on a soft pillow top mattress—something I didn't have on Carina. I'd only been in Gabriella's apartment once, but this was not her bed, either.

An attempt to raise my eyelids failed. The vice pressing between my temples caused me to squeeze them shut for fear that any light might burn through my retinas. My head burrowed under the down comforter, and my hand stretched across the mattress, searching for Gabriella. She wasn't there; I was alone.

With my head under the covers, I attempted to open my eyes. Even shielded by a blanket, sunlight bathed the room in light and, despite squeezing my eyelids shut, seemed to bleed through the skin.

Everything ached as if I had been sleeping for a week. Either that or I dove into two or three bottles of tequila. Normally, that didn't seem like me, but I've gone overboard with alcohol plenty of times in my life. Only a few times ended up with me being blackout drunk. In my defense, most of those happened in my early days in the Marines. Mostly, I've grown out of that.

My fingers reached up and rubbed the bridge of my nose, massaging the area between my eyes. I shoved the comforter off of me, realized I was naked, and scratched at my left elbow.

Everything was quiet at first. Slowly, noises seemed to filter into existence. A ticking from an air conditioner sounded like a time bomb, but there was no other movement. I boosted myself up on the bed, forcing myself to look around. From outside the window, I heard traffic—city noises.

The suite was opulent. More elegant than anything I'd stayed in, even compared to the Tilly Inn with its four-star rooms. The word "palatial" rattled about in my head. I guessed I was in the presidential suite of whatever hotel I had crashed. There was a large wet bar on one side of the room. It was stocked with rums, vodkas, bourbons, and tequila. The long settee stretched across the opposite end of the room, with a lounging area for up to six people. The furniture all appeared to be antiques, or at the very least faux antique. Overall, I described the place as white. The floors were silvery marble, and the walls painted white with tile mixed in certain areas such as behind the bar. The drapes were opaque, so the sun could peek through without neighbors in the next building doing the same. An ornate crystal chandelier hung over the couch and the light played off of the glass like a shallow pool sparkling.

"Gabriella," I called.

No one answered.

The pain in my head was receding, slowly, at a pace I wasn't handling very well. But it was getting better. Unless I was becoming used to it, which was always a possibility.

I swung my feet around and let them rest on the marble floor. I was staring at the double window leading to a small balcony. From where I sat, I saw another building just opposite the window.

Why would we come to a fancy hotel? This was an accommodation neither Gabriella nor I could afford regularly. Furthermore, this was a suite I didn't think either of us would need. Gabriella wasn't simple, but she certainly wasn't the type of person to waste money on this sort of luxury. As for me, the room rate on this hotel would fill my boat stores with beer and rum for at least two weeks on board my forty-foot sailboat.

My brain tried to replay last night looking for clues where or how I got here. I didn't remember drinking that much, but we'd both had a few rum runners and a couple of shots of tequila. Certainly not enough to run off and spend five hundred dollars on a room for a night of passion.

My feet pressed against the floor as I tested my legs, which weren't as wobbly as I thought they might be. I moved them to walk towards the window. As I pulled the curtain back, I realized what I was seeing wasn't another building but part of the same one. The window looked down on the courtyard, and the entire hotel seemed to create a sort of trapezoidal shape. It was hard to really determine from the angle I was looking, but it was definitely a unique design.

Below me, I spotted tables and chairs arranged along a concrete path with small palm trees mixed with a sort of tropical garden, filled with bright flowers and budding green plants I couldn't identify from ground level, much less from up here

Like most things, time seemed to heal, and the pain in my head leveled out. In fact, I was pretty sure that a little coffee and a lot of water would probably go a long way to cure me.

I didn't see a coffee maker in the room. Perhaps it was under the wet bar. My bare feet padded over to the long marble bar, which provided the only actual color in the place with its brown mahogany finish. I bent over and rifled through the cabinets.

No coffee.

No coffee maker either.

It made sense—this was the kind of hotel that offered room service.

Help yourself to your own martinis, but if you wanted to brew your own coffee, no luck.

Instead, I found a crystal tumbler and filled it with tap water. After three glasses, I set the glass back on the marble countertop. An earthy flavor lined my mouth, and I guessed the water wasn't the cleanest in Ponce.

Where the hell was Gabriella?

Maybe she realized we didn't have any coffee and ventured downstairs to find a cafe. If I was lucky, she'd be showing up in the next few minutes with a cup of black liquid caffeine and hopefully a *pan de Mallorca*, the sweet pastry that makes most doughnuts on the mainland loathe their inadequacy.

My eyes scanned the room looking for my clothes because when Gabriella did return, I was sure we would have to consider checking out of this hotel before they charged us for an extra night. At that point, my body suggested it was sometime in the afternoon. My internal clock seemed to readjust, and while I couldn't pinpoint the exact time, I was certain I'd missed lunch.

I never slept this late. Even in my worst blackout drunk days, I was usually up by ten at the latest. Twenty years in the Marine Corps will train an individual to get up before first light, and over the last few years since I left the service, I find I still wake up much earlier than I would like. Even when I'm at anchor on my boat, the body fell into a start cycle time. There was not a lot to do when it wasn't daylight. Once the sun sets, I make a few cocktails while watching that giant orange ball slip into the sea. It didn't take me long to climb up into my berth and drift asleep.

There wasn't a stitch of clothes in this room. Nothing thrown about in a passionate array. Not even a pair of boxer shorts wadded up in the sheets.

Odd.

If it was afternoon, we'd already missed out on most of our day. Gabriella planned to show me the *Museo Castillo Serrallés*. She'd been excited to lead me through the galleries before we took a stroll through the *Jardin Japonés*. Gabriella promised me dinner at a bistro called *El Rastro,* which was run by a couple of ladies she knew.

At this point, we might make it to the restaurant, since the museum likely closed between four and five.

I'd only been in Puerto Rico for two weeks, but I just sailed around the island to the south coast to visit Ponce. San Juan had been too busy, and I'd heard the beaches along the bottom side of the territory were perfect.

So far, I hadn't made it to a beach yet. I met Gabriella the first day I'd sailed into the marina. She was a dive master for one of the charters. When I glimpsed her carrying her scuba gear over her right shoulder with her wet suit stretched down to her waist, I froze in my tracks. Her fiery green eyes cemented the sudden crush I was feeling for her.

Initially, I planned to provision *Carina*, staying only one night at the marina. Normally, I'd rather drop anchor in an isolated cove where I can snorkel and dive without the hassle of crowds and tourists. Suddenly, my plan changed. If this woman was going to be around the dock, I wanted to be close by.

It sounds much stalkier than it should. Before she set her gear down that first day, I slipped over and introduced myself. By dark, we found ourselves in a small cafe where we gabbed until the owner suggested we leave for the night.

The next day, Gabriella drove us to *La Parguera*, about an hour from Ponce, where we spent the morning diving along The Wall. After our dive, we killed the afternoon walking around the fishing village until dark, when she took me out with a few of her diving buddies to see the glowing algae lighting up the bay. The night dive offered an interesting perspective on the bioluminescent surface.

Nowhere in our plans was a night in a five-star hotel room. Now that I was coming around to my senses, I grew worried.

Where was Gabriella?

Better question—where were my clothes?

I turned away from the window. Despite the three glasses of water, my throat remained parched.

Dumbass. The bathroom.

Sometimes it takes a minute for all the gears to get working, and today definitely shaped up to be that kind of day.

When I rounded the bed, I paused. The white marbled floor shined like a mirror, reflecting my own image back at me. In the middle of the reflection of my bare chest, a red glob of blood spread over the smooth tile.

My eyes followed the line from the single drop of blood to the bathroom. The path remained clear, but the hair on the back of my neck straightened.

Dread stuck in my gut like a lead ball. The human body reacts differently to various stimuli, and I was not a stranger to such situations. Usually, terrible events happen in a flash, and the rush of adrenaline pushes me to address the situation. At least that's been my experience.

Right now, I felt sick though. No one was charging me. No battle waged around me. Instead, I was standing in a fine room wearing not a stitch of clothes, and I was panicked. More afraid than I recalled feeling in a long time.

Every second that I stared at that drop of blood dragged that fear out.

I took a step toward the bathroom. The door hung open about six inches. My palm pressed against it, and the hinges creaked as it swung wide.

Bile raced up my throat, and I swallowed hard.

A claw and ball foot tub sat against the wall. Around the basin, a white shower curtain trailed along the round rail, obscuring most of the porcelain basin. However, the leg extending over the lip jutted out past the shroud.

The coppery odor of blood filled my nose, and I leaned against the door frame, catching my breath.

2

"Gabriella," I gasped, pushing off the door.

My hand swiped the shower curtain back. The ringing of the small metal balls rolling along the rod echoed against the white tile.

I stared at the naked form in the tub. A woman. At least, what remained of her. The face marked by a blade that unzipped the skin along her cheekbones. Similar cuts covered the rest of her. Dried blood covered the brown skin. The glassy brown eyes showed no light, but the image of fear still imprinted on the pupils. She'd seen it happening.

I leaned over and glanced at the bottom of the tub. Almost no blood. Whoever sliced her up did not do it here. She was moved.

My knees bent as I stared at her face. My fingers stretched out instinctively, closing her eyes. Cold. More than that though. The skin didn't have any moisture in it. Only that rubbery texture of death remained. She'd not only been killed somewhere else; it didn't happen recently.

Thank God it wasn't Gabriella. My shoulders slumped in relief, and I never realized how tense they'd become. The comfort passed quickly as I saddened at the poor girl's loss.

But who was she? I didn't recognize her face. Even with what little remained, I should have put it to a name or at least a memory. Neither popped up.

I straightened up. The dread and fear that struck me a few seconds earlier returned. Like most things in my life, the emotions didn't live long as others clambered for the surface.

The human capacity to react to danger was usually limited to fight or flight. In this instance, the danger wasn't evident. Yes, someone murdered this girl. But they weren't in the room at the moment. However, they'd be back. Somehow.

Since I couldn't fight, the only logical solution was flight.

Only how far could I go in the nude?

Not very. Which I guessed was the intention. Why though?

It was an obvious frame. I'd seen enough old movies to know a good frame. That meant it would only be a few minutes before whoever started this ball rolling would attempt to bring it to a conclusion.

What would that mean?

Cops. Of course. They'd swoop in and find the only other person in the room with a brutally murdered girl.

Not just murdered. They'd tortured her. Most of these cuts seemed to be made before she died.

I backed out of the bathroom. What had I touched?

The glass at the bar, for sure. What else? The door to the bathroom had been ajar, but I pressed my palm against it. I didn't touch the doorknob.

What would it matter? I wasn't running out right now with no clothes. That wouldn't be obvious at all, would it? Whoever dumped me here must have figured it was a good way to keep me here.

Whoever dumped me here.

How did they get me here? Obviously, someone drugged me.

My fingers traced the itch on the inside of my elbow. The bruising from a needle bubbled up on the skin. Drugged for sure.

I needed a plan. The only way out of this mess was to get out of this hotel room immediately. Even that might not be a surefire method, but it could only be a better idea than waiting for the ax to fall.

First, I need to at least cover myself. My hands tossed the down comforter off the bed before grabbing the top sheet. With a jerk, I yanked the linen off the mattress. It would have to work for the moment.

The sheet draped around me twice like a toga, and I tucked the end into itself. At least, I wasn't naked, exactly.

The glass.

It sat where I left it on the bar. The hotel provided beverage napkins at the bar, because, after all, this must be a classy joint. They didn't want there to be any water rings left on the furniture like some cut rate Marriott.

I wiped the glass down, setting it back in its original position. After that, I wiped down the faucet and bar. For a second, I considered flushing the napkin, but it seemed wiser to stay away from the corpse.

My eyes shifted down to the wadded paper in my hand. I unfolded it to read the words "Hotel Gran Caribe" on the napkin. Underneath the name was the name of the city—Havana.

Cuba!

I let out a string of curse words. What the hell was I doing in Cuba?

It was bad enough when I thought I was about to be arrested for murder in Puerto Rico. That was at least American soil, where the Constitution endowed me with certain rights that ensured I had a chance at least to a fair trial.

Cuba, on the other hand, didn't offer such luxuries. Not that I had any expertise in the Cuban judicial system. What I knew came mostly from cruiser networks discussing the country.

The country, as a whole, had minimum crime. The reason: the citizens had long become aware of what might happen if the *policía* caught up to them. If the punishment for stealing a pack of cigarettes was the same for murder, it made any crime seem less appealing.

Americans abroad have no more rights than the fearful denizens of the country. It's one thing most U.S. citizens don't understand. Once outside of the country's borders, they are subject to the laws of the land. Many countries follow our suit, priding themselves on a fair judicial system. Those tend to be democracies with similar freedoms to our own.

Cuba isn't one of those. It's a great place to visit, filled with wonderful people. But it's also a great place to disappear. It's a country filled with people who mind their own business.

I knew next to nothing about Cuban prisons or their criminal justice system. I understood from other travelers who spent their time here that they were proponents of capital punishment—a firing squad, I assumed.

Of course, hanging might still be the cheaper option.

Don't stick around to find out, I reminded myself.

I stopped again. What about Gabriella? That wasn't her in the tub, but she was with me last. Where was she? Did they take her as well?

My head swept over the room again, as if she might have been hiding behind the sofa. The room was empty, save me.

A voice popped into my head. Sergeant Reuben who shouted at me when I paused to help another Marine over a wall at Parris Island. The young recruit was out of his depth, and after a ten-mile run, he didn't have the strength to climb the barrier. I had draped myself over the top, extending a hand to the kid when that voice broke through the training.

"Get your ass moving, Gordon! Ain't nobody going to stop to pull you up. Ain't your job to pull him up."

Ironically, that wasn't the actual lesson that day. But still, his words prodded me to move. Right now I needed to pull myself up.

My hand gripped around the napkin as I headed for the door.
I cracked the door, peeking around to see if the hall was empty.

A maid came out of a room three doors down, and I pulled
back inside the door. I wondered if she had a robe on her cart,
and I stole another glance. No robes hung obviously off the
cart. The maids at the Tilly Inn, where I work in West Palm
Beach, deliver them folded like towels, so a terry-cloth robe
might resemble a folded towel.

She went into the room across the hall, leaving the door open.
I counted off ten seconds. After that, she should be involved
in whatever tasks she needed to perform, and a toga-clad guest
might not be as noticeable.

I stepped out into the hallway, staring up and down the
empty corridor. The door I held ajar had the numbers 435 in
gold lettering attached just above the peephole. Thick carpet
with colorful palm leaf designs curling along the corridor. The
elevator let out a shrill ding, and I froze for a second.

A man jabbered in Spanish, and the jangle of keys carried
down the hallway. Footsteps shuffled along the carpeted floors
as the Spanish voice grew louder.

With a step back, I retreated into the room and let the door
close gently. My ear leaned against the wooden door, listening
for the guests to pass to their rooms.

The Spanish continued and seemed to pause in front of my
door. I cursed my middle school Spanish teacher for not properly preparing me for these situations. Unfortunately, I only
recalled a handful of words. Most of them wouldn't form a
coherent sentence.

The conversation continued for another second. Then, it
ended. The way it stopped seemed more like a trailing off rather
than the end of an idea. Like the speaker was aware he was
talking too much.

Bang! Bang! Bang!

The beating on the door startled me, and I jerked away, staring at the backside of the door.

"*¡Policía! ¡Abre la puerta!*" came the call from the other side.

"Oh, shit," I mumbled under my breath. I understood "*policía.*"

3

There was this little voice in my head. It sounded a hell of a lot like my mother, too. But it liked to scold me. Which made sense if you knew my mother.

Really, to say it was scolding was being generous. The voice mocked me. Usually, it started up right after I did something stupid, which was far more often than I liked to admit. Often, like now, it simply reminded me I should have done something different.

You could have gone the other way, it remarked. *Away from the elevator.*

I easily argued with the voice. Without being familiar with the layout of the halls, I didn't know what lay in that direction. Unlike the States, it wasn't a safe assumption in other countries that there were fire exits, especially in buildings as old as this one. I might have found myself in a cul-de-sac watching as the *Policía Nacional Revolucionaria* stared at me like a fish in a barrel.

You don't know, though, the voice pointed out.

At least here I bought some time. It was safe to assume the police would not break down the door. On the other hand, the nervous Spanish speaker had likely been a hotel employee with a master key. How long before they opened the door? I considered what would have happened at the Tilly Inn where I worked in West Palm Beach. If there was no answer, they'd go right inside.

"*Un momento,*" I called out, racking my brain for any of that ninth grade Spanish that sounded like an excuse. "*Estoy en el baño, por favor.*"

The banging stopped. I let out a sigh of relief. At least they weren't charging in yet.

Good job. You bought a minute, the voice quipped. Enough time for a drink. What else can you do? You're on the fourth floor.

The voice was right. I didn't have much time. At best, I had two minutes. What do I do?

Like a crazed prisoner, I stalked quickly around the room, searching for some magical portal or secret passage that might lead me out of this snare. There was nothing. I could shove the couch in front of the door, but I'd spend more time moving it than it would slow them down.

The window. It was the only way out.

It's the fourth floor, though.

I ignored the mocking tone in my head, which was difficult. It made a point. Was that any more of a sane idea than hoping for a secret passage? What better plan was there?

I rushed over, opening the two frames. The floor-to-ceiling windows opened out with a creak. Maintenance needed to oil the hinges. Stepping onto the small wrought-iron balcony, I stared below. The lack of an actual floor instead of the barred bottom indicated the balcony was only for show and not designed to stand on.

I scanned the courtyard below me. Four floors up, I confirmed to myself. Why would someone make it easy on me?

The building had a ledge around each side level with the window. I could crawl out there like some ridiculous silent movie star, but it would take the police a matter of seconds to open the window and see me. How far could I go anyway? No matter what direction I took, I was still four flights above the ground.

No, I needed to get to the ground.

Jumping seemed like an epically bad idea. There was no place to land where I wasn't going to at the minimum break a leg. More than likely I'd do more damage than that. A fall like that amounted to a death sentence.

A rope would be nice.

Then I had an idea.

And the voice in my head mocked. That's a stupid idea.

With a quick snap, I popped the fitted bottom sheet off the bed—the one I hadn't wrapped around me. With a jerk, I popped the sheet off the mattress and ran it through my hands.

One sheet would not be long enough to get me to the ground. I stripped the toga off me and took both ends of each sheet and tied them together with a fisherman's knot. It was one of a few knots I'd used on the boat to fasten a couple of lines together. It should hold, as long as the sheet held.

Bang! Bang! Bang!

More Spanish that I didn't understand. Something along the line of "open up." The extra time I bought was gone.

"I'm getting dressed!" I shouted in English, giving up any pretense. The voices outside shouted something. My brain only registered the word, "*rapido.*" That one I understood. They wanted inside now, and I better answer now.

"Just a second!" I screamed at the door. "This is no way to treat a guest."

The response rattled back was Spanish. No time to make any sense of it.

The end of one sheet fed through the railing, and I climbed over the wrought iron, closing the window. My left hand held the metal as I pulled the sheet until both ends at least appeared to be even.

Then I dropped.

My fear had been that the sheets were cheap. The sudden weight against them might tear them somewhere along the middle. In which case, it was going to be a long fall to the ground.

But this was a nice hotel, and these sheets had a thread count higher than the average national income, which didn't offer me a lot of hope in Cuba.

The sheet caught me, and I swung to the next balcony. I released one side of the sheet and pulled it through the upper railing until the other end fell into my hand. I repeated the endeavor, feeding one end between two metal rails, evening up the ends, and dropping again.

If someone glanced out their window now, I'd be the most talked about event of their vacation.

This time when the sheet caught, I heard the tear. A ripping sound that sent fear through my body.

The sheet held up, and my feet touched the next balcony as the fourth-floor window above opened up. I pulled the sheet free, and pressed myself against the second-floor window, praying they didn't see me.

"¿Adónde fue?" a voice above me said.

From where I cowered against the window, I barely saw the police officer from where I was hiding. If he looked down, he probably wouldn't see me, but my attention turned to the window across from me. My reflection stared back, and I hoped he didn't look in that direction. He strained his neck to the left and right.

My breath held as he glanced around, waiting for him to catch the reflection of me across the courtyard. Suddenly, his head disappeared as someone shouted something. Probably someone found the dead body in the tub.

Move it, Gordon.

I laced the sheet through the railing again, dropping before I'd evened up the ends. The rip echoed when my weight hit the end. As the other end tore, I fell the last few feet to the concrete. I tumbled across the rough concrete pad, knocking over a wrought-iron chair and scraping my legs up.

My palms pushed me up off the ground. As I dragged the remaining sheet with me, I crouched behind the planter with those green budding plants I still didn't recognize.

From my hiding spot, I watched as another police officer stuck his head out the window, searching for me. His reflection was clear in the windows across from me, and his head was straining up. He thought I went to the roof. That made sense. Only a moron would jump out of the window.

He shouted something back inside before he vanished.

Go to the roof, I silently urged.

The sheet wrapped around me again. At least now I wasn't naked. I'd stand out but it might be more an oddity than a scream and cover the children's eyes kind of scene.

The only exit from the courtyard seemed to be a large iron door on the other side of the garden. I straightened up and walked as nonchalantly as a man in a toga can. My bare feet tensed as I crossed the scorching hot concrete that had been baking under the tropical sun.

Inside the building, I stared up at the ornate hallways. The hotel had the ambiance of something from the 1920s or earlier. Ornate gingerbread molding skirted along the dark, wooden paneled ceiling. Gothic architecture loomed over me with columns and arches, and in my toga, I might fit into this Romanesque setting. However, prudence suggested I haul ass, so I did.

Without breaking into a run, I located the nearest exit. Two doors swung in, and someone had propped them open to create a wind tunnel through this hallway. Despite the exquisite architecture, this was still Cuba, and air-conditioning was expensive. These builders erected this hotel before indoor climate control was popular, and with strategic doors ajar the breeze made it quite tolerable.

Old school technology, I mused as I walked out the door and onto the streets.

4

Pedestrian traffic milled along *Calle Progresso* as many workers closed up their shops or got off work. On the southern side of the street, a 2014 white Daewoo Tacuma, a hatchback imported after the Cuban government lifted the ban on foreign vehicles, sat against the curb.

The front windows remained up despite the Caribbean sun's constant baking.

"Why can't we turn on the air-conditioning?" the man in the passenger seat moaned in Spanish.

"It's a waste of petrol," the driver acknowledged.

"What do we care, Tomas?" the passenger asked. "The lady paid plenty up front."

"Do you see anyone else running their car on the street?" Tomas questioned.

The passenger took a few seconds to scan up and down both sides of the street. There were plenty of vehicles. Most appeared to be manufactured prior to 1960, when air-conditioning in cars consisted of manual windows supplemented by the triangular window vent that rotated to direct the hot Cuban air through the interior.

Tomas continued, "There aren't any. This little car is already noticeable enough on the street. We certainly don't want to show off more by running the engine unnecessarily."

The passenger sighed loudly. "Can I crack a window, at least?" he begged.

"Fine," Tomas relented.

The man pressed the automatic button, and nothing happened. He turned to stare at Tomas, who grinned from ear to ear.

"Dammit," the man cursed.

"Calm down, Diego," Tomas soothed as he turned the key in the ignition, just enough to power the electrical system.

Diego rolled his eyes as he pressed the button. The passenger's window whirred as it lowered. When it reached the halfway point, Tomas cut the key back. The window ceased lowering.

"Come on, Tomas," Diego pleaded.

"It's low enough," he assured the younger man.

"Why couldn't we get a van or something?" Diego whined. "At least we could stretch out."

Sirens echoed down *Calle Progreso*. Diego's head swiveled around to see two Lada police cars with flashing lights speeding toward them. The two cars whipped through the traffic and slipped next to the curb in front of the Hotel Gran Caribe.

A bellman stepped out of the opened doors as four members of the National Revolutionary Police Force poured out of the two Ladas.

"The police have arrived," Diego announced, in case Tomas hadn't noticed.

His partner didn't respond. His head shook slowly, showing his annoyance at the young man.

"How long do we stay here?" Diego questioned.

"Until we know the American is under arrest," Tomas sighed.

"It looks like they got him."

Tomas turned his head to stare at his companion "We leave when the police drag the American out of the hotel in chains."

Diego's shoulders slumped, and he slid down in the seat, putting his knees against the Tacuma's dash.

His arms folded across his chest as he stared out the window.

"Uh, Tomas," he called, straightening up and pointing across the street. "Is that him?"

Tomas's eyes tracked along the invisible line from Diego's finger to a man vanishing down a side street.

"What is he wearing?" Tomas asked.

"Looked like a sheet."

Tomas snorted. "He's insane."

Diego didn't respond.

"The staff would have seen him," Tomas continued.

"Maybe he took the stairs," Diego suggested.

"This is no good," Tomas uttered. "What are we supposed to do?"

"Better call the boss," Diego offered.

"Follow him," Tomas ordered. "Don't let him see you. I'll call her."

Diego nodded, opening the passenger door. He didn't care what he had to do as long as he got out of the stuffy Daewoo. After a couple of hours, it reeked of musk, something the young man didn't care for. Even if it came from himself.

He paused as a wave of cars zipped past him before he stepped out onto the street. His feet hurried across while his left hand raised up as if it would shield him from any oncoming traffic.

Havana's streets smelled a little better than the inside of the car. There was a constant souring stink that permeated between the buildings. The daily rain washed all the trash scattered through the city into piles in the gutters, which baked in the Caribbean sun. Diego wondered if the odor would subside in the dry season—it didn't matter since Cuba never had a dry season.

Once he reached the other side, he wondered about the American. How did he get out of the hotel? Tomas and Diego helped move him into the room. Diego himself had to strip the man naked. In fact, the American's clothes were in the back of the Daewoo.

Apparently, that didn't stop the man. He must have stolen the sheet from the bed. That seemed to make sense—Diego figured he would have done the same thing if he found himself stranded naked somewhere. Honestly, he wondered why they bothered taking the man's clothing. Perhaps they thought he wouldn't leave the room without clothing. Framing him for murder was one thing, but if the police found him with no belongings, it would seem weird. Besides, Diego thought, if he found himself in a room with a murdered woman, he'd run like hell. Naked or not.

It seemed almost as if the woman wanted to make a big joke. Otherwise, it made no sense. If she just wanted to throw the American off, that would do it.

Apparently, she underestimated the *gringo*. He made it out of the hotel, and Diego wondered how the plan would change. Not that anyone made him privy to the original plan. Leave the American in the room with the dead woman. After that, he and Tomas were to wait until they knew he was in the PNR's custody.

The back of his hand wiped sweat from his forehead. He shook his hand, flinging droplets of perspiration away from him. The endeavor was futile—as soon as the drops hit the sidewalk, more appeared on his skin.

Diego approached the intersection. His head swiveled to verify Tomas was still watching him. The man had his mobile to his ear, but his eyes stared at Diego. He offered a nod from across the street, and Diego stepped around the corner onto the next street.

5

The soles of my feet burned as I crossed the searing concrete. Generally, my feet are tough. I spend most of my time barefooted, or at least in some sort of sandals. No one wants to wear tennis shoes to the beach, and I thrive there. There is a pair of Nike cross-trainers on board Carina for running, some of the only PT I maintain from the Corps. Although, I relegate it to weeks when I'm docked. It's tough to run around the deck of a forty-foot sailboat at sea.

Even though my feet are used to sand and even gravel, the scorching surface of the roads nearly caused me to dance across it. I struggled to maintain my composure, fearing any manic behavior might draw more attention to me. And right now, nearly every eye on the street turned to stare at the *gringo* in the toga.

I've found that if I wanted to get into a place I didn't belong, the best method involved holding my head up and acting like I belonged. The same theory should hold true to my current situation. If I didn't act like I was doing anything out of the ordinary, the public might pass me off as a harmless crank or some silly practical joke. Hopefully, no one would call the police to report me.

As I came off the side street I'd just made my way down, I came out onto a larger road. Down the middle of the street was a tree-lined walkway separated from the lanes of traffic on either side by a small two-foot stone wall. Most of the pedestrians adhered to some sort of organized traffic rule, similar to the States. Groups waited in clusters to cross the street when the light changed, and I slipped into the crowd as the oncoming vehicles stopped.

The center walkway had diamond and square patterns on the ground that seemed to mean nothing except offering a certain aesthetic. Heads turned to stare at me as I started down the middle of the road.

The buildings towering over the street seemed European, with arches, columns, and balustrades adorning the structures on all sides. Small balconies similar to the ones I'd just rappelled from jutted out from several buildings. From the appearance, most of these were personal homes with plants, chairs, and some clothes draped over the railing to dry.

I'm a travel fiend, which is why I live on a boat. Every new destination sucks me in with the culture and sights. I'd only visited a few small fishing villages on the northeastern side of the island, so Havana was an unfamiliar experience. While it was more metropolitan than I expected, I, unfortunately, didn't have the luxury to absorb any of it.

What I needed to do was to get off this street. It would take one roving police officer to wonder why a man was strolling along the avenue in a sheet. I had no intention of going to a Cuban prison, but I needed a plan. So far, I'd been working solely on instinct—reacting to my current predicament in real time. While I work well in a reactive state, it's not sustainable.

My mind worked to lay out a strategy of some sort.

Get off the street. Find clothes. Get out of Cuba.

It wasn't much of a plan, so much as a guideline.

I jumped over the opposite wall separating the median plaza from traffic. I dodged between an old El Camino and a fifties-era Cadillac with a rusted fender. A smaller road cut next to a red-trimmed stone building with several segmented arched windows. A sigh of relief escaped my mouth when I saw there were far fewer pedestrians on this street. I walked close to the building, trying somehow to blend into the wall.

With no passport, getting off the island proved tricky. No airports. That left the only option—leave by boat. It worked for hundreds of Cuban migrants every year. It was only ninety miles to Key West. That's a full-day sail on *Carina*, but she wasn't here. If I could find a marina though, I might find a sympathetic American cruiser. The idea seemed ludicrous. I'd be asking an innocent tourist to break the law and smuggle me out of the country. In some circumstances, I would do it, but I'd have to consider it closely. By now, I was a murder suspect, and that upped the ante a great deal.

Steal a boat. That made sense. I was already up shit creek on a potential murder charge. How much more time could the Cuban government tack on for grand theft? I wouldn't keep the vessel—just long enough to make it to Key West. After that, I'd make arrangements for the owners to get it back. By the time they knew the boat was missing, I'd tell them where to get it back. I'd even pay for the airfare if they wanted.

All of that was three steps down a very tall stairwell. First, I needed to get off the street. The longer I was out in the open, the better the chances of getting caught were.

Along this road, apartments stared down, and I wondered how I could get in one. If I could find an empty loft, I'd buy myself a few minutes. Right now, I was in a buying time kind of mood.

After a block, the road crossed another side street. I glanced back warily before crossing the empty road.

The street wasn't empty, but the man trailing me stood out like a sore thumb. He was Cuban, but his attention directed toward me. As soon as I turned back, he dropped his head in an ill-fitted attempt to appear nonchalant.

He was almost an entire block behind me. From his pace, he wasn't trying to overtake me. Just watch me?

I guessed they wanted to know what I was doing. Someone spotted me leaving the hotel—not difficult since I was donning only a sheet. Now they were reactive too. I suppose that benefited me. If they were trying to catch up, I had a little edge.

Across the street, I saw a sign that read "*Iglesia Metodista Habana*." My Spanish was pitiful, but the cross helped me guess it was a Methodist church. If ever I needed sanctuary, it was now. Plus, if my friend followed me inside, he'd have difficulty maintaining discretion.

Without turning back to check on my tail, I crossed the street. The double wooden doors were unlocked. I pushed open the left door and stepped inside, letting the door close behind me.

The decor of the church was simple compared to most of the ones I'd seen stateside. Twelve rows of simple wooden pews lined the small space. Set in the middle of the far wall was a lighted stained glass display of Jesus with the woman at Jacob's Well. Two arched openings led to another section from this room. Toward the front, a small pulpit stood with a modest-sized cross on the wall. The cross hung several inches off the wall and incandescent bulbs accented it from behind.

An aisle split the rows of pews down the middle, and I paused in the center, listening for anyone else in the building. No sound came from anywhere. I moved up the aisle and ducked through the arched opening into a darkened hallway.

My back pressed against the wall in the dark. My chest filled and emptied as I waited. Two minutes passed before I heard the click of the door. Was it the tail? I couldn't risk a peek without giving away my hiding place. He might be carrying a gun, and until I knew what I was dealing with, surprise was my strongest offense.

Footsteps creaked as the man inched up the aisle. My left foot slid farther left as I increased the distance between myself and the door.

Without putting my eyes on him, I imagined how he was moving. He knew I came into the church, and now he didn't want to give away anything. I guessed he didn't know what to do if I discovered him.

The man's shadow stretched into the darkened hallway as he moved toward the opening. When he rounded the corner, I recognized the face from the street. With a quick step forward, I grabbed him by the shirt, wrenching him forward.

My assault caught him by surprise, but he recovered, throwing an elbow at my face. The blow had little force, and it glanced off my cheek. I threw him across the hallway, slamming him into the wall. My knee came up, driving into his groin. His eyes widened. My head pulled back quickly before slamming forward into this nose. A crack sounded as the man's nose broke.

"*¿Qué está haciendo?*" a voice down the hall called.

I let go of the man, who slid to the floor. The speaker walked up to me, staring at me with a confused look on his face.

The pastor, perhaps.

I lifted my hands up defensively. "English?"

He stared at me for a second before nodding slowly. "Some," he admitted.

"This man stole my clothes and is trying to hurt me," I explained as plainly as I could.

The pastor's eyes turned between me and the unconscious man on the floor. "He tried to hurt you?"

I nodded. "I got lucky."

The man reached over, pulling gently on the sheet.

I shrugged.

"Come with me," he ordered.

With very little options, I started after him. How long before the man on the floor woke up?

It would surprise me if he continued after me. Probably slink off to lick his wounds.

The pastor stopped in front of a door that he opened. Several cardboard boxes lined the little closet.

"*Ropas*," the man said, pointing to the boxes.

I leaned over and opened one of the closest boxes. It was full of clothes.

"Thank you," I told him, and the man nodded.

6

In an alley five blocks from the church, I found an empty bucket—not quite as big as the five-gallon-sized ones we have in the States. I flipped it over and settled on it like a stool with my back against the wall.

Once I'd found some clothes that fit me, I slipped out the back of the church. The man I'd fought was gone, but I suspected he hadn't gone far. The longer I stayed at the church, the more dangerous it would be for the pastor running the place. At least at this point he didn't know he was harboring a fugitive. I hoped that was adequate for the police here.

My stomach rumbled, and I wondered how long it had been since I ate any real food. How long would it take someone to drug me and transport me from Puerto Rico to Cuba? If they had a private plane, less than twelve hours. Of course, there were a lot of extenuating factors to consider. Most of those dots would need to be connected later.

Unfortunately, I didn't have any money—meaning food was off the table for the moment. If I'd had pockets at the time, I'd have gone through the man's pockets after I knocked him out. Spoils of war and such. But, missed opportunities.

I'd had a few glasses of water before escaping the hotel, but those few glasses weren't going to hold me for long in this tropical heat.

At least clothed, I drew less attention. My mind rolled the problem around, trying to probe what was happening to me.

It was a frame-up. I didn't know the girl in the tub, and from the looks of it, she hadn't been murdered there.

I should have examined her a little closer. There were lots of questions forming.

How does one bring a dead body into a hotel?

The answer seemed to be a suitcase. As much cutting as the girl endured, a blood trail would be evident.

A pathologist would know almost immediately that she wasn't killed in the hotel room. At least, one in the States. I was making the mistake so many made—equating what should happen here with what would happen back home.

Cuba might not care. Hell, they might not have a coroner. Or he could be bought.

Bought. I considered the idea. Whatever was happening wasn't cheap.

They kidnapped me in Puerto Rico, transporting me here. The easiest way was either by private boat or plane. Neither are necessarily expensive, but the equipment and drugs to keep me sedated might be. Especially if they wanted to get them outside of normal, official methods.

There had to be bribes. No way they could bring two bodies into that hotel, let alone the country, without greasing someone's palm. Sure, the girl could be a local. Then it's just a matter of bringing her into the hotel.

It was all so obviously staged. Whoever dumped me there didn't care how it looked.

Did I see a knife? A blade or anything?

I didn't remember one.

It wasn't even good high school theater. This was intentionally sloppy—which meant the circumstances didn't matter. Either they intended the police to not charge me or they had some other motive in place. Of course, it could mean the amount of evidence didn't matter since the police didn't need actual proof.

The guy I faced in the church reeked of amateurism. He wasn't the brains behind this. Just muscle.

Who did I piss off so badly?

That list might be longer than I liked, but most of them wouldn't go through something so elaborate. They'd sneak up on me and put a bullet in the back of my head. Not whatever this was.

To what end?

At the moment, it didn't matter. No amount of pondering in an alley would solve this mystery.

Push it aside, Chase.

The only thing that mattered now was getting somewhere safe—preferably on American soil.

My options were limited. There was a U.S. Embassy in Havana. At least, I thought so. It could be on the other end of the country at Guatánamo Bay. That didn't seem convenient though. Honestly, I didn't know enough about the country.

Guatánamo Bay was out of the question. I knew where it was. On the eastern side of the country—several hundred miles away. Key West was closer.

Either I make it to the embassy or swim for Key West. I was a bit hyperbolic—swimming ninety miles wasn't an option. I'd steal a boat.

Make it to the embassy. It was the safest route. If something went wrong while I was stealing a boat, I'd be in a worse situation. Well, the same situation, only arrested. I doubt the charge for stealing a boat added enough to the sentence for murder to worry about.

Time to move. I raised up on my feet. The shoes the preacher gave me were a bit too small. I squeezed my feet into them, but they were twisted tight like a geisha's. Despite that, it was far more comfortable to be wearing something than running through the alleys in my bare feet.

I walked north. With no idea where the embassy was, north felt like the best option. The idea had only a small logical method to it. My goal was to get to the U.S., and no matter where I was in Cuba, my homeland was north of it. It also meant the coast was there. If the embassy didn't play out, I could fall back on the boat plan.

As long as I stuck to the back streets, I hoped to avoid any run-ins with the police. Not to mention, whoever the man in the church had been with. He was easy, but somehow I guessed he was the scout ant. I didn't want to face a whole army.

The next alley widened when I crossed the street. A cherry red Ford Fairlane whipped down the road causing me to press against the wall to avoid being struck. The brakes screeched as it slammed to a stop. Three Cuban men in their twenties jumped out of the car. The one in the front yanked a door open and stormed inside like he was on a mission.

Crossing to the other side, I continued past the Fairlane. The door the men barged into had a small plastic sign hanging over it. The words "*Comida China*" were printed across the sign with symbols I thought belonged to some Asian language.

Through the open door, I could see the back of a kitchen. The three men circled around an Asian woman in her sixties and a young girl in her teens. The lead man shouted in Spanish—the only word I made out was *dinero*.

Keep moving, Chase.

I didn't though. Instead, I slowed just as the man yelling slapped the older woman.

The internal voice scolded me. Don't.

I didn't listen—it should probably be my motto.

When I crossed back behind the Fairlane, I pulled the door open wide and stepped into the door frame. I'm not so big that I fill the frame like some, but I certainly outweighed each of these guys. The leader, a young dark-haired kid with a white scar across his cheek—the result of a burn some time ago—twisted around to stare at me.

He spat something out in Spanish. I guessed it was along the lines of "Who are you?" or "What do you want?" He ran the words together so I couldn't distinguish them even if I understood them.

"Hey guys," I greeted them with a congenial grin. "Anyone speak English? It would make things a lot easier."

The girl's pupils widened a bit. The rest of them stared at me.

White Cheek told the other two something in Spanish, his finger waving toward me. Despite my linguistic inadequacies, I understood the gist of his order—get rid of me.

The other two men obeyed immediately, turning toward me in unison.

In combat, there are numerous theories on how to win a fight against an enemy with more numbers. One could take out the leader. Not really possible from where I was standing. The other is to take out the biggest guy. That was the second guy—the one farthest from me. In cases like this, theory didn't matter. Reduce the number of opponents by any means necessary.

These two men counted on the fact that they outnumbered me. I stepped toward the first one, snapping my right foot up in a front kick that impacted his groin and doubled him over. The second man realized his friend was down and reacted, jabbing his fist out fast.

Reaction was often a dangerous method. In a fight, almost everything one did was reaction, even if it was reacting to the visual cues. Any fight can be a strategy. It doesn't always work. Sometimes reactions come fast, driven by instinct. My gut wanted to block the punch he threw at me, but I resisted. He threw it too soon which caused him to overreach. If I'd blocked the fist, he'd have time to close the gap.

Instead, my right foot stepped behind my left, making him lean forward. Rotating on the balls of my feet, I twisted around and drove my elbow into the back of the man's head. A blow like that was hard, but not debilitating. Unless one didn't have a good footing. He didn't and stumbled forward, away from me. I stepped after him, grabbing him and driving him face-first into a stainless-steel shelf filled with pots and pans. The cookware clattered to the floor, and I grabbed a skillet by the handle.

When I turned to face the leader, he pulled a switchblade from somewhere. The snap of the blade was inaudible among the din of clanging metal.

His eyes burned with rage. It wasn't likely many people around here stood up to him, and he didn't care for that. I emasculated him. Unfortunately for him, I wasn't done.

As he swiped the blade toward my gut, I returned the favor, swatting the skillet into his face like it was a tennis ball. Only he grunted instead of me. The blade skittered across the tile floor, and the man tumbled sideways, landing on the kitchen floor. I leaned over the man, patting him down for another weapon. Instead, I found the keys to the Fairlane and a wad of pesos.

The man who took my foot to the balls straightened up. He seemed the least injured of the party. I locked eyes with him, waiting for him to run at me. He shook his head slowly, and I signaled for him to take his men and go, tossing him the keys I took from the leader.

He looked to the other hand which held the pesos. I wagged my head back and forth, pointing at him as I waved the money at him. He realized what I was demanding, and his hand went into his pocket. The skillet lifted as I watched him, waiting for an unseen weapon. He produced a small stack of bills that he threw on the floor in front of me.

The second man pushed himself up off the floor, dazed still from the avalanche of pots on top of him. He turned toward me, but I waited. He said something to the man with the swollen groin, who responded back. Then the second man lifted his hand in surrender, pulling out cash and tossing it next to the first man's money at my feet. The two men scooped up their unconscious leader. I stood motionless in the kitchen watching as they carried him to the car.

When the engine sound faded around the corner, I bent over and retrieved the money before I glanced at the two women. The older woman spouted something I didn't understand. However, I think she thought I might have made things worse.

The girl said, "Thank you." Her voice held a heavy Asian accent, but her diction remained clear. "Are you hurt?" she asked, each word sounded out distinctly.

"I'm okay," I assured her.

"They will be back," she told me.

"I'm sorry," I admitted, worried I might have made it worse.

The girl shook her head. "They will be back no matter what. They will want their money."

"Shake down?" I asked.

She stared at me questioningly. "I don't know what that means."

"They take money because you work in their neighborhood," I explained.

She nodded. "Every week."

I stepped back, my feet hurting from the cramped shoes. "Is your mother hurt?" I questioned, as I pulled the shoes off. My bare feet were red and marked with the imprint of the shoe.

The girl stared at them. "She's fine," she assured me. "Are your feet hurt?"

"The shoes were a gift," I acknowledged. "They are just too small."

She turned and looked at the older woman, saying something. Then she turned back to me. "My brother may have something you can wear," she told me. "Come with me."

The girl walked out of the back door and waited on me.

7

"I am Mai Thanh," the girl explained as she led me down the street.

"Chase," I told her.

"Chase what?" she asked.

With a chuckle, I explained, "No, my name is Chase."

"Oh," she giggled.

"Who were those guys?"

"They are part of the Brotherhood of Pain," she explained. "They say they are protecting us, but they are the ones we need protection from."

"Did I make it worse?" I asked.

"I do not think so," she said. "I'm not sure how much worse it could be."

"What do you mean?"

"The Brotherhood takes their cut, and our landlord raises our rent. We can't keep it up."

I nodded, as she opened the door leading to a stairwell.

"They think we are stupid," Mai retorted. "The Brotherhood is paying the Russian too."

"Who is the Russian?" I asked.

"Oh, sorry. Our landlord," she clarified. "He controls most of this block."

"So he's sending the gang to terrorize you and take your money?" I asked. "To what end?"

"He knows we don't have the money to pay him," she told me. "This way he gets his money. Still we owe him with...what do you call it? Interested?"

"Interest," I corrected.

"Yes, interest."

"Does the Russian control the gangs?" I asked when we reached the top of the stairs.

Mai used a key to unlock two deadbolts before she unlocked the lock on the knob. The door swung open into a small studio apartment. Small meant only slightly larger than *Carina*, which could get cramped easily.

"Is this your brother's place?" I asked, stepping over the threshold.

She nodded. "We stay here while he's gone."

There was something she held back. There was little room for three people here. I wondered if the idea of staying here "while he's gone" was an excuse they told themselves.

"How long has he been gone?" I asked.

"About six months."

"Where did he go?" I wondered.

She glanced down without answering. I didn't push it. That look said a lot about "while he's gone." Brother likely wasn't coming back from wherever he went to.

"There are some clothes over here," she told me, leading me to a box pressed between a mattress and the wall.

After digging in the box, she pulled out a pair of old boots. They were bigger than what I had on, but not by much. Still, once my feet were in them, I felt instant relief.

"Thank you, Mai," I said.

"You were very kind to help us," she told me.

"Here." I removed the wad of money, pulling a handful of pesos to keep before handing the rest to Mai. "Maybe this can help you and your mother."

"Oh, no," she declared.

"I insist."

The girl took the cash and stared at me. "What is an American doing in this part of Havana?"

"I'm a little lost," I admitted. "I'm trying to get to the American Embassy."

Mai lifted an eyebrow curiously.

"I'm in a little bit of trouble," I admitted. "I don't have my passport, and I need to get back to the States."

"I can take you there," she offered. "I've been there trying to get a student visa. I am trying to go to school up in Miami."

If the police picked me up with Mai, she'd get swept up into whatever I was dealing with. Even worse, if the people who started all this were also out there, she might be in more danger.

"No, Mai. I can go. Can you tell me how to get there?"

"Oh, sure," she gushed. "If you head north until you reach the Malecón, then follow it west. I don't know exactly where, but it's that direction. Big white building."

"Probably the one with Marines around it," I noted.

She shrugged, probably not knowing what I meant.

"You want to go to school in Miami, huh?" I asked.

"Yes, if I can get the paperwork taken care of."

"What about your mother?"

"I don't know," she admitted. "I'm hoping she can go too. I'd be worried about her here."

"Where is your father, Mai?"

She shook her head solemnly.

As if to break the tension, my stomach growled loudly, and Mai stared at me for a second before a grin spread across her face.

"Are you hungry?" she questioned.

"I suppose so," I admitted.

"Sit down," she ordered, and I obeyed, resting on the chair at a small table.

Mai moved around the small kitchen, pulling a small wok out. She threw some oil in the pan, and I watched as she moved the wok over the heat, warming up the oil. Once she was happy with it, she tossed some rice and dried vegetables in it.

"Where are you from?" I asked while she cooked.

"Vietnam," she told me.

"Oh, where in Vietnam?"

"It's a fishing village called Sông Cầu."

I didn't think I could repeat the phonetics it took to say the name, but I asked, "How old were you when you came here?"

"Four," she responded as she tossed the food around the wok with a flourish.

As she plated the fried rice, she commented, "I don't think my mother will leave until my brother comes back."

"How old is he?"

"Twenty," she answered.

"Is he still in Cuba?" I asked.

She only shrugged as she handed me the plate with a pair of chopsticks. "Would you prefer a fork?" she added.

"No, thank you," I replied, snapping the ends of the chopsticks together. "This is perfect."

The adrenaline of the day had abated the hunger pangs, but once the savory aroma hit me, I found myself famished. The chopsticks dug through the rice and vegetables, shoveling it into my mouth. I slowed down after several bites, attempting to savor the meal.

Mai watched me with satisfied eyes.

"This is delicious," I told her.

"Would you like some tea?" she offered.

"No, just some water would be good."

When she returned with a glass of warm tap water, Mai asked, "What actually happened to you?"

I glanced up at her with some curiosity.

"You don't get lost in this part of Havana," she pointed out. "The only tourists who come around here are looking for something bad."

I nodded. "I'm not, I promise."

She shook her head. "I know," she assured me. "I can tell. You risked your life against three Brothers. No one does that. In Havana, it's smarter to look away."

"I'm not always the smart one."

Mai giggled. "You're funny, but you look worried."

I didn't respond.

"Are you a policeman?" she asked. "I mean, at your home. The way you stood up to those guys was something I imagine a policeman should do."

"No, I'm not with the police," I responded with a smile. "I was a Marine once. Nowadays, I work in a bar and sail."

"Oh, I'd love to sail!" she exclaimed. "You fight like a soldier."

"The government spent a lot of time and money to teach me to do that," I said.

"I wish the people here would fight," she stated.

"Fight the government?" I questioned.

She shook her head. "No, the gangs and the Russians who bully everyone around here. The police avoid the Russians, and most of them run the gangs."

There was a tone to her voice. Obviously the gangs affected her, but there seemed to be more to it. At the moment, I couldn't do much for her.

In Afghanistan, I came across a boy in a village. The kid could speak a little English, but he hung onto Tristan like a kid brother. For a few weeks, he became a mascot for us. Every day he learned a few more phrases in English.

Then, after six weeks, we were ordered to move out. The kid begged Tristan to stay. Turned out that while our unit was in the village, we'd been scaring off a small group of men who had been raiding the village before we arrived. Rumors were spilling that they intended to come back after our unit moved out.

We had no options. The villagers were left to fend for themselves. Unfortunately, I never made it back to the town. Now I felt like I was doing the same thing. But the longer I stayed here, the more likely the chances the police would arrest Mai and her mother for helping me.

I needed to keep moving.

Mai took my plate, carrying it to the kitchen.

"If you make it to Miami," I told her, "call me."

She turned to look at me.

I continued, "Chase Gordon. Can you remember the Tilly Inn in West Palm Beach?"

The teen nodded.

"Call there and ask for me. If I'm not around you can leave a message, okay?"

"I will," she promised.

"I'm sure they'll get the visas all worked out."

She offered a nonchalant shrug as if she expected nothing from it. I wondered how often she decided disappointment was the preconceived result of her dreams. Probably more than she deserved.

We stared at each other for a few seconds.

"I need to get to the American Embassy," I said. "I've caused you enough trouble."

Mai shook her head. "No, no," she insisted. "You helped us."

I couldn't help feeling like my assistance had only delayed the inevitable. The thugs would return seeking the same protection money, only now they'd have a vendetta.

"If those guys come back, you'll need that money I gave you," I told her.

She stared at me blankly. Was it enough? They might want some retribution for their embarrassment. I kicked myself for not thinking about that before I jumped in. What had I accomplished? Gave Mai and her mother a day reprieve before the Brotherhood of Pain returned for their protection money. Only now, the mother and daughter would owe the back pay. There was going to be an interest or fee added on for the beating I gave them too.

"Mai, you need to tell them you didn't know me. When they ask, say I robbed you after they left."

She offered a small grin. "They won't care," she said wearily.

Not a surprise. These weren't compassionate protectors. No, they were leeches. It didn't matter how much they took from Mai and her mother. If they bled them dry, it would only be a matter of time before another business cropped up for them to drain. If the corruption climbed up to their Russian landlord, it was a rampant problem.

An urging to stay and help Mai tugged at me. If these punks came back, I'd send them packing. Or maybe I could drag them upstream until I found the man pulling the strings. Remove the head of the snake? Of course, in cases like this, it wasn't a snake—more like a hydra. Create a vacuum of power by eliminating the top dog, and another dog slides into take its place. I might fight this war forever.

And how long before the dead body in the hotel caught up to me?

Not long. Someone was pulling the strings, and if the guy I confronted in the church was any indication, they were watching—at least as far as the church. Now, they would be looking for me. I didn't think it would be as easy as ditching the first guy thrown at me.

I was at a disadvantage. Havana was a stranger to me. Add on the fact that I had no money, no identification, and no way to communicate. If they had enough guys, it wouldn't take long to cordon off the area around the church.

No, there was no way I could stay and help Mai. I didn't like it either, but my presence would draw even more danger to her and her mother.

The sound of cars echoed up the sides of the buildings. I stepped over to the window and peered at the street below. An old Buick rumbled by slowly.

"Is there a way out the back?" I asked.

8

"What the hell happened to you?" Tomas questioned Diego in Spanish.

"The bastard surprised me," Diego mumbled. His hand still clutched his side, but he wanted to cup his groin, which throbbed from the American's knee.

Diego had regained consciousness inside the church, and he struggled to get out before anyone discovered him. The *gringo* was nowhere to be found, and Diego wasn't ready to run into him again anyway. He'd never admit that to Tomas, but he limped back to the car.

"Where was this?" Tomas asked.

"A church," Diego muttered. His face had swollen where the man struck him. The blow split his lip, and the blood crusted over the cut with a red scab. His voice sounded like he had a mouthful of marbles when he talked.

"Damn," Tomas cursed. "We have to find him."

Tomas turned his head away from his bruised companion. His face burned with anger. How could Diego lose him? This was supposed to be a simple job, and the *mujer* who hired him didn't strike Tomas as the type to accept failure. Despite her diminutive frame, the woman offered a fierce demeanor.

She'd found Tomas through a mutual Russian acquaintance. As he considered that meeting, Tomas wondered if Kotov could offer some help to track the American. The American man had to still be on foot and presumably wrapped in a hotel sheet. How difficult would it be to find him?

Moriz Kotov had resources Tomas couldn't imagine—operating throughout Havana. The Russian handled everything from whores to protection. He worked with a few cartels throughout the States distributing cocaine to the over-indulgent Americans. Most importantly, he wasn't about to cross the Asian woman. That much was obvious when Kotov first reached out to Tomas.

"This woman has the power," Kotov assured Tomas. "She has tendrils throughout the government and if she wants to get something done, she will."

Tomas wasn't sure whether the government Kotov referred to was Cuban, Russian, or American. He considered asking, wondering what need someone like Kotov would have. Instead, he held his tongue. Tomas appreciated the woman was offering enough money to ensure he asked no questions. She only wanted him to deliver.

Right now, he wasn't delivering anything. If the *gringo* wasn't found, he'd do more than forfeit his payment. He might endanger his working relationship with Kotov.

In the past, the Russian proved reasonable enough. He'd assist Tomas if it profited him. Tomas just hoped he would understand that it would displease the Asian woman and both Tomas and Kotov might suffer if Tomas did not find the man.

Tomas dialed the number to Kotov's import office, a cover business on Calle Marti near the Havana port.

"Yes," Kotov answered in Spanish. Tomas noticed he'd rotate between Russian and Spanish when answering his phone. Kotov didn't bother to read the number on the display, and he certainly didn't store any details in his address book. Therefore, Kotov just answered and waited to hear which language to proceed with. Tomas wondered how many languages the man could speak. He'd heard him switch to French just like turning on a light bulb. Tomas's tongue was limited to only Spanish. He didn't have the patience or time to learn another.

"It's Tomas," he told Kotov in Spanish.

"Yes, my friend," the Russian continued in the other man's native language.

"I have a problem," Tomas explained. "The American we were watching for our friend has escaped."

Kotov hadn't been privy to the details of Tomas's task. He'd only arranged for the woman to meet him. She'd been specific about what kind of operative she was looking for—local, Cuban descent, and trustworthy. A European or another Russian stood out. A Cuban could stand on the corner all day watching a hotel without drawing much attention.

"I don't know about the American," Kotov explained.

Tomas gave him a quick summary.

"Your man lost him?" Kotov asked after Tomas finished.

Tomas glanced over at Diego, asking, "Where was this church?"

"Off the Plaza," Diego offered. "I believe it was Calle Virtudes. I am uncertain of the cross street."

Relaying the information to Kotov, Tomas stared out the front window and waited.

"Interesting," Kotov commented. "I had a couple of guys run into a man that might be your American. One of them isn't going anywhere for a while. The other is walking funny."

Tomas stole another look at Diego, who was still suffering from the blow to his genitals. "That might be him," Tomas agreed. "Where was this?"

"An Asian restaurant near the church where you say your man lost him. This American seems dangerous," Kotov noted.

"Not what we expected," Tomas acknowledged, realizing as he said this that those unspoken details were why the woman was paying so much for Tomas's cooperation.

"This business never is what one expects," Kotov pointed out. "I can send a few extra guys around if you'd like."

The implication was this good deed would cost Tomas. Kotov controlled men throughout the city. Through Kotov, Tomas dealt with the most notorious in Cuba: the Brotherhood of Pain. The name, like so many, intended to convey fear. Mostly membership in the Brotherhood comprised young men desperate to find a place in Cuba's struggling economy. Legitimate income came about with some difficulty, and men like Kotov paid better. The young men bore very little in the way of scruples and morality. What good did either of those ideals do when it came to putting bread in one's belly?

"The man seems quite capable," Tomas noted, hoping to push Kotov to send his better soldiers.

"The two he fought were pathetic," Kotov complained. "Even the old lady at the restaurant could scare them off if she found the courage."

Tomas's eyes shifted to Diego. His companion wasn't the toughest associate of Tomas's, but he'd seen Diego handle himself. The man wasn't the smartest, and Tomas assumed Diego's ego allowed him to be caught offguard. After all, following the American wasn't part of the plan. They were just supposed to set the scene and wait.

"You think we can find him?" Tomas asked.

Kotov chuckled, remarking, "Havana is not so big a city that a desperate American can hide forever."

Tomas breathed a sigh of relief.

"Besides," the Russian continued, "We know where he is going."

Tomas perked up, somewhat confused. "We do?"

"Of course," Kotov explained. "He has no identification, and he must assume he's being hunted by the police. He'd want sanctuary, and the only place an American can go within several hundred kilometers is the American Embassy."

"Of course!" Tomas exclaimed.

His mood brightened. Why hadn't he thought of that? He started the car and shifted into first gear.

"Moriz, if you'll send your men out, we'll set up near the embassy. He'll have to come past us if he somehow gets around your men."

Kotov grunted in agreement before hanging up. Tomas smiled, relieved he had a plan of action. Diego slunk down in the passenger's seat as the car pulled off the curb.

9

The alley reeked of soured wet garbage, reminding me of the few times I'd been to New Orleans in the summer. Mai led me down the stairs and to the back of the building. She offered again to take me to the embassy, but I told her to go back to her restaurant. I worried that if she were seen with me, the Brotherhood of Pain might take it out on the two women. As it was, I already worried I'd caused them too much trouble.

I was able to follow the alley the next two blocks. The new-to-me boots worked wonders as I worried less about wading through the puddles of oily water that scattered along the street.

When I reached the next intersection, I clung to the side of the building, straining my neck to glance around the street. A small sign on the side of the building read "*Animas.*" The street seemed busier with several cars rambling along it in both directions and pedestrians moving along the sidewalks.

My feet stepped back, moving me deeper into the alley. If it had been me on the other end of this jaunt, I'd expected my quarry to do exactly what I was doing. With no options, the embassy seemed to be my only refuge. That might mean I was walking right into the people following me. They might actually funnel me there.

The smart thing would be to find a place to hide out—wait until dark. The number of things that could go wrong was too high, not to mention a limitation on funds. I couldn't exactly rent a hotel room.

The safe assumption was they calculated a radius from the church to watch. Once I poked my head up, they'd spot me.

I didn't like not having options. While I didn't mind uneven odds most of the time, it put me at a bigger disadvantage. At some point, it might be the PNR coming after me in an official capacity. It would be one thing to argue my way out of a murder charge, but if I took on a contingent of police officers, my defense would weaken.

As a kid, I was perpetually going places a kid shouldn't be: R-rated movies, bars, even a strip club two days after my seventeenth birthday. The key was always to act like you belonged. If I skulked in, trying to keep my head down, I stood out to whatever authorities looked for that sort of thing. People notice the odd behavior. Don't avoid eye contact, just don't offer it to everyone. That's just as bad. The best move is to belong. In the Corps, the running gag was to carry a clipboard—no one paid attention to the clipboard.

I took a deep breath and stepped around the corner, heading west on *Calle Animas.* My head aimed forward with only a few slight swivels, allowing my eyes to scan the crowds ahead. As each car passed by, I let my eyes shift to register the occupants.

After a block, I sighed with some relief. Another block put me at ease. I continued to scope out any potential danger, but I began noticing the people wandering around the street. These were the locals who made their way to and from home and work every day. Most appeared to be Cuban, but like Mai and her mother, there were several immigrants who made their home in Havana strolling along the avenue.

If the image of the woman in the bathtub didn't linger in the front of my mind, I might enjoy the stroll through the old town. The architecture reminded me of old European cities with stone buildings set almost next to each other. Each building sported its own color, ranging from turquoise to weathered gray. Terra-cotta tiles decorated the corners. In some places it seemed like the reddish-brown tiles were used to patch or cover up damage from years of neglect.

Above me, nearly every window offered a small balcony overlooking the street. Flaking concrete on some of the rails offered very little encouragement about the structure's ability to support much, if any, weight. From the street, I saw several rooftop terraces. A handful were occupied. Most seemed to be women with cigarettes held between their two fingers, staring down at the activity on the sidewalks.

A white Toyota passed me as it headed in the opposite direction. The driver was a Caucasian, and based on the hairstyle and attire, I guessed European. The way the man peered along the sidewalk like he was searching for the address on a building stood my neck hairs up on end.

My relaxing walk ended, and I quickened my pace without looking like I was quickening my pace. It was a subtle distinction, but I hoped it was sufficient.

I didn't want to glance over my shoulder—worried such a gesture might give me away. However, the alert system along the back of my neck was clanging its alarm. I paused long enough to throw a nonchalant glance back the way I came.

The white Toyota was coming off one alley where it had circled the block. Now, my nerves screamed out their anxiety. He must have spotted the one guy on the street that appeared to be American. Even the secondhand clothes weren't enough to disguise that American swagger. I'd seen other soldiers who weren't able to hide it. The military trained us all to be one thing, and subtlety wasn't part of that. It's like disguising a crowbar as a cane and expecting no one to see the obvious differences.

I'd only seen a driver in the car. I counted that as a positive. I could handle one guy. Even if he was armed. In fact, sometimes when the enemy thinks they have the advantage—thanks to a gun or other weapon—it makes them too cocky.

The Toyota cruised slowly up the street toward me. He was still a block away, and even from that far away, I could see the phone up to his ear. His gaze pinpointed on me.

On the ball of my left foot, I spun back around and took several long strides away. Ahead of me, the street continued to a busier intersection. There were still several alleys on either side of the road that I could dart down.

A second car, another white Toyota, turned at the crossroads. With no evidence, I knew in my gut this guy was with the other one. They probably bought the Japanese cars at the same time. I figured they were Russian—again with nothing to point to that conclusion.

Two were manageable, but the smarter move would be to dodge them.

I stepped up three crumbling steps to a thin, six-story building. The front door opened, leading me into a small foyer which hadn't had a fresh coat of paint, let alone a decent cleaning, in a decade. The once yellow walls were brown and sticky like the walls of an old diner. A metal security door that was little more than square steel tubing welded together in the shape of a door blocked the entrance to the rest of the building. With enough time, I could get through the lock, but by then the drivers would be on me.

The distinctive clip-clop sound echoed in the stairwell on the other side of the security door. An older Cuban woman in a faded but colorful dress descended from one of the apartments upstairs. I watched as she came through the security door, gently offering her a gracious nod before stepping through the gate. I pulled the metal frame back until the lock clicked. My feet bounded up the stairs, taking two steps at a time.

Below me, the front door opened and closed. The metal gate rattled as one of the men shook it. There was some obvious griping that I couldn't understand as it spewed out in Russian.

I could kick in the door of any of these apartments, but I hoped there was another way out. At the top of the stairs, I found a single door on a landing.

The sound of metal clanged as the men below pounded on the gate. It wouldn't hold long, especially if they were using brute force to go through it.

The door on the landing pushed open, and I spilled out onto the roof. Plastic chairs and tables littered the area. My feet stepped over mosaic-styled terra-cotta pieces, broken and mortared together. I ran to the western side of the roof and peered over the balustrade at the next roof which was about two stories below me. The gap between the building spanned only five feet, and I scrambled up on top of the stone barrier. The roof below rushed up as I dropped. My feet landed, and my body rolled to absorb the momentum of the fall.

On my feet again, I continued across that roof, bounding over the raised edge and landing on the next building's stair-step gabled roof. It was only a few feet higher than the last roof, and by the time I reached the peak, I glanced back to see the two men on the first roof.

I slid on the side of my leg down the other side of the gable before the men saw me. If they couldn't put their eyes on me, I'd have a few minutes of reprieve.

Tires squealed on the street below. More shouting in Russian.

My head lifted over the peak to see one of the men on the roof shouting to someone on the street. Reinforcements.

My hands and feet scooted me down the roof. If I stayed still, they'd eventually find me. The embassy was still several miles away, and the farther I got from these guys, the better my chance at getting there was.

As I stared over the edge of the roof, I estimated the distance between the two buildings. The next one was another apartment building, but it was taller. Not to mention, the gap between the two was wider than the last two. By almost double.

A ten-foot jump was a bit much. Even if I made the jump, the only thing across from me was an old television antenna. The screws holding it into the wall were already pulling out of the stone, and it was a guarantee that my weight would jerk them the rest of the way out.

I scanned the rest of the building. There were several stone balconies along the side. The closest was a story below me.

Russian voices echoed off the buildings, muted only by an occasional passing car. It was impossible to tell where the shouting originated. The only thing of which I was certain was that it wasn't coming from in front of me.

Without taking the time to consider any of the factors or even guess at the mathematics, my legs sprung up and forward.

There's a split second after someone does something so utterly stupid that time virtually stops. That micro-moment occurred about two feet away from the edge. I hung over the concrete alley four stories below me. Everything stopped—sound, wind, me. As if the entire universe came to a screeching halt for me. I realized there was a pile of trash in the walkway between buildings—something I didn't notice when my feet remained planted to the roof.

The frozen second ended, and I flew across the gap and down. My chest slammed into the stone edge of the balcony. As the wind rushed out of my lungs, I wrapped my arm around the concrete railing, gripping for my life. I heaved myself over the balcony and collapsed. My chest sucked in a gulp of air. A sharp pain stabbed at me when I inhaled.

My fingers felt around my chest. Nothing moved, but when I touched the third rib on the right, the pain returned. Cracked rib. Nothing too serious.

Sitting up, I looked at the window I hunched in front of. Two glass panes swung out to open it, however both were closed. Luckily, the latch on the inside was up. The crack between them was tight, but my fingertips pried the right one back enough to open it.

It was obvious why no one secured the latch. The hinges hadn't moved in years, and it took a great deal of pulling to open the right side. The left would have been more difficult except I had enough room to grip the edge and leverage it open.

Seconds later, I was inside the apartment. The two windows pulled close, and I turned to examine the home where I was taking refuge only to find myself facing a woman holding a baby.

10

The woman's eyes widened as she stared at me. She was in her twenties with dark, almost olive-colored skin. Her silky black hair hung down over her bare shoulders, and I blinked twice before I realized she was only wearing a pair of white panties.

I turned my head and raised my hands. "I'm so sorry," I blurted out.

The woman didn't respond.

"I'm not going to hurt you," I assured her again, trying to keep my voice as calm and as soothing as possible.

Still no response.

Idiot, she doesn't speak English.

I ran through the small amount of Spanish I still retained from the eighth grade.

"*No hablo español*," I said. "*Lo siento*."

She started talking. In Spanish, of course. Whatever she said came out in quick staccato manner like bullets from a gun.

"I can leave," I said. "I don't want to hurt you. Men are chasing me."

"*¿Americano?*" she asked,

I nodded.

Her eyes narrowed as she studied me. I kept my head turned away from her so that I wasn't staring directly at her breasts, even though one was firmly attached to the baby's mouth.

"*No hablo inglés,*" she said.

No surprise there.

I needed to leave, but I didn't want her to throw up the alarm as soon as I was out the door. If she understood I was in trouble, she might let me sneak out.

"I need to go," I told her, motioning with my hands the best I could muster. I pointed out the window as if that would explain everything.

Good going, Chase. Can't even tell her what I need.

Despite the lack of communication, the woman stepped past me and looked out the window. She said something else. This time, the words came out softer—a little more empathetic. She turned and looked into my eyes. I didn't look away. Her irises were dark brown, like milk chocolate. Soft and understanding. Without a word, she pulled the baby off her nipple and handed the infant to me. It was a boy. She motioned for me to burp him, and I lifted the child onto my shoulder and patted his back.

The boy cooed in my ear. I had no idea how old he was. Kids weren't something I was around a lot. He was young, though. He strained to lift his head, but to no avail.

While I urged the kid to burp, the woman stepped into the bathroom. I listened for anyone else who might have been hiding in there. All I could hear was some movement. Then she came back out wearing a simple cotton dress. Either she or someone close to her sewed the garment, but someone perfectly crafted it.

As if on cue, a belch erupted from the baby. Her hands extended, asking for the baby back. Without letting her ask again, I returned him to his mother.

I scanned the small apartment. It had one room which functioned as the bedroom, living room, and kitchen. The bathroom where she'd gone to change was just off the main room and separated only by a thin cloth curtain. I didn't think anyone else lived here.

I nodded to her, saying, "*Gracias.*"

She didn't respond.

At this point, I was running out of Spanish phrases I remembered.

My hand pressed against my chest again. "I need to go," I said slowly, motioning my hand from my chest to the door. I held my finger up to my lip, signaling her to keep it quiet.

She gave me a nod.

"*Gracias,*" I repeated.

"*Tenga usted cuidado,*" she said.

I hoped it was something nice. My head lowered as I backed out of the room. With an appreciative smile, I slipped out of the apartment into the hall.

All that effort left me less than a block from where I'd ducked into the first apartment building. I descended the steps to the first floor. This building, like the first, used a security door to block entry past the small foyer. I propped the security gate open and stepped to the front door.

I counted four cars in total. All of them were Toyotas. At least the last two weren't identical—they were different colors and possibly different models.

Three men paced along the sidewalk. They'd spread out. If I exited out the front door, there was no way they wouldn't spot me.

Four cars. I figured the first two guys were still in the first building, trying to figure out which direction I took. I guessed there had to be at least two more somewhere. They might have been checking the buildings on either side.

If I'd been running this operation, I'd leave one guy on the street. Two would secure the entrances on either side. I'd send two around back to make certain my quarry wasn't slipping out the back. That would leave the original two to search and secure the first building. Although they might have a good idea I went to the roof, so it might be prudent to be the eyes in the sky.

On top of all that, I'd bring in more people. Tighten the circumference of the area—squeeze me out.

I didn't want to stay around long enough for them to do that. I stepped back through the security gate and closed it, ensuring it locked behind me.

The bottom floor of this building extended around the staircase. There were three apartments on the east side. I followed the hallway behind the stairwell, only to run into another apartment on the back side. No exit.

It seemed I could go out the front or I could go out on the roof again. I didn't love the idea of the roof, having just gotten off it. But from there I could survey my escape and possibly locate the Russians hunting me. Better to avoid them.

I climbed the steps two at a time, pausing at the floor of the girl and her baby for no reason. I continued up the stairs to the top floor. It always seems there are certain aspects of architecture that come across universal. The building was only five stories tall, a little shorter than the first roof I'd escaped on. When I found a door leading to the roof, I expected it. However, the tenants set up a similar patio-like setting with chairs and tables. Someone strung lights around the roof. I'm sure at night, the ambiance created an escape from the doldrums on the ground.

I peered back toward the other buildings. No one was on the first roof.

No. Wait. There he was. One Russian circled the edge of the roof, staring toward the streets. His attention was directed below, but I didn't want to take the chance he'd glance my way. I crouched down and watched him, using a chair to hide behind.

When he passed along my side, I waited until his back faced me before standing to check the street. Two guys now watched the road. One must have split off to either search a building or a side street. They remained clustered around the first building. I guessed when I disappeared, it left them too many options. Was

I still in the building or back on the street? They didn't have enough men to search every building.

Why hadn't they called the police? If the goal was to frame me up, the smart play would be to alert the authorities, who certainly had the manpower to shut down and search the entire block.

That made little sense. Of course, none of today made sense yet. Someone was out to get me, and I didn't have a clue.

A horrifying thought occurred to me, too. No one would know I was in trouble.

That wasn't an unusual feeling. I'd sailed across the Gulf of Mexico and the Caribbean Sea alone several times. Most of the time, no one had the slightest idea where I was in the world. I'd drop an email to Missy or Jay occasionally when I was in port with decent internet. But they were used to me being gone for months at a time when I was out cruising.

Gabriella might miss me. But our relationship was new—she might assume I'd ghosted her. That's not my style, but she didn't know that yet.

The first people to notice I was missing would be the harbormaster at the marina where I docked Carina. When I didn't pay my bill, they'd wonder what happened to me. After several months, they'll take possession of my boat, declaring it abandoned, and sell it.

Even then, no one would come looking for me. They'd move on like I'd just walked away from my home. In a month, Jay might wonder why I hadn't reached out. This trip was going to be at least three months, I'd told him. However, I didn't have any pressing reasons to rush back to Florida. He knew as long as I had money in my cruising kitty, I might wander around the islands until I got lonely—something I didn't do often.

There was the hope that the marina in Puerto Rico would try to contact me at the Tilly Inn before they sold *Carina*. That would set off the alarms. But I'd guess that would be at least four to six months from now. Possibly longer.

Jay would look for me. He was a hell of a detective, and with the resources of the Palm Beach County Sheriff's Department, he might get somewhere. Once he located Carina, he'd realize I didn't sink somewhere in the Caribbean.

He'd suspect something. But whoever kidnapped me did so with some finesse. No matter how good they were, they left behind some clues.

That thought led me down another path. In order to grab me, they needed to be prepared. It would require watching me and knowing exactly what I might do. Unless.

I paused. It wasn't something I wanted to consider.

Without sounding too full of myself, I'm not a pushover. Obviously, they expected that too. That was why they drugged me—a lot easier than fighting me.

It was possible they spiked a drink at the club. Maybe they had a bartender on the payroll.

But it could have been Gabriella.

That thought made me a little sick. I had gotten to like her a great deal. If I was being honest, there was at least a stray thought about "what if" with her. Those sentiments didn't come to me often. For years, my only relationship was with Missy, an unhappily married woman with no intention of divorcing her husband. Not exactly the healthiest of relationships.

But there were a couple of moments with Gabriella I didn't want to end. Was she playing with me the whole time? Just trying to get close to me?

I'd like to consider myself smart enough to sniff that sort of thing out, but I would assume most people who get conned think the same thing.

My head shook as I cleared those thoughts out. I needed to move.

On my hands and knees, I crawled toward the opposite side of the roof. When I lifted my head over the balustrade, I smiled. The next building was only a few feet away. Hanging off the side of it was a rickety fire escape—one of the few I'd seen on these structures. As I studied the old metal stairs, I considered how unlikely I'd attempt it on a normal day. No one had maintained the ladders and railings since their initial construction. However, human nature being what it is, I assumed someone, probably a kid or two, had used the walkway recently. The cup filled with cigarette butts one level down confirmed my assumption.

With a swivel of my head, I located the Russian on the other roof. He had a frustrated glare about his face as he patrolled this side of the roof. As soon as he turned away, I vaulted over the balustrade and landed on the roof of the neighboring building.

11

The metal creaked as soon as I stepped onto the grated platform. Everything on the structure shook from the roof to the ground as the anchor bolts struggled to hold the frame to the stone wall.

I put a lot of trust into century-old construction, but it was my quickest way to the ground without walking out the front door. As I climbed down, I moved quickly for a couple of reasons. Despite being several buildings away, the Russian still had a clear line of sight on me, should he turn my direction. The sooner I was below the roofline, the quicker I solved that problem. Second, there was some logic, whether faulty or not, in my brain that told me if something seemed dangerous, then it needed to be accomplished quickly. Other people thought the opposite way—more care in the task meant they moved slower, hoping everything remained stable. I figured if I got closer to the ground faster, when the fire escape broke away from the building, I'd have a shorter distance to fall.

Truthfully, I'd already convinced myself that the odds of all the anchors failing at the same time were fairly low. Even if a few pop out of the wall, the rest should hold for a minute or two at least. If I already jumped from one building to a balcony on another, then descending a dilapidated ladder was a piece of cake.

Halfway down the ladder, I stopped as the entire cage-like structure wobbled violently. After it stopped and I realized it hadn't dropped to the ground, I pushed down. The bottom section—usually a ladder that slides to the ground—was missing, leaving me a twelve-foot drop to the concrete below.

Once my feet were back on solid ground, I glanced back up at the fire escape and breathed a sigh of relief. I moved away from *Animas* to one of the cross alleys. The passage between these two buildings barely deserved to be called an alley. Perhaps a motorcycle was small enough to squeeze through, but with the piles of trash flowing out of every receptacle scattered along the way, it would be slow going, even for a bike.

At least, it meant no one was going to be running me down, and it offered plenty of cover, should I need it.

From what I'd seen of Havana so far, the streets were clean. This neighborhood, though, didn't have regular trash pickup. Or the building owners didn't see a need to pay for such extravagances. I thought about the small apartment Mai and her mother lived in, wondering what the rent for a place like that was.

Mai mentioned the Russian landlord, and since there was a coordinated effort by several Russians to hunt me down, I wondered how much of the city was controlled by Russians.

The country had long been had an ally with Russia, and if the United States continued to prevent its money from going to the Cubans, it made sense that power-hungry men with money grappled for that control. It just happens that Russia had no issue with dealing with the Cubans.

While I was nothing more than a boat bum, I wondered what effect the U.S. might have on Cuba if we opened up trade fully. At the very least, we wouldn't be rescuing as many Cuban refugees off the coast of Florida if they were allowed to come and go freely through the immigration channels. Instead, America remained divided by ideology that left those "hungry masses" dying because we didn't want to let them in. Even when they come into the country legally, seeking asylum for themselves and their children, our politicians make a mockery of everything America stands for, shipping them off to other states like some fraternity prank. Every time I see something like that, my stomach turns at the inhumanity.

I moved between the buildings, stepping over puddles dripping from the garbage. The alley didn't have any drainage either, and all the moisture collected, soured, and stank. A few times, I forced the bile back down my throat as I gagged at the smell.

Much like coming down the fire escape, I wanted to clear this area fast. Unfortunately, if I didn't take a little time, I'd end up splashing through water that no doubt carried dysentery. Or at least caused it.

After the first block, I took a right down a wider alley. This one was large enough to accommodate a vehicle, but only one. While there were still mounds of trash, the sewer drains in the middle of the street allowed the afternoon rains to rinse the ooze out to sea.

A voice shouted in Russian, and I turned back to see a man three buildings back. He pointed in my direction as he alerted his companions.

I broke into a run, glancing back to see him start after me. There was a quarter-mile distance between us, and I had the head start.

While running is far from my favorite activity, it was something the Corps drilled into me. While I don't train every day, mostly because it's difficult to run laps on a forty-foot boat, I do it when I'm parked at the Tilly. Sometimes, I'll run while I'm cruising, although I'd dropped the ball on this trip.

Nonetheless, I bet I was in better shape than he was, which meant he would not catch me on foot.

One of those Toyotas might be more difficult. When I passed the next alley, I cut left and leaned into the run. He had three building lengths to cover before he made the same turn. By then I doglegged my way deeper into the neighborhood, using the alleys and streets like a maze.

At the next intersection, I went right into another small alley that barely allowed me on foot. As I passed a small doorway, I stopped running. After moving onto the step, I pressed myself against the door, hiding in the inlet.

Sixty-three seconds clicked by in my head before I heard the echoes of footfalls slapping against the pavement. The sound of feet running stopped, and I wondered if he was standing at the intersection wondering which way I might have gone.

By now, I assumed the guys with the cars were moving around to tighten the circle around me. Once they spotted me, that was inevitable. There still weren't enough of them to manage that efficiently, and I hoped I could slip out of their bounds.

Come on, I silently urged the man.

I didn't enjoy being on the run. Next to sitting and waiting, I hated being on the defensive. It was time to find out a thing or two. If that didn't work, I'd take one of their men off the board.

It took him several seconds, and I heard him talking in Russian—probably on the phone. Finally, he chose. Based on the sound of approaching footsteps, he picked the right alley.

My ears pricked up as I tried to determine if he was still alone. I heard his heavy breathing. It was just him.

The huffing came closer. He was definitely in worse shape than I was.

His feet splashed in a puddle, and he groaned softly. He was almost to the doorway, and I shrank back more.

When he stepped past, my hand shot out, grabbing his shirt and jerking him into the wall next to the doorway. It wasn't the most effective blow, but it stunned him long enough for me to move out of the alcove. My right fist shot out, hitting him in the throat. I repeated the punch to his face, and the Russian gasped. His hands moved to his nose that I crushed.

Every movie I'd seen portrayed fights that lasted several minutes, with the good guy always offering his opponent an honorable attempt to defend himself. In reality, that's the way to lose a fight. The key to coming out victorious in any close-quarter combat was to never let your opponent have a break. It's the best way to ensure success in any battle.

I did just that. After breaking his nose, I grabbed his shirt and pulled him to me. My head and my knee struck simultaneously. His broken nose took the brunt of my forehead while my knee rammed into his groin. The Russian almost went limp as the nerves in his face and crotch overloaded his body.

My forearm wrapped around his throat, and I dragged him back into the doorway. If his friends came looking, we would not be obvious.

I took a second to stare at the man. He was skinny—the kind of thin that comes from regular cocaine use. Overall, he was a decent-looking chap. The barefaced boy was in his early twenties. If he was traipsing around alleys, then he wasn't too high on the food chain. Sometimes those guys knew the most. Their bosses overlooked them like they were just the background.

"Do you speak English?" I asked.

The Russian blinked twice before he nodded. Blood dripped out of both nostrils, coloring his chin red.

"Good," I said, tightening my arm around his throat to remind him I was still in control. "Who are you?"

"Alexey Lavrin," he rasped.

I shook my head. "Why are you after me?"

"Tassie tell me to find you."

"Who's Tassie?"

"Uh," he stammered. "He's like the boss."

"The boss?" I repeated. "Boss of what?"

Alexey swallowed, and I felt the muscles in his neck constrict. He said, "He works for Mr. Kotov."

"Kotov?"

Alexey tried to nod, but my grip prevented his head from moving.

"Does this Kotov want me?"

The Russian moved a little, trying to shrug. "I'm just told to find you."

"What do you do when you find me?" I asked.

"Take you to Mr. Kotov's warehouse."

"Who the hell is Mr. Kotov?"

"He's a businessman," Alexey answered, saying "business-man" the way someone might describe Tony Soprano.

"Like a gangster?" I asked.

Alexey's face twisted as if I'd just told him a joke. "Maybe," he said. "Like Al Capone."

Like Al Capone. I had to give Alexey credit—at least he didn't refer to him as Scarface.

"Where is Kotov's warehouse?" I demanded.

"Other side of the bay," he replied.

I let out a gruff breath. The other side of the bay might have been anywhere as far as I knew. My bearings were completely off. Even now, after dodging these bastards for the last half hour, I'd turned myself around from the directions Mai gave me.

The way Alexey made it sound, though, this warehouse was more than a few miles from me. The embassy was still closer, and while the thought of finding this Kotov and some answers sounded good, it was impractical. I couldn't get out of this neighborhood, much less make it across the bay.

"Where's your cell phone?" I asked.

"My pocket," he answered.

"Take it out slowly," I insisted. "If anything else comes out, I'll snap your neck before you can use it. Understood?"

Alexey nodded. He moved his right hand down to his pants and pulled out a cell phone.

"Unlock it," I said.

He keyed in six numbers. Seven-two-three-five-zero-two. When the phone showed the home screen, I snatched it out of his hand.

"Here's the deal, Alexey," I explained. "I'm going to let you live right now. If I see you again, our deal is off. I'll kill you before I kill anyone else. Do you understand me?"

Alexey nodded.

"Do you know why Kotov wants me?" I asked, knowing he didn't know the answer.

He shook his head. "No," he said.

"I'm guessing I killed someone he knows," I growled in Alexey's ear. "It's what I do."

My voice sounded more dangerous than normal. I wanted to instill enough fear in Alexey that he might help me out of his own instinct for survival.

"My suggestion to you is you get as far from me as possible. Because from here on out, I'll kill every damned Russian that crosses my path."

He nodded furiously.

I shifted my arm and tightened. The boy panicked, slapping at my arm. The struggle lasted only a few seconds before the lack of oxygen sent Alexey into unconsciousness. I slid the Russian to the ground and patted him down. He had a switchblade, almost five hundred pesos, and his wallet. I took it all. A simple barter for his life. He got the better end of the deal.

12

With Alexey sleeping off our encounter, I hurried down the alley. The next street was empty, and I ran west down the narrow road. After two blocks, I cut left again into another alley to catch my breath.

I wanted to get off the streets for a few minutes. Alexey might follow my suggestion, but once the threat wasn't present, it was easier to follow the people he dealt with every day.

As I moved down the alley, I searched for another door. Even another fire escape might work. Just some place I could get out of sight and figure out what my next move was.

Another zig right at the next crossroads, and I was on another two-way street. My eyes scanned for any street signs, but nothing stood out. Based on Mai's directions, I needed to get to the Malecón and head west. The Malecón was to the north. But how far?

I stepped onto a stoop as a white Toyota crossed the street ahead. He didn't see me, but they were obviously making a circuitous route around me. Eventually, one would spot me.

Sprinting, I headed toward the next alley. As I passed a building, a rotund, graying man ambled out of a door. I offered him a smile and a nod, followed by "*Hola.*"

"*Hola,*" he responded as I caught the door before it closed, stepping inside as if I belonged.

I felt his eyes follow me. Perhaps he knew everyone in the building. That wouldn't be a surprise. Even though I had a deep tan, I didn't pass for Cuban. The blondish hair and blue eyes probably gave that away. But I'd seen plenty of immigrants on the street, so hopefully he wondered about me but wasn't too suspicious.

This apartment didn't use a security gate in the foyer. Just the front door provided protection, and I'd made it past that. I rushed up the stairs. Three flights to the top.

I stopped when I ran out of stairs. There was no door to the roof. Only six apartments.

While the hallway was clean, nothing had been updated in years. Paint had browned, flaking off in wide swaths. Brown patches, where moisture came through the roof, shone on the ceiling.

I dropped to sit on the top step. With Alexey's phone in my hand, I keyed in his passcode.

The home screen was a naked woman stretched across a Lotus Emira. I'd seen a similar one in West Palm Beach several weeks back. It was a few years older than this model. Not the girl, though.

Everything else was in Russian. Cyrillic letters I couldn't make out.

Symbols I knew though. I found the phone and opened it. The keypad had Cyrillic letters, but thankfully, the numbers were all Arabic. I dialed the country code for the United States and tapped in Jay Delp's phone number.

After several seconds, the phone connected. The ringing on the other end sounded like it was in a box buried under a pillow.

"Delp," Jay answered.

"Jay, it's me."

"Flash," he replied with his thick Mississippi drawl. "Are ya back?"

"No, listen. I'm in trouble."

I pictured him sitting up straight wherever he was at the moment. That was his go-to move when he switched from jovial to serious.

"What's up?"

"I'm in Havana," I explained. "Cuba."

"Uh-huh," he replied.

"I woke up in a hotel this morning in Cuba. The last thing I remembered was being in Puerto Rico. Someone drugged me and kidnapped me."

"Shit!" he blurted out. "Why would they do that?"

"No idea, but they left me a present in the bathroom. A dead girl."

"Oh, shit. What do you need?"

I paused for a second. There wasn't much he could do. Certainly, the Floridian sheriff's deputy had no jurisdiction in Cuba.

I said. "I just wanted to tell you what was going on. In case I can't get out of here."

"Did the police arrest you?" he asked. "Are you in jail?"

"No, I got out of the hotel, but I have a Russian gangster after me. He sent a crew to track me down."

"What the hell are you into, Flash?"

"Jay, I wish I had the slightest clue. It took a lot of effort to get me here, but the entire scene looked staged—badly. No cop would believe it. They didn't kill the girl there. I could see that just with a quick look."

"Well, no cop here would buy it, but that doesn't mean it won't buy you a world of trouble."

I told him, "Right now, I'm trying to avoid the police, just in case."

"What can you tell me?" he asked, switching into his detective mode.

"To start with: I was in Ponce, Puerto Rico. I hope *Carina* is still there. I'd been out with a girl named Gabriella. She's a divemaster there. We'd gone on a night dive in La Parguera. After that, we drove back to Ponce and hit a dance club. I don't remember the name, either. Just some back street joint."

"Next thing I remember is waking up in the Hotel Gran Carib in Havana."

"The girl. The dead girl. Was that this Gabriella?"

"No, I didn't recognize her."

"Okay," he acknowledged.

"Once I got out of the hotel, I realized I was being followed. I took him out, but I couldn't ask him any questions."

"He was the Russian?"

"No, he was Cuban, I think."

"Then the Russian?"

"It's about six guys trying to corral me. I lost them in the maze of alleys, but they seem to circle the area. I talked to one of them. He works for a man named Kotov."

"What else?"

"They are supposed to take me to this Kotov in his warehouse on the other side of the bay. That's really all I have gotten so far."

"Damn, Flash," Jay said.

"I'm trying to get to the embassy," I told him.

"Good," he agreed. "This has to be easier than the run we made from Sangin."

I didn't answer, remembering the three days we trekked across the Afghan desert, hunted by nearly thirty Taliban. We moved after dusk and hunkered down during the day. When we almost reached Kandahar, the Taliban launched an ambush. We lost Saunders when a grenade landed beside him. The smell of burning flesh seared into my memory.

"I need to move," I said.

"I'll see if I can do anything on my end," Jay promised, but I understood the limits he faced would hamper most of his efforts.

"Thanks. I'll call you as soon as I can."

Without a long goodbye, I hung up.

A sigh of relief escaped my lips. At least, I didn't vanish without a trace—Jay had an idea what happened to me. There was an odd comfort in that. People have a need that crosses the line between humans and animals. We want to be remembered. It was why death rituals have always developed. No one wanted to be forgotten.

It also offered a sense of finality and closure. There is always a glimmer of hope if a person goes missing. Loved ones have searched for decades after authorities give up on the hunt. It's always a question of what happened. We, as humans, needed to understand either the "how" or the "why" even if one or the other remained a mystery.

My finger swiped over the screen, searching for a maps app. Everything was in Russian, and none of the symbols resembled what I expected a map to look like. I found the internet browser, but the keyboard was Cyrillic. No chance of searching for anything on it.

Frustrated, I got to my feet and pocketed Alexey's phone. For a minute, I wondered if I needed to dump it—wondering if the police or even Kotov could track it. The Cuban police might could, but there was no way they were on to his phone. It seemed unlikely Kotov could, at least in real time. I chanced it in case I needed it.

With no roof access, I climbed back down to the first floor. As I stepped off the building's stoop, I spotted a Toyota down the road, turning east toward me. The front door of the apartment building had closed, leaving me no retreat inside.

The engine on the Toyota revved as the driver sped up. He must have spotted me. I sprinted away from him, heading back the way I'd come. At the next alley, I rounded the corner, barely slowing and barreled down the street. Seconds later, the car bounced into the alley with a scraping sound as the front fender dislodged a trash can.

I skidded to a stop as a second car pulled into the alley in front of me—another damned Toyota. They had me trapped. Both cars moved toward me.

My gaze turned back and forth between the two vehicles. Two people sat in the front seat of both cars.

My brain whirred into motion. Alexey said his bosses ordered them to take me somewhere. That meant, they wanted me alive. While there were four of them, it gave me something of an advantage. They didn't plan on killing me. My options weren't so limited. I only hoped they worried about Kotov's reaction if they did.

The Toyotas pressed forward, and the gap between them shrank. It left me with no options. The buildings on either side of the alley had nothing but stone walls from the ground to the second-floor window about fifteen feet up.

The cars stopped, almost simultaneously. Four doors opened, and the driver and passenger from each car stepped out. The back door of the second car opened too. I watched as Alexey climbed out. He glared at me with a satisfied smile. While most was wiped away, streaks of dried blood still marked his face. His nose had doubled in size since I'd left him in the alley, swelling from the broken cartilage and smashed flesh.

"You will come with us," the driver from the first car demanded. If it weren't for the broken nose, he might have been a stunt double for Alexey. In fact, all five of the Russians fell out of the same mold. Skinny but not gaunt, short black hair, and pale almost jaundiced skin. If I guessed, they all bought their clothes at the same European outlet. Or Kotov imported last year's styles from across the pond for the boys to enjoy. Maybe it was part of their compensation package.

I ignored the driver, turning to Alexey. With a wry smile, I taunted him, "I warned you, Alexey."

The two Russians from Alexey's car glanced his way. The kid's smirk vanished with my threat.

"We don't want to hurt you," the first driver said again, assuring me with a mocking sincerity none of us believed. After the trouble I'd caused and the beating I gave Alexey, they all wanted to hurt me. Besides, it was exactly the thing a gang of sociopaths enjoyed doing.

"Do you guys collect all the protection money?" I asked, guessing they were associated with the two men I'd met in Mai's restaurant.

"We know about those two," the driver told me. "You got lucky."

I smiled. It's not a practiced thing I do. When I was in the Corps, Tristan commented about the face I made when someone challenged me. It was right after a couple of Army Rangers grew upset over a pinball game in a bar. He told me it was like something creepy spread across my face begging for my opponent to charge. Tristan called it the "fearless grin." It wasn't actually fearless. Jay explained to him once it was confidence.

When I considered it, I might agree, but it was more than that. Against a couple of Rangers, I knew two Marines would come out on top. Right now, with five Russians facing me, I didn't think it was a battle I'd win, right now. But they still had a disadvantage—Kotov wanted me alive. If that was the case, I intended to make them work for it.

My hands moved to my hips as I waited for them to approach. Despite their numbers, they exhibited some apprehension, creeping toward me. They flanked me as they closed in, and I watched Alexey walk toward me.

Even if he hadn't telegraphed his move, I expected what was coming. His fist smashed into my face, and I didn't react. Instead, I let the blow knock me back. It was a powerful hit, but he missed my nose by a fraction. He swung again, unhappy with the first strike. This one connected with my nose, but he didn't put enough effort behind it. The pain shot through my cheeks but it didn't break the nose.

My hands came up as if to reach for my face, but my right snapped forward. A nearly inaudible click sounded as the switchblade popped out just before the blade embedded in Alexey's throat. My aim was exact, and the other four gasped a warning as he pulled the blade free.

Blood spewed from the carotid artery as the blade came out. Alexey's eyes widened when he realized what was happening.

I stepped back as two of the Russians moved forward to their collapsing friend. He stared up at me as the life spilled out onto the alley.

"I told you I'd kill you," I said flatly.

Then the blow to the back of my head sent me tumbling to the ground in blackness.

13

There was a throbbing in my head. The sensation was common after someone clubs another into unconsciousness. I'd have a massive headache for a bit, but I hoped I'd be all right.

I bounced around in the dark. Another trunk.

My hands weren't bound. That was a mistake, but these guys were amateurs. They'd run around together in a gang so long they bought into the machismo they portrayed. When the target of one's abuse was defenseless people like Mai and her mother, one might believe they are as tough as they act.

But I saw the reaction when I killed Alexey. The move shocked them. After all, there were five of them and only one of me. How dare I stand up against them?

My body shifted as I rolled around in the cramped quarters. Once my arms were no longer pinned beneath me, I searched the dark for a weapon. Nothing. My fingers felt over the empty clasp where the jack should be. At least these idiots thought to take the jack and tire iron out first.

None of them brandished a gun, but that didn't mean they didn't have one. After Alexey, I doubted they'd be as careless. If someone had one, he'd have it out. A silent threat to do what I was being told.

The Toyota turned, and I rolled to the side. I felt my pockets. The cell phone was gone. So was the cash.

Nothing much I could do but wait until we arrived. I wished I could visualize how the city of Havana was laid out on a map. It might give me an idea of how far they'd be taking me.

It didn't matter. Once we got there, I'd have to find my way to the embassy again. I could always take one of their cars. It might not help me much since I didn't know how to get there.

In the dark, I considered how long I'd been unconscious. The internal timer in my head estimated twelve minutes—give or take a minute.

The car moved at about thirty miles an hour, so we'd covered about five to six miles if I factored in turns and stops. Or they had just dumped me in the trunk, and we were only a block or two from the alley.

Did they leave Alexey in the alley? I supposed it depended how they viewed those things. How close were they to Alexey? Would his body trace back to them? Despite whatever influence Kotov carried in Havana, he wouldn't want the PNR in his business. Too many hands in the cookie jar made it difficult to hide the cookies. Eventually, someone waved their cookie at the wrong person, and everyone would want their turn.

Something told me that the other four took Alexey's body. I bet it was in the other trunk. At least they didn't drop it in here with me.

As the car bounced along, I considered my course of action. A plan was difficult to set with so many variables. How would they take me out? Would it be all four? There was no chance they'd let me get a quick kill before they dragged me out. How many other people would be there when we arrived? At the moment, I had no weapon. I could kill a man with my bare hands, but it was nowhere near as efficient as a .45-caliber bullet to the brain.

Another thing floated around my mind. What did Kotov want with me? Why would he go through the trouble of kidnapping me and setting such a sloppy frame job up?

If I came out fighting, I might not get those answers. The same thing held true about humans wanting closure—I wanted someone to tell me what the hell was going on.

The car turned again with a bump. We were in a driveway or parking lot. The bounce and slight angle of the car told me that.

After a few more minutes of crawling, the Toyota came to a stop with a modest jerk. Without the engine and road noise, I could hear the two men up front jabbering in Russian.

I waited. The doors opened, and the Russian sounded fainter until both the passenger and driver doors slammed. The Russian voices grew louder as they approached the rear of the Toyota. I counted three distinct voices.

"American," one called through the trunk. "If you try anything, Yasha will shoot you dead."

Guess they have a gun.

"I won't," I assured them.

The latch inside clicked as the lid popped up an inch. One of them threw the trunk open and stepped back. Bright light blinded me for a second, and my hand shielded the afternoon sun from my eyes. After a second, my eyesight cleared. Three of the four Russians stared at me from a respectable distance—far enough, I couldn't lunge for them, but close enough to maintain control. The one in the middle held a nine-millimeter Makarov pistol at me. The stock was a deep tan wood grain, and the barrel had blackened over time. No one was cleaning the weapon the way they should. For a second, I wondered if they bothered to load it.

My left hand gripped the edge of the opening, pulling me over the bumper. When my feet touched the ground, I straightened, letting the blood flow back to my feet after the cramped ride.

I studied the three faces, pausing only a second on Yasha with the Makarov. When I said the words in my head, it sounded like a USSR propaganda kids' book from 1976. Yasha with the Makarov.

"That way," the same driver who did the talking back in the alley ordered.

I obeyed, turning to face a stone building on the edge of a dock. From where I stood, I viewed the bay where tankers and freight ships were moored, waiting to be loaded or unloaded. On a nearby pier, cargo boxes were being unloaded by tall cranes from a small freighter. Old forklifts zoomed around in the distance.

The building he pointed me to was old and run down. The exterior was of wood construction, and as pieces rotted and fell away, they'd replaced them with incongruous wood slats. None of the patches matched the old structure. Most felt like it was simply a quick fix-up, the way someone throws a sheet of plywood over a busted window after a storm. Only the owners of this building allowed the fixes to be permanent.

I marched toward the door with Yasha several steps behind me. The other two flanked me on either side, just far enough out of reach. They figured at best I might get one of them before Yasha shot me. I guess they hoped I realized that, too.

The inside of the building was vastly different. As soon as I stepped through the metal door, I felt transported to a modest real estate office. Nothing too extravagant, but compared to the decaying shell on the outside, it was amazing. Someone didn't want to advertise themselves.

We marched down a hallway lined with prints of paintings from museums around the world. Kotov had the good sense not to put up the Mona Lisa or Water Lilies, but most were at least recognizable. There were even three flourishing tropical plants in the office. It seemed like overkill, unless Kotov just enjoyed the ambiance.

"In here," the driver ordered, pointing me into an empty room with only a table and four chairs.

When I stepped inside, the driver locked eyes on me. "You'll stay here," he said sternly. "If you try to leave, Yasha will shoot you. He wants to do it after what you did to Alexey."

"Alexey deserved it," I quipped. "I told him I would kill him."

His eyes narrowed.

"What's your name?" I asked.

He didn't answer. I offered him my "fearless grin," saying, "Fine." My head turned toward Yasha, who held the barrel of the gun directly at me. "I'll put you next on my list, Yasha."

To his credit, he didn't flinch. The driver pulled the door closed, and I heard the clunk of a deadbolt securing me inside.

As soon as the lock latched, I spun around in the room, scanning the walls and ceilings. There was a smoke detector in the corner with a small lens—hidden camera. It wasn't overtly obvious, but I think everyone has gotten a Facebook ad about these things. They weren't scarce, apparently even in Cuba.

I grabbed the chair, dragged it away from the table toward the smoke detector. With a quick swing, I hoisted the seat above my head and hammered the little spy camera with the chair's foot. The plastic cracked and chunks of debris rained down on me. When all I could see were the two wires hanging out of the ceiling, I returned the chair to the table.

The rest of the room was devoid of anything. The walls were simply painted drywall. A neutral eggshell white. Not even the glossy kind. Kotov went with the flat texture. The ceilings were also drywall. I'd hoped for acoustic tile because there was often a space above the metal grid. With drywall, I'd have to tear an opening big enough to fit through. Yasha would have time to bust in and shoot me.

Frustrated, I kicked a different chair away from the table and slumped into it. My arms folded across my chest, and I stared at the door. Somewhere on the other side were some answers. It seemed the only thing I could do was wait.

If I'd been on board *Carina*, I might spend the entire day
lounging in the cockpit, especially if I was making a passage.
Somehow, sitting here unsettled me. There were too many un-
knowns at the moment. Kotov left me to stew in those mysteries. It's a classic trick used by cops around the world. Create im-
patience, and the subject will rush to fill the void left by waiting.
It worked with silence, too. Stare at a subject in an interrogation
long enough, and eight out of ten will start rattling on about
anything. People hate a void.

Since I knew that's what was happening, I should be able to
gird myself against it. In theory, that is. Unfortunately, I am
aware of my weaknesses, and even armed with that knowledge,
it rarely eases my mind.

Funny how staring down five men willing to beat the shit out
of me bothered me far less than waiting here.

However, nature armed me with something else—innate
stubbornness. I might want to fidget or pace, but I was going to
let that anxiety loose only in my head. It's nerve-wracking, but
I sat motionless, staring at the door. Waiting.

The second hand in my head clicked away, and I tried to
watch it move around the clock, attempting to find some peace.
After two hours and thirty-nine minutes, two shots echoed
through the walls. The drywall muffled it, but I recognized the
sounds of gunfire. It wasn't the Makarov. Something smaller.
Maybe a twenty-two. It resembled the pop of an enormous balloon. The nine-millimeter Yasha carried should have boomed,
even through the walls.

I didn't move. Something was going to happen soon, and that
fact eased the tension in my head. I hated the waiting around.

Now, I plotted. If I was right, the driver, Yasha, and Kotov
would come through the door any second. Yasha's job was to
cover me with the Makarov. With his threat already defined, the
logical play was to keep my attention on him. Either the driver or

Kotov had the twenty-two. I figured they both had something, though.

My mind began counting the seconds. The little hand on my internal clock paused at 187 seconds. The deadbolt on the door clunked as someone unlocked it from the other side. It swung in, revealing Yasha still holding the Makarov. He moved into the room with the driver right behind him. A third man stepped through the door. He was in his sixties with a thick gray beard sculpted into an arc just below his chin. His hair was less gray, but time was evening it out quickly. He towered in the doorway, and his broad shoulders filled out the suit he wore. Under the jacket, he appeared to have once been quite muscular, but now the bulk had faded with age. He still portrayed a dominating image as he crossed his arms.

"Mr. Kotov, I presume," I said, without shifting the slouch I'd been maintaining for almost three hours. "I don't suppose someone brought me a sandwich or anything."

The big Russian smiled, amused at my snark. It was understandable, sometimes I was quite amusing.

"You are Mr. Chase Gordon," he announced in a raspy, accented voice.

"That wasn't a question," I pointed out. "If it was a declaration of my identity, then I hate to break it to you. I already know who I am."

He cocked his head sideways, surveying me. "It seems no one wants you," he said bluntly.

I straightened up in one quick fluid motion, causing Yasha to tighten his grip on the Makarov. "Good, I can go then. Any chance someone could drop me at the American Embassy?"

Kotov chuckled, glancing at the driver. "Americans," he said to the man. "They are so demanding."

"Oh, my apologies," I offered sarcastically. "I didn't realize when your boys knocked me over the head and dragged me here against my will that you meant it all as a request. Obviously, it's one of those cultural things we just don't understand."

"I don't think you'll be going anywhere," he muttered.

"You just said you didn't want me," I pointed out.

"No," he corrected. "I said, 'no one wants you.' Since that is the case, I believe Yasha here has some thoughts about what you did to his cousin, Alexey."

I stared back at him. "Why would you drag me to Cuba just to play this stupid game?"

Kotov shook his head, clucking his tongue against the roof of his mouth. "I didn't bring you here."

My brow furrowed.

"To Cuba, I mean," he amended. "I just found you when you got lost."

"Who the hell brought me here?"

He smiled. "It seems it doesn't matter anymore."

Yasha said something in Russian.

Kotov responded with a nod.

As Yasha raised the barrel to my head, I saw a glimmer of mirth in his eyes.

Then the gunfire erupted.

14

Kotov shouted something in Russian, and the driver grabbed Yasha by the shoulder. As his head twisted toward the driver, I drove my hand up, catching his wrist and redirecting the Makarov from my face. Yasha turned back to me as I slammed my forehead into his face the same way I'd incapacitated Alexey earlier. Stunned, he couldn't get his footing as I barreled into him. We slammed against the wall. I rolled him around to shield me from the other two as my free hand punched into his gut.

Over his shoulder, I saw the driver pull a gun out, trying to aim it at me. With Yasha blocking him, he couldn't get a clear shot.

Outside, the tat-tat-tat of gunfire continued to grow closer.

I pounded my fist into Yasha's torso until I felt a rib break. As he gasped for air, I pushed off the wall, shoving him toward the driver. The other man fired his weapon. Yasha's body jerked as the bullet punctured his back. The two of us collided with the driver, who had the good sense not to shoot his friend again. Unfortunately, he had the bad sense not to continue firing until he dropped me, no matter what happened to Yasha.

The three of us crashed onto the table, and the structure collapsed in the middle. Yasha finally released his grip on the Makarov, and I slammed my head into his face again before scrambling for it. I rolled off the two Russians, wrapping my hand around the handle.

My forehead throbbed from the blows to Yasha's face, but ignoring the pain, I shifted my focus to Kotov, standing to the side with a gun pointed in my direction. I straightened up, staring at the bewildered Russian. The two men on the ground weren't moving much.

There was no way I could get my gun up before he shot me. I dropped the Makarov and stepped toward Kotov, who raised a pistol I couldn't identify. A newer model, judging from the condition. The Cyrillic lettering on the barrel clued me it was likely Russian.

The gunfight in the hall was closer.

"Who is that?" he demanded. The gun in his hand quivered. He'd been in charge too long. Someone like Yasha had been doing his heavy lifting the last few years. Still, the gangster's eyes glazed over with a steely resolve. I didn't doubt he'd pull the trigger, but for the moment he was weighing something. My value, perhaps. Whoever was shooting up the front was an unknown.

"What makes you think I know?" I retorted. "You never even told me why you wanted me."

The Russian growled. "Are you some American spy?" he mumbled.

"I'm a bartender," I told him. "You dragged me here."

He said something in Russian, and while I don't speak the language, I was certain it meant "bullshit." Or at least some derivative of it.

I stepped toward the gun. If that man was going to shoot me, I'd at least press him for some answers first. "Who brought me here?"

He scowled at me.

"She refused to pay for you," he remarked. "You aren't worth this."

"She?" I questioned. "Gabriella?"

He narrowed his eyes, and I realized the decision he was about to pull the trigger. In the movies, the hero would snatch the gun out of the villain's hand, and sometimes that can work. It requires the person with the gun to hesitate, but when the eyes behind the barrel were as determined as Kotov's, there would be no hesitation.

The gun fell limply in his hand, and his eyes lost not only the resoluteness but the life. He slumped to the floor, and I reached for the gun.

I never made it. A thick man stepped into the room. His arm held an M45, almost identical to the one I kept hidden on board *Carina*. He wore a flak jacket over a tight gray shirt. His arms bulged underneath the sleeves, and I paused when I saw the eagle with two sniper rifles crossing. Around the eagle in clockwise formation were the words "Death Before Dishonor Semper Fi."

My hands raised in the air, and the soldier studied me for a second.

"Gordon?"

I nodded, wondering how the hell Jay got a Marine in to rescue me.

"Leo Taylor," he introduced himself with a familiar accent. "Wanna get out of here?"

"Do I ever," I responded. I pointed at the gun on the ground. "May I?"

He pursed his lips as if he knew I would ask that question. "I'd have been disappointed if you didn't," he quipped.

I bent over and scooped up Kotov's gun before following Taylor out of the room. The foyer was a mess. I hadn't seen that many of Kotov's men, but now I counted nine, including the driver and passenger from the other Toyota. I stopped for a second when I recognized one of the men on the floor. He was the Cuban who followed me into the church. Next to him was another Latino. The only two locals in a pile of dead Russians.

As we passed the bodies strewn about in the lobby, I studied Leo Taylor. The man was in his forties—at least ten years older than me. He moved like a soldier. A Barrett Rec7 Gen II automatic rifle hung over his back from a strap. He kept the M45 in firing position as he swept over each room, prepared for additional combatants to join the fray.

The office was empty.

"We'll need to take one of their cars," he told me.

"Pick the one without the dead body in it," I suggested.

Taylor looked over his shoulder at me with a wicked grin. "Nice," he muttered, and I pinpointed the accent he had. I bet it was a mix of boot heel Missouri and Midwest.

As we stepped into the last remnants of dusk, I pointed at the Toyota I'd been stuffed inside. "Take that one," I suggested, wondering if we should have taken the keys off the driver.

"Shit!" I muttered, spinning back to the building.

"What?" the Marine asked.

"There's a guy still in there," I told him, remembering the driver was both alive and uninjured. I couldn't know what happened to Yasha, but even if he didn't die, he wasn't running after us with a bullet in his back.

"Leave him," Taylor said. "Just cover the door while I start the car."

The Russian pistol raised in my hand as I watched the door. It took Taylor thirty-three seconds to start the Toyota.

"Come on," he called, and I jumped in the front seat as he let off the clutch.

The car jerked forward, and Taylor ground the gears as he shifted into second gear. I glanced his way with little judgment. It had been a while since I drove a stick myself. Overall, I wasn't much of a driver, either. Too many years without a car.

When the tires squealed on the road, I asked, "Not that I'm looking a gift horse in the mouth, but who the hell are you?"

"I told you. Leo Taylor."

"Marine?" I questioned, knowing what the answer was.

"Yeah. You too?"

I nodded. "Did Jay send you?"

His lips pursed as he shook his head. "Jay who?"

"Jay Delp?"

His brow furrowed, as if he was searching for a connection. "He won the Scout Sniper Competition?"

"Yeah," I answered warily.

"I think I beat his score," he commented off the cuff.

My eyebrow lifted.

"You aren't active?"

He shook his head. "Not exactly. I can't answer your questions yet. My job was just to get you."

"Who sent you?"

He shrugged, a reminder that he said he couldn't answer my questions.

I sighed. "Can you tell me where we are going?"

"Safe house."

With a deep breath, I let my current predicament roll over in my head. Should I trust him? He seemed to be a Marine. At least a former Marine, if you can call us that. But if someone wanted to lure me into complacency, a fellow Marine would put me at ease.

Ultimately, it didn't matter. I was in a better position right now than I had been before Leo Taylor showed up.

That didn't change the fact that there was going to be a bill to pay. Someone sent him to get me. No one did that out of the kindness of their heart. Whoever sent him wanted something. Hopefully, it wasn't my head on a platter.

I still held the pistol in my hand, and while I considered slipping it under my waistband, it gave me some comfort.

"Where are you from, Taylor?" I asked.

"Call me Leo," he said. "I was born outside St. Louis, but like most of us soldiers, I don't stay in any one place too long. Right now, I'm living in Memphis."

"I thought I heard some Missouri in your voice, but I was guessing somewhere around Kansas City."

He shrugged again. Most conversations would involve him asking me the same question, but he didn't. Since he knew my name, he might have read a file on me. Leo didn't strike me as the small-talk type of guy.

I took a moment to stare out the window as we drove along the port. The lights from the ships in the bay reflected off the water. The last twenty-four hours had been nonstop. I considered that it hadn't even been that long. I woke up midmorning, and now it was only pushing seven in the evening. Nine hours. Twenty-four hours ago, I'd been driving back with Gabriella.

"What day is it?" I asked Leo.

"Friday."

Two days. Gabriella and I were together two days ago.

It made sense. To transport me from Puerto Rico to Cuba would require a little time. They kept me drugged while they flew me to Havana. Possibly, they brought me in a boat. That might explain the length of time. Even in a plane, they wouldn't need that long. But a boat is much more covert. The authorities watch them, but not nearly as tightly as they do airport security. All it takes is picking an empty beach, dropping a dinghy to shore, and taking the boat out again. Unless a patrol happened by, one could infiltrate the country without alerting anyone. If they were moving an unconscious boat bum, it would be far less conspicuous.

Leo maneuvered through traffic as we drove away from the water. The streets grew more crowded with buildings and pedestrians as we entered an area that resembled the very neighborhood the Russians pursued me through. If I hadn't checked a few of the street signs to see they were different names, I might have been fooled. It was an older area with the same style buildings dotted with balconies and crowned with railings. Clothes lines, filled with the day's laundry fluttering in the breeze, stretched overhead.

My eyes felt heavy after the adrenaline in my body dropped. I forced myself to sit up straighter. While I didn't completely distrust Leo, I had no intention of drifting off to sleep with him. It was a dumb concern—he'd had ample opportunity to kill me before now. Still, I fought off the slumber, trying to remain alert.

To my relief, he pulled onto a small side street and slowed until the Toyota came to a stop on the curb.

"We are going to hoof it from here," he said. "I don't want the car found too close to the safe house."

Curious, I asked, "How'd you get there without a car?"

"I hitchhiked," he answered, grinning the same wry smile.

We left the car and hiked west along the sidewalk. After two blocks, Leo cut across the street and down an alley. He took three blocks and turned right, covering another block. At that intersection, I followed him down an alley to a metal door. He unlocked it with a key, and we slipped inside, where a narrow staircase led up to a landing and a blank wooden door.

I waited as he knocked twice on the door. A second later, it swung open, revealing a muscular man in his late thirties. He wore a tight tank top. The tattoo on his shoulder showed a bird with a trident in its talons. Navy SEAL.

"This him?" the sailor asked.

"C'mon, Gordon," Leo told me as he stepped inside.

I followed him in to see a second person in the apartment. A dark-haired woman in her thirties was seated at a small kitchen table. A laptop sat on the top. Three monitors connected to the computer, and she was wearing headphones. Her gaze lifted from the screens to me, and she pulled the headphones off.

"Chase Gordon?" she asked.

Without answering, I scanned the faces of the other three people in the room. She didn't fit. The others were military. So was I, I suppose. But she wasn't. This woman was government, though. I had an idea exactly what department she belonged to.

"I'm Danielle Wallace," she introduced herself. "CIA."

15

"You do like to make a splash," Wallace remarked as she rose from the table. She was young for an agent in charge. Dark brown hair hung over her shoulders, and her face seemed younger than she probably was. Her skin was pale, like she avoided the sun, and I noticed some barely visible freckles peeking out under her eyes.

I didn't speak yet. Sometimes it's best to hold the tongue until more cards are on the table. What I could surmise was easy. Danielle Wallace was in charge. The other two answered to her. I'd seen operations like this before. Small-scale and tight. That usually meant it was so far below the radar even the agent in charge didn't comprehend what was going on fully. These were also the most dangerous. The agent in charge wants results, and the men doing the grunt work are far more expendable.

Leo already confirmed he wasn't active-duty, and unless I was mistaken, the SEAL wasn't either. They might work directly for the CIA, but I bet not. Mercenary?

"You're all over the radar," Wallace continued when I didn't respond. "The Russians are calling around about you. Everyone is talking about some guy who has clogged the wheels of progress for them. So to speak."

I continued to stare at her.

"The PNR is also looking for a foreign tourist fitting your description. Seems the PNR found a murdered woman in the Hotel Gran Caribe."

"First I'm hearing about that," I replied.

Wallace nodded as she paced around me. It was a tactic someone once told her to use to put a subject off guard. The circling felt predatory. It worked the same way silence did. Eventually, the prey reacts. In the wild, it might sprint from its hiding place—which is exactly what the predator wants. If, instead, the prey remains still and hunkered down, the hunter might grow weary and move on.

If I'd been an asshole, I'd lunge at her—see if she flinched. However, I might have her to thank for sending Leo in like the cavalry.

"It seems you got yourself into a bit of a pickle, so to speak," Wallace remarked. "Why don't you tell me your story?"

I cocked my head. Slowly, I moved my eyes over the room, stopping in the tiny kitchen. My stomach grumbled. Mai's fried rice had been delicious, but it wasn't cutting it now. I stepped away from Wallace, walking toward the little refrigerator in the corner. When I opened it, I spotted several pre-made yogurt parfaits with granola piled on top. Danielle didn't buy this at the corner market. I pulled one out and looked back at the other three people staring at me. Lifting it up, I motioned towards the others the unspoken offer. Instinctively, the SEAL shook his head. Leo and Wallace just watched me.

The plastic top popped off, revealing a small plastic spoon that reminded me of the sample spoons every ice cream shop has. I carried the yogurt to the table, pulled the chair out, and sat down. With a spoonful of yogurt in my hand, I said, "It's a lot of single-use plastic here. I hope someone is recycling."

Wallace folded her arms while Leo grinned widely.

"Ms. Wallace," I said with a mouthful of strawberry and granola, "why don't you tell me what you know first? It's going to be more than I do."

She let out a harrumph in frustration. Then she sat across from me. Leo and the SEAL exchanged amused looks.

"I'm betting you were at that hotel today," she commented. "Nothing in your file indicates you would kill a woman like that, though. I spoke with General Shaw."

My eyes lifted at the mention of my former CO.

"Shaw?" Leo asked. "She was your CO?"

Wallace waved him off, ignoring his question. "She confirms what your file states. Shaw went further to say that even if she saw you cut a woman up, she wouldn't buy it."

"That doesn't sound right," I said, spooning more yogurt into my mouth.

"Oh, she told me exactly what you were capable of," Wallace confirmed. "She actually used the words 'innocent woman.'"

I shifted my gaze back to the yogurt.

"If I take her at her word, and she is a general."

"Generals never lie," I said flatly.

Wallace stared at me before she repeated, "If I take her at her word, someone else killed the woman, and the blame is on you."

"Great, can you clear that all up?" I questioned, placing the empty yogurt container on the table with the spoon and lid inside it.

"That doesn't really explain the Russians or why you started your own minor war with them."

I shrugged.

"Look, Gordon, I can help you," she said. "But I need to understand what happened."

Again, I looked at the other two men. They had been decidedly quiet, and I had a sick feeling that I might not find out what happened to me without telling someone. The CIA had a farther reach than Jay did.

"Someone kidnapped me from Puerto Rico two days ago," I explained.

Wallace leaned forward and folded her hands, listening.

"I woke up in the hotel this morning with no idea how I got there. When I found the girl, who, by the way, didn't die there, I realized I was in trouble. I escaped out the window when the PNR showed up at the door."

Wallace nodded along. "And the Russians?"

"I'm not sure," I explained. "When I left the hotel, I picked up a tail. I ditched him in a church—he was one of the two Cubans Leo killed at the warehouse."

"Wait," Leo interjected. "I didn't kill the Cubans. They were already dead when I came in. Single gunshot to the back of each of their heads."

My brain rolled back time, remembering the two shots I heard before Kotov came into the room. He killed the Cubans. Why? Because the one failed to get me in the church?

"They must be connected to Kotov. I think he's the Russian mob here."

Wallace said, "Not so much the mob, but yes, he's a crime boss. He is...or rather, was taking over most of the city."

"He was strong-arming businesses for protection money," I said. "I stepped into a shakedown today. That might be what got his attention, but it doesn't explain the Cuban. Two guys at the restaurant bullying an old woman."

"Was Kotov involved from the start?"

I shrugged. "I have no clue what happened from the start. This Kotov guy and I have never crossed paths. At least as far as I recall."

"He could have been doing it for someone else."

She refused to pay for you.

Those were Kotov's words. *She.* My eyes flicked up at Wallace. *She.*

"It doesn't make a lot of sense," I said. "Why not just kill me?"

"It was a game," the SEAL remarked.

Wallace and I turned to look at him.

"Sorry, man. I've seen how the Russians work. They like to make examples."

Wallace lifted her palm to stop him. "I'm sorry, Gordon. This is Aaron Watkins. You already met Leo."

I gave Watkins a nod. "What do you mean?"

"It's how they are raised. The threat of the iron fist and all. They've always governed by fear. If they make an example of you, then word spreads. People, years from now, would talk about how this crime boss, Katolva…"

"Kotov," I corrected.

"How this crime boss, Kotov, kidnapped and ruined this American's life. It will be like this legend, and Kotov's name will be synonymous with fear."

"I still don't know him," I explained.

"Doesn't matter now," Leo pointed out. "He won't be coming after you again."

Leo was correct. Kotov wasn't a threat anymore. Leo ensured that.

She refused to pay for you.

I wasn't sure now if he was ever the real threat. If that's the case, she was going to show herself again.

Wallace shifted in her seat.

Maybe she already had.

"That's all I know," I finished.

"I can fix the issue with the hotel," she assured me.

"In exchange for what?"

"We need an extra body, and, like I mentioned, your CO suggested you would fit the bill."

"I don't do that sort of thing anymore," I remarked.

Wallace laughed. "Of course you do," she said. "Look at what you've done today."

I nodded. "Let me rephrase that. I'm retired. I don't do that sort of thing for anyone else."

"The way I see it," Wallace remarked, "is you need some help. This is a little quid pro quo, so to speak."

My head shook. Typical Agency bullshit. They want something but have to package it up as if I owed her something.

"Listen, Wallace, I appreciate the help today," I said, shooting my right index finger at Leo. "But I enjoy being a civilian."

"I don't buy that, Gordon," she refuted. "Your record indicates, for being retired, you have a lot of kills."

My arms folded across my chest. "How about you just drop me at the embassy?" I asked. "They can sort me out with a passport."

"Then what?" she asked. "You plan to hop a plane? Don't you think the PNR might want to prevent their murder suspect from leaving the country?"

"This sounds a lot like blackmail," I remarked, looking over at Leo and Watkins. "Is that how she got you?"

"Oh, no," Wallace interjected. "These two are being well compensated for their time."

"Why?" I asked. "Whatever this operation is, you have a plethora of active-duty SpecOp guys who can do it. As far as I know, America doesn't have any significant wars going on. Those guys are sitting around twiddling their thumbs. Hell, there are probably a dozen or more SpecOps at Gitmo right now."

"The United States government cannot sanction this op."

I smiled. "There it is," I said with a chuckle. "I suspected that. Why else bring in a couple of retirees? No offense, guys."

Leo waved off the comment as he moved to the worn couch. Watkins didn't acknowledge it.

"General Shaw told me you would never volunteer to work with me."

"Does she know what is happening here?" I asked.

Wallace shook her head. "She doesn't have the clearance for that."

"But I do?" I almost laughed. Shaw worked at the Pentagon now, running top secret projects every day. It made little sense for me to have access to something she couldn't.

"This isn't a government job," Wallace explained. "You are a contractor."

"No, I'm not," I insisted. "If I let you pull this shit with me now, the next thing I know, you'll be showing up, demanding I fly to Bahrain to execute some political leader."

"The CIA doesn't do assassinations," she denied.

"Right," I retorted. "And I piss liquid gold. Leo, there, shits diamonds."

"Damn right I do," Leo quipped.

Wallace reached into an attaché case and removed a small stack of papers. She tapped the bottom of the pages on the table until every individual sheet lined up and squared on all four sides. Her hand extended to pass the pages to me.

"What is this?" I asked.

"Orders from the Secretary of the Navy," Wallace explained.

I took the paper, scanning the words. "What the hell?" I demanded.

"Keep reading," she urged.

I flipped through the pages. "What the hell?" I repeated. "You can't do this."

"I didn't. The Secretary of the Navy issued those orders. As of right now, the United States Marine Corps has officially recalled you back into active duty with the rank of lieutenant."

I stared up at her, letting the papers hang loosely.

"What the hell?"

16

I stared at the paper in front of me. My brain couldn't register what was in front of me. Of course, I remembered there was an addendum to my discharge paperwork. Every soldier and sailor was reminded of that. For the life of me, I couldn't recall what the actual code was. In effect, the Marine Corps could recall me to active duty if they saw fit.

But that never happened. Not one person I ever served with had been recalled. The tailor of that code designed it, I assumed, during times of war or crisis. However, leave it to the CIA to pervert its intent.

"This can't be real," I muttered. "I can fight this."

"Sure you can," Wallace agreed. "In fact, why don't you head over to Washington and file an appeal?"

I stared at her.

"Of course, you'll need to get there, won't you?"

I twisted to glare at the other two men in the room. "Did she do this to you, too?"

Both men shook their heads.

"No, these men volunteered," Wallace said.

"To be paid?" I questioned.

"Of course," she answered. "You'll be receiving your mid- and end-of-the-month pay too."

"Somehow, I imagine the private option pays more," I quipped.

Danielle Wallace shrugged. "That was an option."

My eyes narrowed. "I might just wait for the court-martial," I retorted.

"Another option," Wallace conceded. "Again, the United States will wait until whatever judgment you receive from the Cuban government concerning the woman found in your room has been finalized. On the plus side, I believe the Cubans are quick to reach a decision and execute the sentence."

The emphasis on "execute" was heavy-handed but effective.

"I intend to appeal this no matter what," I informed her.

"Your right to do so. However, until this matter concludes, you have orders to answer to me."

I shifted uncomfortably in my chair.

"Man, I hate to break this to you, but I don't think you have a lot of options," Leo consoled.

A sigh escaped my lungs. For the moment, I feared he was correct. The worries rolling around my head centered on what I'd gotten into. So far, I did not know what the op was, but with a small three-man team, it might have verged on suicidal.

"Fine," I relented. "What's the operation?"

Wallace suppressed a smile. Still, her pupils dilated with satisfaction.

"Right now, William Thompson is being held by Russians in Cuba. The three of you are going to locate and rescue him."

"William Thompson?" I questioned. "The president's son?"

"That's the one," Wallace confirmed. "He has been working in the energy field, and his dealings with the Russians have come under some scrutiny. Unfortunately, it seems he overstepped his bounds. He began working with Valeri Mikhalov."

My head shook. "Who is that?" I asked, adding, "The only Russian political name I know is Smirnoff."

She rolled her eyes slightly.

Leo chuckled, saying, "Smirnoff might make better decisions."

Wallace continued, "Mikhalov has a home here."

"Why would this Mikhalov kidnap the president's son?" I asked. "Surely, that's a diplomatic disaster waiting to happen."

"If it weren't for the fact that Mikhalov has documents indicating William Thompson has spearheaded a push to drill for natural gas in the Danube Delta."

"I hate to beat a dead horse, but I don't follow the news," I pointed out. "There's very little internet on the ocean."

"That's not exactly true anymore," Wallace corrected.

I shrugged in conceit. Nowadays, while it was a struggle to get high-speed internet in the middle of the ocean, there were many options for slow-speed. With the way technology is advancing, high-speed will be available within years, if not months.

Wallace continued, "The Danube Delta is a marsh land between Romania and Ukraine. Geological studies have shown it to be quite rich in resources."

"Why does that matter?" I asked. "Thompson works in energy. Can't fault him for doing his job. Be like complaining because the CIA is a bunch of bitches."

She ignored my jab. "The Danube Delta is a protected marine environment. There are many people who find this troublesome, including both the governments of Romania and Ukraine."

While I rarely followed the world political cinema, it was hard not to miss Russia's invasion of Ukraine this past year. The United States took a mostly staunch stance of staying out of it. Although we offered some missiles and tanks, that generosity seemed more like an obligation to appear to side with Ukraine. Even the president's condemnation of Russia was perceived by the American public as little more than disingenuous admonitions.

Connecting the dots, I said, "If the press proved the president's son had been profiting from the Russian absorption of the Ukraine, the American people might suspect the president's apathy toward the war to be connected. Which, of course, it is."

"We can't say that," Wallace snapped.

"Sure we can. Two plus two equals four. It doesn't matter that three plus one does, too. Once one of the news outlets picks it up, it becomes truth. Besides, if neither of the Thompsons realized there would be a backlash from this connection, then they deserve to be raked over the coals."

I'd been to the Black Sea once when I was on leave. It was three days in a little village in Romania, and the area was beautiful. I'm not an ecological warrior, but my life is on the water. It's hard not to see the effect even a little trash has on marine life. No matter what precautions these companies make, there are ramifications to any drilling operation. Just the construction alone will disrupt sea life around it. But if something goes wrong, like the Deepwater spill or even something less disastrous, the damage to the area would take decades to fix. If it could even be done.

"Why would they keep him prisoner?" I asked.

Wallace didn't answer right away.

I nodded with realization. "Because he's not, is he?"

"Not that he is aware," she answered.

"You want the proof," I said. "Mikhalov has the evidence connecting to the president, and we are going to take it."

"Along with William Thompson."

I leaned back in my chair, considering what I now knew. In all my years in the service, I never met a single CIA operative I trusted. Inevitably, each one proved me right, too. I doubted Danielle Wallace was about to break that streak. However, it seemed, at least for the moment, she and I remained locked together. At the first available moment, I intended to call someone in Washington. I'd keep at it until I found the right person who could get me out of this predicament.

Not that I had any affinity for Thompson, Russia, or the Danube Delta. However, if I were to take a leaning, it would be to protect the Delta from pointless pollution. Somehow, I doubted the facts laid out by Wallace were, in fact, facts. Even if they were, Russia long proved they don't give a shit about what the public thinks of them. They'd steamroll the rain forests with a smile on their lips. All the while asking the United States, "What are you going to do about it?"

I'm no geo-political expert. Hell, I don't even know what goes into that. I've always been a soldier. I did what I was told. If I found myself recalled to duty, I'd do the same thing. What I wanted, though, was something more official than a sheet of paper in a hovel in an obscure barrio of Havana.

Some days, one can never get what they want though. I'd go along for the moment. If everything was legitimate, I still had a duty. When I left the Corps, I didn't disavow the duty I had. I'd pick up the flag and run with it if the Corps told me to.

"Where is William Thompson?" I asked, forcing myself into the present.

"We aren't sure," Wallace said. "What we do know is that he's in Cuba. We have two possibilities."

Leo leaned against the wall. "What are those possibilities?"

I made a note to get Leo to the side. He might be a mercenary now, but he was a Marine. I hoped he shared that same sense of honor. A few guys I'd served with turned into mercenaries or security work. They loved the action, but it just didn't pay enough. Sometimes, though, it was the standards they couldn't cut. My gut told me that Leo had no trouble with that. He seemed to be cut from a similar cloth as I was.

"The most likely location is somewhere at the Russian Embassy, however, Mikhalov has been staying at a house in Miramar. We can't establish who the owner is, so it's likely an asset buried in a holding company."

I suppose my face contorted because Leo explained, "Miramar is the fancy-schmancy neighborhood on the northeast side of town. All the well-to-do keep their manses there." His voice shifted into a badly imitated New England accent.

"I guess I hadn't made it that far," I remarked.

"How do we determine which one?" Watkins asked. "I don't think we can hit them both with only three people."

I almost pointed out that Wallace made four, but it seemed ludicrous. The agency doesn't get involved themselves. Too easy to get their shoes smudged. We were lucky Wallace was in the same country as the op.

"We're going to set up surveillance on both," Wallace told him. "I need you and Taylor each to recon around the buildings. Leo, you take the embassy. Aaron, the house in Miramar. I want eyes on all 360 degrees around each building. We'll work on getting inside for a look after that."

"What do I get to do?" I asked.

"You are going to need to get cleaned up," she explained. "You and I will be going to a dinner party tomorrow night at the Russian Embassy."

"Damn!" Leo whistled. "You get to doll up and have some of that nice Russian caviar." He let the word "nice" stretch into nearly three syllables.

"He can have it," Watkins murmured. "Russians can't cook to save their lives."

"But the vodka," Leo reminded him.

"I drink American whiskey," he retorted.

"Tough gig, Gordon," Leo verbally jabbed.

"Someone's got to do it," I replied with a shrug.

It was a natural ribbing that brings a team together. But these guys weren't part of my team. It takes time to bond a unit together. Right now I didn't trust Wallace, and that, in turn, meant I couldn't trust the other two yet.

I wanted to point out that I was more of a point-and-kill type soldier—not the undercover espionage kind. It didn't matter. Right now, I was walking from one lion's den into another.

17

The Russian Embassy seemed much odder than I'd expected. Other than a visit to the American Embassy in Turkey, I'd never stepped foot into a diplomatic house like this. The U.S. one was much bigger, and I figured the Russians would build a comparable one in Cuba, if only as an escape to the Caribbean.

Instead, I stared at an oddly shaped tower with a spire-like structure on top. From the video feed, I couldn't tell if the spire section had an interior or if it was just some strange architectural design.

Today had been a dull day of waiting. While she did not forbid me from leaving the apartment, Wallace pointed out that she hadn't cleared up the mess from yesterday yet. Her emphasis on the word "yet" intended to be the dangling carrot. If I braved the streets, I might find a Cuban officer with a rough description of a murder suspect just ready to drag an American to prison.

Wallace took the one bedroom, and that relegated the three of us to the various corners. At least there was a rolled-up foam mattress and pillow to ease the discomfort.

When I woke, I found Leo and Watkins had left. Within an hour, the first delivery arrived. Wallace never asked for my assistance as she unpacked several monitors and arranged them on the table. After two hours, she turned the screens on and waited. Images filled the screen. On four monitors, I counted twenty-four video feeds of two buildings. It wasn't hard to distinguish the embassy from Mikhalov's mansion. The Cyrillic lettering and Spanish translation on the sign outside the smaller of the two structures gave me the clue I needed to solve that.

Like I said, it was definitely smaller than I expected. Of course, the one embassy I'd been in looked like a sterile office building. At least the Russians used the Spanish architecture to class it up.

After an hour of watching the monitor, another delivery arrived. A three-piece black Armani suit—apparently my dinner attire.

"You'll be my date," Wallace explained at one point. "I'm going as a representative of the Calypso Hotel Group."

I stared at her.

"It's a boutique hotel company with locations all over the Mediterranean and throughout the Caribbean," she explained.

"And I'm your date?" I questioned.

She handed me a piece of paper. I scanned the top. Clayton Trenton.

"What am I, an intern?" I asked, reading the back story for Clayton Trenton. "Don't you think I'm a little old for that?"

"Not an intern," she sighed. "You are the corporate manager for food and beverage. Your stint as a bartender might help with that."

My head shook. "I deserve a raise for this."

Wallace shrugged. "We are in the planning stages of placing a hotel on the northeast part of the island. I've secured the invite under the guise of expanding into Russia and along the Black Sea."

"Sounds like a lot of fun," I commented.

"We mingle, talk about the area, and look for Thompson."

"What do we do if we find him?" I asked. "Take him with us?"

Wallace's head shook. "Not without the documentation."

"He could always deny it," I said. "If someone leaked it, he can tell the press it's a forgery or that they pressured him to sign it."

"It would still be a melee in the press," Wallace told me. "The public doesn't care how true something is nowadays. Whoever draws first blood is the victor, so to speak."

"First blood?" I questioned. "What happens if we can't get both?"

"We have to."

There's a thing about going to battle. Every soldier must bring with him the absolute confidence that he'll walk away a victor. Doubt is deadly. It might be the deadliest thing. It must be a foregone conclusion to the men fighting that they will win.

But the commanders had a different perspective—something that came from experience. They see the overall action instead of the distinct instance. Their position requires them to understand the war matters more than the men. Sure, Marines don't leave anyone behind, but that's just a belief. It is unfortunately not always true. I'd known too many soldiers left behind.

No, the commander should know better. The best laid plans fly out the window when the battle starts. There must be a contingency.

"What happens if we can't?" I asked her again.

Her eyes rolled up to stare at me without lifting her head. "We cross that bridge when we get there, so to speak," she assured me.

As if signaling the end of the discussion, she turned back to the monitors. I carried the Armani suit over and hung it on the door frame between the bedroom and the living room.

I didn't like the tone she had. Wallace had a contingency plan—she just wasn't sharing it. At least not with me.

Wallace sat staring intently at the screens. I didn't like the itchy feeling she gave me in my gut.

"I'm going to get some air," I announced.

Her head lifted to study me. "Are you sure about that?" The unspoken threat that if I didn't remain close, I might fall prey to the Cuban authorities.

"I'll take my chances," I said, walking out the door.

The longer I was around the CIA agent, the more I distrusted her. The paperwork to recall me into the service wasn't a quick job. That would need to go through someone in Washington, and bureaucracy was never that fast. Did she have it all along? Which made me conclude she had something to do with my kidnapping.

When I hit the streets, I paused, letting the tropical sun beam over me. Kotov's guys liberated the cell phone I'd stolen earlier, meaning I couldn't easily reach out to Jay or anyone. I walked east on the sidewalk, wondering what the hell I was going to do and hoping I'd find a phone.

The embassy was still an option. If this op was going the way I thought it would, blowing the whistle on it was a good way of getting out of it. On the other hand, an attempt to find asylum there could blow up in my face. That outcome seemed the most likely, too. Historically, whistle-blowers in the government didn't end up on the right side of history. Or if they did, it was long after it did them any good.

Besides, if I was active duty again, I had orders to follow. So far, those orders weren't unreasonable. While they might violate some diplomacy and a few treaties that I didn't know about, they seemed legit.

However, I'd developed a sixth sense for knowing when a shoe was about to drop. I couldn't see it, but I sensed it floating around above me.

I turned the corner and walked down the block. My eyes swept across the street ahead of me. Somehow, I doubted Wallace would let me get picked up unless she wanted to. Suddenly, it occurred to me I never spoke to the police.

My feet froze in place.

Was this all a setup?

I never saw a cop. Well, I caught a glimpse of the officer looking over the railing from the room.

But was it an actual PNR officer?

The human mind tends to fill in the gaps when it sees fit. During moments of panic or high adrenaline, the details added might be only figments of the subconscious. Often the vision turned out to be nothing more than what the brain expected to see. If someone nudged the subliminal thoughts up, perhaps by dressing like a police officer, then the brain has a lot less work to do.

Dammit. There was no way to be sure—without marching up to a PNR officer and surrendering.

The hotel. The answers would be there. I hoped, at least.

In my mind, I flipped through the data like each fact was an index card.

First, I didn't walk into the Hotel Gran Caribe. Even if I'd just been drugged enough to walk but not remember, I didn't have the wherewithal to check in myself. There shouldn't have been an employee at the hotel who saw me.

Second, I'd never seen an actual cop—not counting the glimpse of one peering out my window.

Third, if it was a setup to get my cooperation, Wallace didn't want undue attention. She'd clean up the body without police intervention. It left the threat of getting caught looming over me.

Fourth, why would she need to recall me to active duty then? She could manipulate me. Even without the paperwork, there was a strong chance I'd help her just to save my hide. Add in the president's son, and anyone who knew my record would expect me to do my patriotic duty.

Her mistake was trying to force it. That alone made me suspicious, but the agency tended to operate in that manner.

It didn't make sense to go overboard to set me up though. My shoulders slumped as I realized I still didn't know anything.

Something had to be at the hotel. It verged on foolish, but I've said many times how much I hate inaction. The defense was never a position I wanted to take either.

Of course, I had no idea where I was in the city in relation to the Hotel Gran Caribe. Plus, I only had a few dollars, or rather pesos, that Kotov's guys didn't take from me.

It might get me to the hotel if I could flag down a cab.

That turned out to take me half a block before a white car with the word "Taxi" across its hood passed me. I let out a whistle, turning as it drove past. The brake lights brightened as the driver stopped.

Keep the conversation to a minimum, Gordon.

"*Hola*," I announced as I climbed into the back seat. "*Hotel Gran Caribe, por favor.*"

"*Sí,*" the driver said. "*¿Como está?*"

"*Bien.*"

I'd exhausted the extent of my Spanish without, I prayed, cluing him into the fact this *gringo* didn't understand anything. My head turned to watch out the window, hoping the driver took the clue to drive in silence. He seemed to understand, as the only noise came from the radio. The singer sang in Spanish, but the melody wasn't bad.

I pulled the wad of pesos out of my pocket. If I listened carefully, I might be able to translate whatever number he spat at me when we stopped. But I didn't want to take too long. I peeled off two hundred-peso notes off. I had no idea what the conversion was, but I hoped that would cover it. It left me with two more hundred-peso notes and three twenty-peso notes. If it sounded like more than two hundred, I'd throw it all at him. I'd have to figure out how to get back later.

The drive took twenty minutes, and I wondered how I was going to overcome the language barrier once I reached the hotel. That was a bridge I'd cross when I got there.

The cab slowed as we drove along the plaza where I'd crossed, wearing only a bed sheet. He turned and stopped in front of the hotel.

Before he said anything, I added a third hundred-peso note to the stack and passed it to him. A second later, I was on the street before he had time to count it.

18

There weren't any police officers waiting in the lobby to arrest me.

I didn't expect there to be any, but it didn't mean my stomach hadn't climbed into my throat just in case. It's odd how I can face a barrage of bullets with no anxiety, but the mere possibility of a police presence unnerved me. Everything came down to training. They built Marines to face battle. There wasn't a lot of training for avoiding being falsely accused.

There wasn't a lot of time yesterday to appreciate the architecture of the hotel. The building was old, but its construction had been solid. The concrete walls, like so many in the islands, could withstand most hurricanes, and given the age of the hotel, it had done just that. Ornate metal light fixtures hung from the ceiling. They had a more rustic appearance than what I considered a chandelier to be, but they projected an elegant ambiance. Like so many buildings in Mexico and Latin America, the Spanish influence was notable with maroon tiles along the adobe-style walls and floor. A fountain in the middle of the lobby offered a soft trickle to soothe the travelers.

Was there some history to that? So many hotels place a fountain as the centerpiece, and I wondered if the point was to offer comfort. Unless one had an urgent need to evacuate their bladder, the babbling brook or dripping rain conveyed a sense of opulence. It must be subliminal, and I reminded myself to research that at some point.

Now, however, wasn't the time.

There were a handful of guests milling about the common area. Behind the front desk, three employees shuffled papers, nodded to whatever guest was in front of them, or answered phones. My ears strained to listen to them talk.

Everything was in Spanish.

It wasn't unreasonable to assume that at least one employee spoke English. At the Tilly Inn, I knew Daniel, our concierge, spoke Spanish, French, and some German. Bilingualism was a selling point for front-facing employees in this industry.

However, I didn't want them to remember talking to an American about anything suspicious. It might send up a red flag, and at the very least, it might be something the police ask about in the future.

"We ate at that little bodega around the corner." The voice wafted across the lobby, and my eyes scanned around. "I thought the beans and rice were amazing."

"Beer wasn't bad either," another voice responded.

"Dell, you never met an ale you didn't like," a third joked.

Laughter erupted, and I spotted the source, a foursome of middle-aged travelers. Two women and two men. Married couples, I assumed. Caucasian, and—judging from their accents—British. I made my way toward them.

"Hello," I greeted.

One woman glanced up at me. "Oh, hello there."

"I'm sorry to intrude. I overheard you guys talking. Is it okay if I slip over for some conversation? My Spanish has been atrocious, and you are a welcome respite to drop back to English."

"But of course," one man said. "Pull up a chair. I'm Dell."

"Ah, the beer lover," I acknowledged, and the foursome chortled.

"Aye, that's true. I'd tell you I appreciate it because of my background. Forty years teaching chemistry to secondary students, but it'd be a lie."

I smiled. "I don't know. That we can take grain and turn it into something as beautiful as beer has always amazed me. Who wants to eat a handful of barley or hops? Not me. But wet it down and let it go sour, and now I'm on board."

"That's true," the other man howled in laughter. "I'm Chip."

His hand extended, and I took it graciously before pulling a chair over to the group.

"Are you all on vacation?" I asked.

"Oh, yes. Well, we are all retired, so it's a holiday with no set end."

"Same here," I explained.

"You seem quite young to be retired."

"I was in the military," I told them. "Now that I'm out, I'm trying to see the islands."

"RAF myself," Chip announced proudly.

"Pilot?" I asked.

The older gentleman shook his head. "Nothing that fancy. Glorified mechanic is what I tell everyone."

"Someone has to keep those birds off the ground," I said, to which he nodded with appreciation.

"Is this your first time in Cuba?" I asked.

"Only for us," Chip's wife admitted. "I'm Phoebe, by the by."

"And I'm Aggie," the other woman introduced herself.

"Chase," I told them. "How are you liking it so far?"

"Oh, it's delightful," Phoebe replied. "The weather has been perfect. While the city seems a little run down, it's been quite nice. The people are so friendly."

"*Simpatico*," Chip interjected with pride.

"He's just showing off," Aggie quipped.

Phoebe laughed. "Chip only knows a little bit of Spanish."

"More than the rest of you," he boasted.

"I bet it's more than me, too," I admitted. "Were you around yesterday?"

"Oh yeah. Some of us slept half the day away," Aggie commented, rolling her eyes toward Dell.

"The beer?" I asked playfully.

"The rum," he corrected. "Too much of it."

"I feel you there, Dell," I offered. "Someone said I missed the excitement yesterday."

"Oh?" Aggie questioned.

"Something about the police being here. One of the bellman thought someone died."

The two women glanced back and forth. "I didn't see anything," Aggie said.

"Me either," Phoebe agreed.

"Well, I didn't either," Chip stated boldly.

"You were passed out until the midafternoon," Phoebe pointed out.

"I still heard nothing."

Everyone laughed again. The old mechanic had a sense of humor, and he wasn't afraid to use it.

"Maybe it was just a rumor," I admitted. "I didn't get in until late."

"I'll have to ask Marcos," Phoebe suggested.

"Who is Marcos?" I wondered aloud.

"That's him," Aggie said, pointing at a tall, thin waiter in a crisp white uniform that would shame many a Naval officer. Marcos was no more than twenty-two, and he was somewhere between boyish good looks and Latino hunk. I wasn't sure how the scale worked, but judging from the two women sitting with me, he produced some steamy thoughts. Aggie and Phoebe both watched the man carrying a tray with four martini glasses.

As the man delivered what appeared to be vodka gimlets to the four retired Brits, Phoebe asked, "Marcos, we heard someone might have died here yesterday?"

The man's brow furrowed. This wasn't a question he expected.

"No, *Señora*. I never heard of anyone dying here."

She glanced around. "I guess it was a rumor," she said, as if she'd solved one of the greatest mysteries.

"Were you working yesterday?" I asked.

"*Sí Señor*. All day."

"There weren't any police around?"

His face shifted as he considered the question. "There are usually one or two who come through every day, but nothing out of the usual."

I nodded with some relief.

"Chase, you need a gimlet too," Aggie announced, motioning for Marcos to bring another. Neither mine nor Marcos's opinion on the matter seemed important.

The server nodded and vanished. I watched the two women admiring the young man as he left. Their husbands didn't appear to notice the affection.

"Hear, hear," Dell blurted out, lifting his glass up.

"We should wait for Chase," Phoebe said.

"No, no," I insisted. "It's always better to toast twice."

I gave her a wink, and she smirked before lifting her glass to clink them with the others.

Marcos wasted no time in returning with another gimlet, which I obligingly clinked with theirs in another toast. Although Dell's and Chip's enthusiasm waned slightly. We sipped the lime-flavored cocktails, and the foursome shared some sights they'd seen in Cuba. They planned to spend another three days here before catching a chartered boat from a small port on the southeastern side of the island to Jamaica. The ninety-mile journey, which they touted as 150 kilometers, would take them a full day. But then they'd be in Montego Bay.

"Montego Bay is a fun city," I assured them. "Be sure to check out the straw market and grab some dinner at the Pork Pit."

"I read about the Pork Pit," Dell told me. "Supposed to be on that list of things to do before you die."

"I don't know about that, but it's quite delicious."

For a brief second, a gloom passed over me as I remembered my last visit to Montego Bay. I pushed the thoughts aside, bringing myself back to the present. Much like inaction, I despised dwelling on the past. Unfortunately, it's a fault nearly all humans have.

"How long are you in Cuba?" Aggie asked.

"Not long," I told her. "I hope to get back to Puerto Rico very soon."

This time, the feeling washing over me was mixed. I wanted to see Gabriella, but the lingering fear that she had somehow been involved in my kidnapping worried me. At the least, I wanted to know if she was involved. And safe. I worried if she hadn't been involved, then my kidnappers might have hurt her while they took me.

"We haven't been there yet," Dell told me. "I don't think that's on our agenda this time."

"It has a lot of beautiful sights to see," I assured him, imagining Gabriella the last time I saw her. She would have been as alluring to Dell and Chip as Marcos seemed to be to their wives.

We talked a little more while I finished my gimlet.

"Do you want another one, Chase?" Dell asked.

"No, I need to get going," I responded, glancing around for Marcos.

"Oh, it's our treat," Phoebe informed me.

"Thank you," I said, taking her hand. I shook everyone's hand before I extricated myself from the group.

Once I was away from my new friends, I moved to the elevator. The old lift reminded me of something from an old black-and-white movie. The door was nothing more than an accordion-style gate that could manually slide open and shut. I stepped inside, pulled the gate shut, and pressed the number four. The panel on the elevator wall was the newest addition to the quaint device. Above me, a whirring sounded, and the lift shuddered as it rose from the first floor.

Without stopping, I passed the second and third floors. When it stopped, there was no ding like some of its more modern siblings. Instead, the elevator jolted to a stop.

On the fourth floor, I took a second to get my bearings. I'd only stepped into the hallway for a second, and I was certain it was down to the right. I laid out a mental map of the building in my head, tracing my route from the entrance to the table of Brits, and then to the elevator. At the same time, I calculated my route backwards from the street to the courtyard. While there was a slight margin for error, I was certain the room I woke up in yesterday was down this hallway.

Number 435. I stood in front of the door and glanced to my left and right. The corridor was empty. My knuckles rapped on the door.

A few seconds later, the door swung open, revealing an Asian woman around my age. She stared at me, and I noticed she was only wearing a robe. For a second, I wondered where the robe was when I woke up yesterday.

"Can I help you?" she asked in an accented voice.

"I'm so sorry," I admitted. "I think I have the wrong room. Have you been here all week?"

Her brow furrowed. "No, I checked in last night."

With a nod, I apologized again. "I think I'm on the wrong floor."

"Okay," she responded, pushing the door closed.

Staring at the number on the door, I was certain this was the correct room. Unless the woman had some weird tendencies, I didn't think there was a corpse in there. And while I didn't know how the PNR investigated things, it seemed unlikely the room would be available to rent the same night they found a body in it.

19

When I stepped onto the curb, I spotted Aaron Watkins across the street. He sat in a beat-up Volkswagen Beetle that had seen better days. The paint job was a combination of dirty yellow and rust, with several patches of metal succumbing to the oxidation. He drummed his fingers on the steering wheel, watching the front entrance.

He offered me a two-finger wave, signaling he wasn't there to watch me. Wallace must have sent him to pick me up.

At this point, I was still pretty confused. While there was no proof, I wondered about the whole setup. Was it staged to put me off-guard? Send me running for help? Even if I made it to the American Embassy, was Wallace going to be there waiting to enlist me?

It hadn't all been faked? The police—possibly. Not the dead girl. No matter what machinations they used to manipulate me, she was definitely there. And she was definitely dead. No, everything about her was real.

How hard is it to get a dead body? Most morgues don't have the best security, and I doubted one in Havana was the most vigilant. If they brought me in without being noticed, a corpse might prove easier. Once I was on the run, they could wrap it up and take it with them.

I'd been too preoccupied with the interaction in the room. I don't know what I expected, but a tourist wasn't it.

"Wallace send you?" I asked when I got into the Volkswagen.

"She figured you might come here."

That wasn't a guarantee. Leo might be sitting outside the American Embassy right now, waiting for me to show up. Wallace would not hedge her bets.

"I was curious," I admitted.

"Can't blame you," Watkins agreed. "I'd be a little more freaked out than you seem to be."

I shrugged.

"What did you find out?" he asked.

"Nothing," I admitted. "I tried to get into the room but couldn't."

It wasn't a lie.

"Think Wallace fixed it for you?" he asked.

Did Wallace fix it? Was there anything to even fix? She mentioned the PNR looking for me, but what if she made that up?

There was no way to trust him any more than I could Wallace. Instead of answering, I asked, "How did you get involved with her?"

"I retired from the Navy about ten years ago. Did some work for Pacific Security for a bit. You know, overseas protection. Even some kidnappings. We'd swoop in and grab the victims from the kidnappers, not the other way around. Started doing some off-book jobs for the company. It gets pretty lucrative."

"How lucrative?"

"This job will net me 50K if we finish this week. If it rolls over to Saturday, it's a hundred. Can't say I'd mind waiting a day for another fifty thousand."

"Damn," I whistled. "I don't do that in a year behind the bar."

"After this, you might score a few gigs."

"I don't need a few," I remarked. "One would keep me in beer and chips for a year or more on the boat."

"Not a bad way to live, huh?" he questioned.

"Before yesterday, I thought it kept me off the grid where no one could find me."

"That's your mistake," Watkins retorted. "Someone is always good enough to find you."

He wasn't wrong. The last two days proved that.

"I'm hoping after this, I can get my ass re-retired," I said.

"Yeah, that was some bullshit," he commiserated. "It's not that I didn't love being a SEAL, but, damn, once I was done, I was done."

I nodded.

"She must've really wanted you," he pointed out.

"That's what I was thinking," I replied, wondering how far she'd have gone to get me. "Why not just ask me? For fifty thousand, I'd consider it."

That might not have been true, but it was at least something to keep him thinking.

"Can't say," he said. "She strikes me as a tough bitch, though. I mean, not tough like she can fight, but more like she's going to get what she wants, and damned anyone who gets in her way."

"What was going to happen if I didn't get in the car with you?" I asked him.

"Nothing," he told me. "I was just supposed to give you a ride back."

He might have been telling the truth. Or it could be a lie. He and Wallace had to know if I didn't want to go, forcing me might get ugly. Watkins seemed formidable, but that didn't mean I couldn't take him. In fact, I'd bet the house that he'd go down in a hand-to-hand with me. That's not to say he wouldn't put the hurt on me, too.

Like I said, it would get ugly. Ugly enough for the cops to show up.

"Where's Leo?" I asked.

He shrugged. "Guess he's back at the flat," Watkins suggested. We drove back through the city.

"You risked a lot to come back here," he said.

"I don't know," I replied. "It might depend on if anyone was actually looking for me."

Watkins's eyes flicked toward the rearview mirror. "What do you mean?"

"I'm not sure yet," I admitted. Luckily, it was the truth, but even if I knew what was going on, the best plan was to never reveal everything.

A nervous energy coursed through me. My fingers twitched with the desire to tap against the door handle. I resisted. If Watkins had any psychological training for interrogating prisoners, a tic like that might be telling. Better to hold it in—keep my cards tight to my chest.

"You never really said," I remarked. "Is this the first time you worked with Wallace or Leo?"

"Taylor, yes," he answered. "I've done three jobs with Wallace before. Although, this is the first one she's run lead on."

"So you trust her?"

Watkins laughed. "She's a company man—I mean, woman. I wouldn't trust her to tie my shoelaces. How many of those agency types you ever meet that you could trust?"

It was a strange bedfellow to cozy up with. I'd trust almost any Marine at first. They'd have to prove themselves untrustworthy. However, whether it was CIA, NSA, the Office of Compliance, or even the IRS, I'd carry a hefty load of distrust for them. Enough that getting out from underneath it would take a near miracle.

I'd seen too many of the shitty outcomes from bureaucratic ops run by the Alphabet Agency du Jour.

"Did you see any sign of Thompson?" I asked, changing the subject.

"Not a peek," he replied. "It was quite a fancy house, though. I kinda hope we go in just so I can scope out the bathrooms."

I turned to stare at him, expecting a smile.

"Seriously, I'm building a house in Virginia," he told me. "It's nice to see how the rich do things."

"I suppose," I remarked, somewhat dumbfounded. "You sure you don't want to check out the dude's pool?"

He chuckled. "No, I already have that planned out. Kidney-shaped with field stone walkways around it and a big outdoor kitchen attached."

"For the kids?"

"Yeah," he responded, and his eyes drifted off the road for a second.

I said nothing else. At fifty thousand a week, it wouldn't take long to build an enormous mansion like that. Who cares how big your shower is? Bigger, as a general rule, was better.

Watkins interrupted the silence after about ten minutes. "I think he's at the house, myself. The document is going to be at the embassy."

"That makes sense," I acknowledged. "I have a feeling that Thompson isn't quite the prisoner Wallace is making him out to be. Better to keep him comfortable in the big house. The files are safer on Russian soil."

"She's going to want the files first," Watkins pointed out.

After the conversation I had with her earlier, I didn't doubt that. My concern was what the contingency plan was going to be. My gut told me I would not like it one bit, though. I hoped I was wrong.

Watkins stopped two streets over from the flat. We hiked back, and I let the sun warm my back. If I'd been out here for much longer, sweat would have formed under my shirt.

"Good, you're back," Wallace greeted us when we came through the door. "Any luck at the hotel?"

"Some," was all I said. I felt Wallace glare at me with a curious look.

"Leo's on his way back," she told us. "I haven't located Thompson yet. However, Mikhalov arrived at the embassy about two hours ago. He just left in his car."

I didn't respond. There wasn't a question to it. Watkins seemed to follow suit.

"Aaron, I'm putting you back on the house tonight. If you spot Thompson, let us know."

"Can I make entry?" he asked.

"We'll make that call when the time comes. Take some cameras with you just in case. If we can get picture and sound, that may help us."

"Do you plan to do the same thing tonight at the embassy?" I asked.

Wallace pulled a small case off the floor. She unzipped the canvas bag, removing several small devices no bigger than a quarter. I counted twelve of them.

"These are audio microphones," she explained. "They'll connect to the embassy's wireless network and transmit audio."

"So bugs," I said.

She nodded. "But state-of-the-art bugs. They are made from a polycarbonate material, so they'll pass through a metal detector. The mics will pick up any sound within a fifty-foot radius, and normal speaking voices up to two hundred feet. They have a resin which allows them to be stuck anywhere. And because they work off the network, they are more difficult to detect with normal sweeping methods."

"We each get six?" I questioned.

Wallace nodded. "We'll work the building together. It's going to be tough getting into the more secure areas, but I'm sure we'll manage."

I wondered how secure an area she was thinking. Wallace handed me one of the coin-sized devices. I spun it around in my fingers, examining it. There was a thin, clear film on one side. I assume it peeled off like a Band-Aid to reveal the sticky side.

"That building is big," I reminded her. "We can't cover it all."

"We'll avoid the office areas where the public has access. The party will be in their ballroom, which connects to the living quarters. I want to cover that area, and hopefully the ambassador's offices.

"What do we do if they catch us?" I asked.

"Don't get caught," she responded.

Watkins snorted, and Wallace cut her eyes to him. "Something funny?"

"It's just the agency way of thinking," he replied. "As if the plan has no flaws."

"Of course it has flaws," she snapped. "But this is an unsanctioned operation. If they catch us, the United States will disavow us. Russia can cart us off to Siberia if they want. So, don't get caught."

"Just so you know," Watkins informed her. "If it comes down to it, I don't go down easy. There will be either one dead Aaron Watkins or a slew of dead Russians between me and the gulag."

20

Against the darkening Caribbean sky, the Russian Embassy glowed from every window. The outline of the building illuminated the sky as the light reflected against the low-hanging clouds creeping over the island.

Wallace arranged for a car to carry us to the party—part of the disguise. We passed through a gate, and the driver announced us. Miranda Cole and Clayton Trenton with the Calypso Hotel Group. The Russian guard checked our names against a list he had. He nodded to the driver and the other guards who stepped out of the vehicle's path to allow us to enter.

"You ready for this?" Wallace asked.

I didn't respond. My fingers felt around the knot of the black bow tie on my neck. I straightened it again, knowing it was probably going to be an obsession if I didn't get a grip on it.

"Just follow my lead," she told me again. She was reminding me that even our cover stories required me to be her subordinate. It was something she seemed to continue to do. Her own tic—a need to assure herself she was in charge and capable.

The car stopped in front of the building, and I climbed out, holding the door open for Wallace. She wanted to go the extra mile, dressing to impress. The long black dress poured around her curves, making it impossible to know for sure where her skin ended and the fabric began. The plunging neckline ended in a V in the middle of her cleavage. Around her neck, she wore an emerald necklace the size of a half-dollar coin with gold skirting around its edges. The bright green jewel glowed against her pearly white skin.

Despite an intense distrust of the woman, I had to admit she was stunning. While she seemed to doubt her leadership capabilities, the lady knew exactly what she looked like. It was probably a fear she had—worrying that her career success might hinge on her appearance rather than her talent.

I offered her my arm, and she hooked her wrist through my elbow.

"Are you ready for this?" I asked her in turn.

"Always," she replied, offering a smile.

A server in a white tuxedo stood sentry with a tray of champagne flutes. He offered one to Wallace, who took it with a smile. The man lifted the tray toward me, and I picked up a glass. The temperature of the glass was warmer than I'd prefer my champagne, but it was, no doubt, a struggle to keep the wine chilled in the tropical night.

Still, I sipped the champagne. The bubbles escaping to the surface tickled my lip.

Another tuxedo-clad gentleman ushered us inside the doors. Bronze stanchions with red velvet rope lined the walkway to the elevator, where another man donning an identical suit as the rest guided us onto the lift.

When we were inside the lift, I leaned toward Wallace, pressing my lips next to her ear. "Elevators often offer a certain privacy," I suggested.

Her eyes scanned the interior and stopped on a small camera eye at the top. She stretched her neck over, kissed my cheek, and responded in a hushed voice, "Already being watched."

The doors opened on the sixth floor, and we found the heart of the party. A string quartet sent notes of what I thought was Vivaldi across the room. However, my classical training remained limited to what played in Missy's office in the basement of the Tilly Inn. I enjoyed the music, but I had never taken the time to study it. Since my musical talents comprised singing three keys off in a shower and playing the radio, it never seemed like something I could fully grasp.

We stepped out, and several eyes followed us as we entered. Really, the eyes followed Wallace. I expected she was going to have her pick of conversations tonight as men vied for her attention and the women narrowed down their competition.

"Why don't we divide and conquer?" Wallace suggested.

"We need to do it with some grace and discretion," I advised her. "We can't just split up. People would wonder what was wrong with me."

"You're supposed to be my employee," she reminded me.

"Don't you know much about Russians?" I asked. "They don't mind a powerful woman, but they'd question a man who wasn't trying to sleep with her."

"Fine," she relented. "How do we do this?"

"Let's make the rounds," I suggested. "Start with the bar."

I led Wallace to an ornate bar built from clear blocks. The theme must have been something to do with crystals. Large quartz nodules decorated the top of the bar. Bottles of Cristal champagne stood sentry around the rocks.

As one would expect from a Russian Embassy party, bottles of vodka adorned the back table. The most prevalent was the Jewel of Russia Black Label, a clear squarish bottle with a round black label.

"Martini?" I asked Wallace.

"Please," she replied, her head twisting slightly so she could examine the partygoers.

I held up two fingers and touched the martini glass on the bar. From his manner, I assumed the bartender was Russian. Since I spoke neither Russian nor Spanish, I opted for the universal signs.

The man poured an ample amount of the Jewel of Russia vodka into a stainless steel shaker. He shook it vigorously before pouring it up into two glasses. He garnished both with a sliver of lemon peel.

When we stepped away with our drinks in hand, a silver-haired man in his fifties stepped up to Wallace. He took her hand, saying something in Russian.

"Miranda Cole," she introduced herself.

The man switched to English, which he spoke clearly and with only a slight accent. It was practiced, something he endeavored to do.

"Yes, with Calypso Hotels. I'm Yura Turchin."

"Of course," Wallace bubbled. "The Minister of Foreign Affairs. Just the man I wanted to talk to. This is my associate, Clayton Trenton."

I bowed my head in greeting and extended my hand. The minister grasped it like a vise, only squeezing for a second. I returned the handshake firmly without some masculine need to one-up his grip. He grinned with satisfaction, which I allowed him to enjoy. The man was a beefy individual, and his strength wasn't just for show. I didn't know what sports Russians took part in, but this man reminded me of some rugby players I'd seen in Kuwait—like they'd run through a brick wall without stopping.

"What do you do, Mr. Trenton?" Turchin asked.

"He's our executive food and beverage director," Wallace interjected.

"Indeed," Turchin mused. "How do you like our choice of vodkas?"

I lifted the glass. "Jewel of Russia is a fine vodka," I told him. "I'm looking forward to pairing it with some of the caviar I saw on the table."

"Excellent," Turchin remarked. "It's a fine beluga. Perhaps you should consider it for your hotels."

"I believe we are already pouring this fine vodka," I lied. "I'm certain the caviar would make an excellent addition—if we can keep the chefs out of it."

Turchin bellowed with laughter. "Every chef we've had here sampled the finest products we brought in, usually at my expense. How they can manage a kitchen confounds me. Imagine what they would do with an entire country?"

"The only oil they'd be importing would be truffle or olive oil," I quipped.

"Indeed," he agreed.

"Minister Turchin," Wallace interrupted, "we should surely talk about expanding our hotels into Russia. Calypso Hotels would be an excellent fit for those seeking a more exclusive holiday."

"Miss Cole, I believe they would," he replied. "We would need to go over the logistics and hurdles you might encounter."

The man drove straight for the meat of the matter—money. How much would it take to build a hotel? What would she be willing to do to ensure a seamless transition?

"The night is young, Minister, but I'll be here all night. Perhaps we can find a private place to discuss the matter."

"Of course, my dear," he readily agreed. Only a fool wouldn't want to find himself in a more private place with a woman like Danielle Wallace, or rather, Miranda Cole. "I must speak to a few people first, but please don't leave without our having talked."

I think if the minister thought he could have gotten away with it, he would have winked. Instead, I saw the twinkle in his blue eyes.

As the man excused himself, I touched Wallace's arm gently. "I'm going to venture toward that caviar," I told her. "Perhaps you could sparkle your way across the room."

"Sparkle?" she remarked with a half-smile.

"Yes," I conceded. "If everyone is going to watch you, then let's make the best of it."

She leaned in, pressing her cheek against mine. It was a simple gesture, but it turned a few heads. The woman had some talent in the field. Although, as Missy likes to remind me, being a woman was training enough.

I intentionally didn't watch her go. First, she wanted me to. If I had, she'd consider it a victory. Second, she needed to continue to appear unencumbered. A longing look by me might be enough to steer others away from her. It was a tricky balance to appear attracted to her while allowing her enough space to mingle.

A server passed near me with a tray of caviar along with other hors d'oeuvres. My free hand scooped up a water cracker with the black caviar spread across it. The delicacy has never been a favorite of mine. As soon as the salty flavor hit my tongue, I remembered why. Salt was a perfectly good seasoning in moderate proportion. Caviar decided to triple down on that adequate amount of salt, and the result reminded me of swallowing a mouthful of seawater.

The martini washed my tongue free of salt, and I noted the vodka paired well with the gourmet treat. However, I'd veer toward the cheese tray after that. I didn't need to remind myself of my opinion of caviar, but if I was playing the part of a food and beverage executive, I needed to act it out.

"How did you like it?" a woman asked me in a soft Russian accent.

Turning to face her, I saw a slender red-haired woman in her early thirties. Her green eyes would have matched Wallace's emerald, and the rosy-white skin almost appeared breakable. The red dress matched her bright red lips.

"It's quite delicious," I remarked.

Her head tilted about ten degrees to the right in disbelief. "Your face said otherwise."

"As caviar goes," I admitted, "this one seemed a little subpar. I would never want to insult our hosts, though."

Her face lit up, showing off a perfectly straight pearly smile. "Oh, I won't tell. However, I have to question your taste. This caviar is exquisite."

My grin widened. "Trust me, my tastes run to the exquisite."

"Indeed," she quipped. "Do tell."

"Fine vodka, French cheese, a decent Bordeaux."

"Have you never had a fine Plechistik? I prefer that to a French red of any variety."

My face didn't flinch, but I did not know what a Plechistik was. Based on her comment, I hoped it was some Russian varietal.

"I can't say that I have," I admitted. "Perhaps I should go find one to sample."

"No need to go far. I know for a fact there is one in the wine cabinet in the study."

My smile spread, and I offered a small bow. "Please, lead the way. I'm never one to avoid a new adventure."

She spun around on the heel of her left red shoe. Her head almost seemed to remain motionless, staring at me as her body pivoted.

This woman was a tiger, and she considered me an antelope. Don't get me wrong, it was the kind of death most men would dream of. It also provided me with an opportunity, not just a carnal one.

"You never told me your name?"

"Lidia," she answered over her shoulder as she led me down a hallway.

We passed a few small clusters of people mingling together. When we reached the end of the hallway, we stepped through a large wooden door. On the other side seemed to be a library. Dark wooden shelves lined three walls, filled with books. The aroma of tobacco lingered in the air and emanated from the leather sofa in the middle of the room. A small bar jutted out from the wall with an array of cognacs, whiskeys, vodkas, and liqueurs. She stepped behind the bar and smiled.

"I seem to have misled you," she admitted. "There isn't any wine here."

With two steps, I leaned on the bar, staring into her green eyes. "What do you have to offer me?" I asked.

Her head tilted with a wry smile before she turned and examined the bottles behind her. My fingers slipped into my pocket and picked out one of the coin-sized microphones. As I pulled it out of my pocket, I peeled the back off and reached across the bar, pressing it to the underside of the mahogany top.

"Do you care for a cognac? Or a sherry?"

"I thought you told me your name was Lidia," I joked.

She beamed as she stepped from behind the bar, holding a bottle of Louis XIII cognac. The bottle runs close to $10,000 in the States. Lidia stepped closer to me, pressing her breasts against me and easing her mouth closer to mine.

"Why don't we try this one?" she breathed as her lips skimmed across mine.

Without moving, I asked, "Don't you need a couple of glasses?"

The Russian woman pulled the top off the bottle and took a swallow directly from it. As she held the cognac in her mouth, she leaned forward and kissed me. She swallowed the liquor, but the sweet aftertaste filled my mouth. Her tongue tickled my own before she pulled back.

"Do you want a drink?" she asked, extending the bottle to me.

I obliged, taking a healthy swig from the crystal decanter. Lidia took the bottle from me and kissed me again. For a split second, I realized she was about to drop a ten-grand bottle of cognac, and the bartender in me caught the glass neck with my right hand. As I continued to kiss her, I set the bottle back on the top of the bar.

"My, you are good with your hands," she remarked.

Without a word, I wrapped my hand around the small of her back and continued to kiss her. Besides the cognac, the woman tasted like cherries.

When the door knob clicked, she stepped back from me just as the wooden door swung inward.

A man and a woman stopped in the doorway. The woman, a young blonde in her twenties, muttered something in Russian. Lidia responded with a waving gesture—the universal "don't worry about it sign."

The couple, obviously seeking a similar hiding place, stepped back out of the library. Lidia's smile returned.

"Perhaps there is someplace more private than here," I suggested.

"Only my bedroom," she offered. "If you don't mind that."

"You live here?" I asked.

"I'm staying here," she told me. "With my husband."

"Your husband?" I questioned. "Who is he?"

Given my relationship with Missy Seine, I didn't normally care about a woman's marital status. However, sometimes, it's better to get those details out first.

"Yura Turchin, the Minister of Foreign Affairs."

21

"That was... how would the Cubans say it? *Divertido*?" Lidia whispered as she fell over on to her back.

"Oh, yes," I agreed. "*Muy divertido.*"

Her manicured fingers still trailed down my chest playfully. She rolled to her side and smiled at me.

I knew the danger of following the wife of the Russian Minister of Foreign Affairs to her, and by default his, bedroom. However, I justified it. After all, if I wanted to plant a bug in the Minister's quarters, I needed a reason to be there. It was a matter of duty.

She kissed me, letting her tongue flick at mine, before she rolled off the bed and padded toward the bathroom. I studied her naked form as she trod across the marble floor. The woman glanced back playfully.

"We'll need to get back to the party," she reminded me as the door closed.

"Of course," I remarked as I slid off the bed and found my tuxedo jacket.

Quickly, I removed one of the listening devices and attached it to the back of the bedside table. While I grabbed my clothes, I scanned the room. The faucet in the bathroom gushed as Lidia freshened up.

I didn't know if I'd have another opportunity to be in the Minister's sanctum, and any chance to search it was going to be now. Most people think they are sneaky when they want to hide something. However, in a secure place like an embassy, there is a presumption of security in place. It makes people complacent.

Nonetheless, secrets are secrets, even from one's colleagues—or spouses. My eyes drifted to the bathroom door.

As I buttoned my shirt, I opened the closet, revealing an expansive walk-in closet complete with drawers, an accordion-style hanger that swung away from the wall, and shoe racks. In the back corner, I saw a small dresser with a lock.

I turned to check the bathroom. The sound of water continued from behind the closed door. I didn't know how much longer she'd be in there, but it wouldn't be much. She left her dress draped across the chair next to the bed, and her shoes sat at the foot of the bed where she'd kicked them off.

Reaching down, I tugged on the drawer—locked.

After closing the drawer, I stepped out of the closet. My pants slipped over my legs, and I tucked the shirt into the waistband as the door opened. The naked Lidia walked out. Her eyes lingered on me.

"You look so much better out of the suit," she remarked.

My face brandished my most charming yet lecherous smile. "I'd say that holds true for you too," I quipped, moving toward her to pull her against me. "I'm in no rush to get back to the party."

She kissed me. "Unfortunately, some consider me the hostess, and I have to check with the caterer about the subpar quality of the caviar."

"I'll show myself out," I suggested. "No point in everyone seeing us return together. It might raise questions."

A wry, playful grin appeared on her lips. "I should hope so."

"Do you mind helping me with this tie before I go?" I asked, lifting the loose bow tie in my hand.

She took the fabric and wrapped it around my neck. "Do you not know how to tie one?" she questioned.

As she looped the ends around each other, I said, "Of course I do, but I like the way your breasts press against me while you do it."

Her green eyes glanced upward at me as she pulled the last bit tight. "I hope you come to more of these events," she told me.

"Trust me, this was far better than the caviar," I said, kissing her and slinging the tuxedo jacket over my shoulder.

When I stepped out of the bedroom, I was in a long corridor. She'd finished dressing and should leave the room in about five minutes. I wanted another look inside the Minister's closet, and now that I'd gained access to the private section of the embassy, it seemed unwise not to take advantage.

The best option was two doors down. Far enough from Lidia for her to not hear me enter the room, and close enough to get back once she left.

It was another bedroom—as large as Lidia's room. However, it had more of a permanent resident feel to the room. Lidia and Yura's room portrayed the aura of temporariness. Like they hadn't set a permanence to it. Sure, everything was in its place, but it didn't seem lived in. More like a second home that was kept clean of the day-to-day drudgery of life.

When in Rome, I might as well eat the pizza. The closet was on the opposite side of the room than Lidia's, but its layout was similar. The light popped on, and I found it was missing the same locked cabinet at the back, despite the matching features. I rifled through the drawers, finding only socks and underwear. The next drawer offered neatly folded shirts. There was no women's clothing in the closet.

In Wallace's notes, I learned the ambassador's wife died three years earlier. Perhaps I'd found his quarters.

Two more drawers garnered nothing. Of course, he was a permanent resident with his own office, I assumed. He'd likely keep any important documents locked away there.

Wallace had a rough sketch of the layout of the embassy, but she'd warned it was old. The CIA knew there had been some renovations last year, but no one verified the new specs. But based on that rough sketch, the ambassador's office was on the ninth floor. Two below me.

Lidia circumvented the security to the private residency. It was something I suspected she'd done more than a few times. My ego didn't mind not being the first man she'd pulled from a party like that. I was just happy to be included.

My guess had been that the woman was mostly stuck. Her husband held a high-powered and visible position in the Russian government. Based on how he eyeballed Wallace, he had his own bevy of side quests. Forced to tag along, Lidia likely never got out of the embassy to do anything. Any of her entourage was likely made up of people who would roll over for someone like Yura Turchin.

When I put everything back in its place, I closed the closet, turning to the bedside tables. There was a novel translated into Russian in the right drawer, along with a bottle of pills. I stuck one of the listening devices to the back of the headboard, and when I was sure I'd given Lidia enough time, I stepped back into the hallway.

Since security regulated entry on to this floor with a keypad in the elevator, it seemed the residents didn't bother to lock the bedroom doors. Again, complacency. It grew tiresome to have to unlock the door every time one came and left in their house. It felt secured, so why bother? I'm sure it wasn't always a conscious thought. Often it just happens a few times, and when nothing goes wrong, it becomes acceptable.

I stepped back into the room where I'd just left that beautiful Russian woman. As I suspected, she'd headed back downstairs. Lidia remade the bed, and while we hadn't done more than tussle the comforter on top, she'd pressed out the wrinkles as if no one had been here.

Before I went into the closet, I checked the bathroom. I hoped to find something I could use to pick the lock, but unfortunately luck wasn't with me. However, I noticed a flat metal shoehorn with the spoon-like curve at the base to ease the heel of one's foot into a tight-fitting shoe.

With the shoehorn in hand, I returned to the closet, closing the door behind me. The light clicked on, and I knelt by the locked drawer.

This wasn't a sophisticated safe. If I wasn't concerned about destroying the face of the drawer, I could pry the drawer open, either splintering the wood or bending the latch. However, I preferred my search to go unnoticed. The flat end of the shoehorn slipped into the crack next to the lock. With some gentle leverage, I pried the drawer down away from the top. The cabinet was old enough that time had worn the edges on the guides, leaving literally a little wiggle room. I rocked the face of the drawer up and down. Each time, I tried to slide the latch back from the catch.

My hand moved the shoehorn up and down as if I was trying to get water from an old dried-up well. After a couple of minutes and countless prying, a small crack bounced off the suits and shoes in the tiny room. I tested the drawer, pulling it open to reveal the broken brass latch. A crease formed just below the hasp in the frame, and the piece folded like a piece of cardboard, making it easy to slide out.

In the drawer, I found a stack of files. Most were in Russian, making them impossible to read. I flipped through them, searching for any English words I might recognize. I paused when I read two words—William Thompson.

It was a signature at the bottom of a page. The rest of the document was indecipherable to me.

I pulled the contents of the folder out. There were six pages.

Before returning the folders, I sifted through the other four files. All total, I counted sixteen pages. I divided them into two stacks before folding them in half. I repeated the folding until each stack was a little thicker than a wallet. Now one fit into my back pocket while the other into the inside pocket of my jacket.

Pleased with myself, I rose and cut the light off. As I stepped back into the bedroom, the door hinges gave a barely perceptible squeal as they swung open. I retreated into the closet, pulling the door closed. It felt like a cheesy episode of Remington Steele, but I pressed myself into the rows of suits in the dark.

Out in the bedroom, voices sounded through the door.

I recognized Wallace and Minister Turchin. Apparently, Turchin had a similar idea as Lidia. Without a doubt, Wallace planned to use the same opportunity I did to drop a bug in the Minister's bedroom.

I guess I sacrificed my body for nothing after all.

While I mused about this, I had no choice but to listen to the sounds of Wallace and Turchin.

Honestly, I thought Lidia and I might have put on a better show, but then David Lee Roth was sure he sounded better than Sammy Hagar.

22

Despite my best efforts, I still noticed how quickly Turchin and Wallace finished. The minister gave her very little time to put herself together before he ushered her out the door. The two spoke solely in Russian, so I did not know what was being said. It wasn't a shock to find out Wallace knew the language. Most agents had a grasp of other languages before the CIA recruited them. In fact, the CIA had a reputation for searching out bright, shining linguistic and mathematic stars while they were still studying in college. Hidden in the dark closet, I wondered if that was how Wallace found her career.

I imagined he was telling her how important it was he get back to the party. At least one of them visited the bathroom for a minute, but judging from the sound, the door never closed. That seemed like something a man like Turchin would do. No couth whatsoever.

Once they were gone, I crept out of the closet. For a second, I considered taking the bug I'd planted, assuming Wallace took the time to drop one as well. However, given that Turchin didn't leave her side, I wasn't positive she'd succeeded in it. Besides, it was her own fault if she didn't set out a better strategy.

In the hallway, I checked out the last two rooms. Both appeared to be guest rooms. The first had no personal items. It looked like a vacant hotel room waiting for its next guest. The second had a small suitcase and three suits in the closet. All the suits were Italian, but one had a dry-cleaning tag from a shop in Bethesda, Maryland. The luggage only contained a few pairs of boxers and white undershirts.

Someone neatly made the bed, making it hard to tell if the staff cleaned up or no one had slept here. When I checked the bathroom, I found a toothbrush and razor. The soap in the shower was dry. So was the toothbrush. No one had used either today.

I slipped back out into the hallway and made my way toward the elevator. The door opened up, and I stepped back as a brutish man walked out of the lift. I pressed myself into an alcove, waiting for the man to pass. Thankfully, he was walking the other way down the corridor.

Stepping out of the corner, I squeezed past the closing doors of the elevator without drawing his attention. I pressed the ninth floor. The lift descended, and when it opened, two men stared at me from the hallway—guards.

The closest guard stared at me for a full second before saying something in Russian.

"*No comprendo*," I replied in Spanish. "*Seis?*"

The guard rolled his eyes, stepped into the elevator, and pressed the six button. I lifted my hands apologetically, moving away from the door as they slid shut.

So much for getting into the offices.

The doors opened on six. The sounds of the party drifted through the building. I moved back into the room. Lidia, leaning into another gentleman near the bar, laughed flirtatiously. I crossed to a table of food, where I found some roasted pork with some diced pineapple on a sliced piece of toasted baguette.

A hand touched the small of my back. "Where have you been?" Wallace whispered into my ear.

I leaned into her with a slight grin. "Locked in a closet while you and Turchin wrestled awkwardly on the bed.

Her eyes widened.

"Don't worry," I remarked. "It felt like you were performing at your best. It's not your fault your sparring partner wasn't prepared to parry."

Wallace grunted. "You were upstairs?"

I nodded, taking a piece of the pork appetizer and putting it in her mouth. "Yes, I made it to the library, too. As well as the other bedrooms."

"How did you get up there?" she asked.

I smiled again.

"Ugh, whatever. Did you find anything else?"

I handed her the dry-cleaning tag from Bethesda. She studied it. "You think it's Thompson's?"

My shoulders shrugged. "I don't think anyone's stayed in the room. At least, in the last twenty-four hours."

"I couldn't get Turchin to take me to the offices," she whispered.

"No point," I warned her. "They have guards on the ninth floor waiting for wayward guests."

"I'd like to get up there and drop a bug," she said.

"Unless you plan to take out the guards, it ain't happening," I told her.

She sighed. "Fine. Maybe I'll take a run at the ambassador."

I stared at her.

"Not like that," she murmured. "The man might be interested in a career change. I don't believe diplomacy pays as well as the hospitality industry."

"Good luck with that," I told her. "He doesn't have a wife or family. That might limit his aspirations."

"I'm pretty convincing," she insisted.

My hand swooped down for another pork toast thing. My stomach was warning me that all my earlier exertion required some refueling. Plus, the damn things were so tasty.

Wallace vanished into the crowd, and I eased my way around the room, searching out any conversations in English. It took passing three groups until I heard an Australian accent talking about a football match last night.

I moved into the group of four and introduced myself. The voice I heard belonged to the chief of staff for the Australian ambassador.

"Clive Sanders," he said, extending his hand. "Are you new to Havana?"

"A little," I explained honestly. "We are about to build a new resort on the north shore."

My brain hiccupped as I attempted to remember the exact location of the proposed hotel. Hopefully, it wouldn't come up.

"Do you have any resorts in Australia?" he asked me.

Again, not knowing the answer, I made it up. "Not yet," I told him. "However, I do believe that may be on our ten-year master plan. We'd like to expand to all the continents."

"All of them?" one of the other men in the group asked.

"Well, all the consequential ones," I corrected. "Although, I imagine there might be a good reception from people wishing to visit Antarctica in luxury."

"For sure there are," Clive agreed. "But the logistics, man. That would be a bloody nightmare."

"Absolutely," the other man replied. "There'd need to be an airstrip or port of some sort. Construction could be done, but the cost. Goodness. It would be a fortune."

"But we could charge accordingly," I pointed out. "If people will go to a hotel in space as some are looking to develop, why not Antarctica?"

"Well, sign me up," Clive announced. "I'd love to sleep with a bloody penguin."

The skinny woman who hadn't spoken yet blurted out, "Clive, you'd sleep with anything."

The chief of staff blushed slightly. "Not what I meant," he scolded her.

I interjected, "Don't worry, there won't be a petting zoo."

Everyone chuckled.

"It was nice meeting you all," I said as I moved away from the crowd.

By now, I'd enjoyed all the partying and socializing that I could stand. I moved to the bar for another martini. Once I sipped some of the ice-cold vodka, I moved off to the corner and watched the party.

Most of the time, I spent my days alone. When I'm docked at the Tilly, I'll spend it with a select group of people. Large crowds often overstimulate me. Not always a bad thing, but when I'm sitting in enemy territory, my senses work overtime. I'd counted four men and two women in the crowd who could be dangerous. The problem was that didn't mean they were. Likely, some of them spotted me too. People who are battle-worn carry themselves differently.

"You are hiding," Lidia commented as she sidled up to me.

"Once the party has peaked, it's tough to focus on the chitchat."

"Peaked, huh?" she remarked with a sparkle in her eye.

"Well, it will not get any better than that, will it?" I responded.

She smiled back at me. Ice tinkled in her empty glass.

"Do you need another drink?" I asked.

"Please," she replied. "Vodka and grapefruit juice. The one bonus to being here is the fresh juice. I'd have to settle for soda water in Moscow."

"They don't have juice in Russia?" I asked.

"Of course they do, but it's like drinking juice in—what's the state with Kevin Costner? Montana?"

I chuckled. "Depends on which Kevin Costner, I think." I took the glass from her hand and left her in the corner.

When I returned with her drink and fresh martini for myself, I found her finishing the rest of my first drink. My eyebrow cocked up.

"These events should not be endured without a constant influx of inebriation."

As I handed her the vodka and grapefruit juice, I replied, "Glad I refreshed mine, too."

"I knew you were an intelligent man."

We clinked our glasses together.

"I take it you don't love it here?" I asked.

"Oh, at least it's not covered in snow," she replied. "But I wish it were more cosmopolitan."

"Old Yura doesn't take you out much?"

She laughed, "Old Yura doesn't do much, period. Just as well, though. He's like a wet pig, rooting around and grunting. Best thing he could do is wander into a butcher's shop."

The visual hung in my mind for a few seconds as I envisioned Wallace wrestling a large pink pig.

"Do you get out of here ever?" I questioned.

"Into town?" she asked. Without waiting for an answer, she offered only a nonchalant shrug. "Sometimes I go to the beach or for lunch."

"Without the pig?"

She smirked. "Oh, Yura would never be caught at the beach, and he finds the food around here to be more than his delicate stomach can handle."

"That kinda deflates your pig analogy," I told her.

She stared at me questioningly.

I continued, "Pigs are omnivorous. They eat anything."

She sighed. "I think you are missing the point."

"How about you get out and meet me for lunch tomorrow?" I suggested.

"Just lunch?"

"How about I promise you that nothing is just lunch?"

"Do you know La Guarida?" she asked me.

"I'm sure I can find it," I promised her.

"Let's do a late lunch," she offered. "Around one. They have excellent cocktails there."

"It can't do to face life uninebriated," I pointed out.

She took a sip of her vodka and grapefruit juice. "No, it can't," she agreed.

When she finished her cocktail, she leaned in, pressed her cheek to mine, and whispered, "You have been a delight in what would have been a rather drab event."

"I assure you, the delight was as much mine."

The emerald eyes sparkled back at me.

An odd sensation filled the room, like a rain cloud pressing across a sunny sky. I turned to see a large man with his own entourage move through the party. He was wearing a black suit. When he walked, he held a straight path, expecting anyone in his trajectory to move. The man could have been an asteroid or a comet, set on a direct course. If one wanted to avoid the collision, it was up to them to move out of his way.

"Who is that?" I asked.

"That is Valeri Mikhalov," Lidia murmured. "He'll be the death of us all."

My eyes shifted from the Russian to the man tagging along like a remora—William Thompson. He didn't act like he was a prisoner.

23

"This isn't a vacation, you realize?" Wallace complained. "You don't get some allowance to take a date out to lunch."

"It's not just any date," I told her. "Lidia Turchina is the unhappily married wife of your grunting minister."

She rolled her eyes at me. "How is that going to help us?"

"She will not be as tight-lipped as a Russian official. And she knows enough to distrust Mikhalov. I think she'll happily spill the dirt on her husband and Mikhalov, if for no other reason than spite."

Wallace sighed. She recognized I was right. After all, the CIA wrote handbooks on how to turn family members based on things like spite. Wallace just didn't like that it had been my idea. Right now, we were sitting on seven bugs in the embassy. Two she duplicated on top of mine in Turchin's room and the library. While I at least added the ambassador's room and the room we suspected had been Thompson's, she'd only dropped one more in the main room of the party.

Last night injured her pride, and she needed a win. I didn't share the documents I found in Turchin's room. I explained I'd let Lidia leave before me under the guise of discreetly returning to the party. When she and Turchin arrived, I told her I ducked into the closet and waited them out.

I still didn't trust the woman, and I had no intention of giving her anything until I learned what she intended to do. Especially after seeing Thompson strolling around unencumbered.

"You see, I'm right," I pressed.

"Yes," she conceded. "What's your plan?"

"She said last night that Mikhalov would be the death of them all. I think she both doesn't trust him and fears him."

"Would she know what he and Turchin might be up to?" Wallace asked.

"The woman strikes me as quite intelligent. You met her husband—is he the type to realize that?"

Wallace shook her head. "No, he's certain no one is smarter than him."

I nodded. That type filled the ranks of all governments. They were dangerous because they were often the easiest to manipulate.

"She'll know Turchin's secrets," I promised. "The woman is basically alone and miserable. I bet no one says anything in that embassy that she doesn't hear."

"Like where we can find William Thompson?" she questioned.

"He seemed in pretty good health last night," I told her again.

"Are you sure it was him?" she also asked me again. According to Wallace, she missed the parade of Mikhalov and his minions. I wasn't sure how that was possible. The man's presence sucked the energy from the room like a vacuum.

"I promise."

We were alone in the apartment. Wallace stationed Leo and Watkins on both of their respective targets.

Wallace scoured the video feeds of the embassy, searching for Thompson coming out. But even with the exact time, the best she could see was a black SUV pulling up to the front. Whoever got into the vehicle remained hidden by the car itself.

Watkins, posted on Mikhalov's house, hoped to spot the same SUV. So far, he'd seen nothing.

"We haven't determined where they went," Wallace moaned.

"Exactly why I need to meet Lidia," I explained. "Unless you think you can get something from the bugs."

It wasn't a jab at her. Surveillance is a long-winded project, and it takes a special person to sit by the receiver listening to hours of droning silence for the one minute of conversation that usually amounts to "What's for dinner?" It's not something I'm cut out for.

Wallace breathed in exasperation. "Fine."

She walked to a bag and retrieved a stack of pesos. "This should be enough," she told me.

"Lidia is a diplomat's wife," I reminded her. "She has better tastes than the Cuban equivalent of McDonald's."

"I think it's just McDonald's," she said, but she peeled another small stack off. "Make it worth my while."

"Whatever, this is Uncle Sam's money. You don't need to worry about how much is there."

Her hands moved to her hips. "I do have to account for it."

"Yeah, call it the price of being a spy," I quipped. "I never saw James Bond fill out an expense report."

She groaned.

"I'll need a car," I said.

"Take a damned taxi," she snapped.

I lowered my head and backed out of the apartment. As soon as the door shut, I ran down the stairs and onto the sidewalk. When the first cab rolled by, I flagged them down.

"¿Hablas inglés?"

"Yes," the man replied. "A little."

"How much to go to La Guarida?" I asked him.

"Four hundred fifty pesos."

I peeled off a 500-peso bill and handed it to him. "Do you have a cellphone?"

"*Sí.*"

Another 500-peso bill passed to him. "May I use it to make a collect call?"

He took the bill and stared at me in the mirror. "Collect?"

"To the United States," I explained. "But I'll pay for it."

He shook his head. I glanced at the wad of money in my hand. It was still more than enough for lunch, so I pulled another bill off, holding it up for him to see in the rearview mirror.

"Okay," he agreed, passing his phone back and taking the 500 pesos. I guessed this call was costing me about sixty to seventy bucks before I dialed.

When I punched in the number, I waited until an operator came on the line. After giving her my name, I waited until Jay answered.

"I need to make this fast," I told him. "Can you reach out to Shaw? You remember Code 688?"

"Code 688? Wait, isn't that the recall one?"

"Yes, an agent with the CIA gave me my active-duty paperwork."

"Shit, Flash, what the actual hell?" Jay whistled into the phone.

"Don't get me started."

"What does this have to do with your current situation? Have you figured out how you got to Cuba?"

"Not yet," I told him. "Find Shaw. The agent's name is Danielle Wallace. She mentioned talking to Shaw directly. I'd like to determine if it's legitimate."

"I'll try, but you know her. You're her favorite, and even you can't get through to her."

"See what you can find out about Wallace through whatever means you can," I told him, adding, "Please."

"Can you say what she wants you to do?"

"Officially, no," I replied. "But since I don't give a shit, she says the Russians here are holding William Thompson captive.

There's more to it, but it gets too convoluted to share right now." My eyes cut up to the driver, who was obviously listening. Hopefully, his English wasn't strong enough to understand what I was saying.

"Dang!" Jay exclaimed.

"There are two other guys on the team. Mercs. Guy named Leo Taylor. He was Marine Recon too. A sniper."

"My kind of fella," Jay quipped.

"Yeah, he said he recognized your name. He's got us beat by about ten years—give or take a few. Other guy is a former SEAL. Aaron Watkins."

"I'll see what I can get. Just remember those wheels don't turn too fast," Jay warned.

"Listen, I'm not sure when I can call you again. I have one more favor, though," I asked.

"What is it?"

"You don't have to do it," I assured him.

The man on the other end groaned. "What is it?"

"Scar."

I could hear him breathing. "Velasquez?"

"He might have some contacts here. I'm feeling a little alone out here."

"Chase, that's climbing into bed with the devil."

I knew Jay would feel that way. Scar was a nickname I'd given Esteban Velasquez several years ago. He was the head enforcer for the Andale Cartel, led by Julio Moreno. Moreno, a Cuban national, grew his drug empire into one of the largest in the Southeast United States. While I considered myself on the other side of the line from Scar and Moreno, there was an odd mutual trust and respect we'd developed. Not that either of them wouldn't gut me and string me up if it benefited them. However, I'd proved early on that I wasn't easy to kill.

Jay's worries were justified. On more than one occasion, Moreno offered me employment. He performed favors for me in the hopes I'd find myself obliged to help him. What Moreno wanted would never happen. While I understood the dynamic between us, I had a certain code I wouldn't violate for a drug dealer, no matter how personable he was.

But if he had someone in Cuba, I wasn't willing to ignore it. The deal with Wallace continued to taste bitter to me, and if I either could get out from under the order to return to active duty or find proof it wasn't legitimate, I wanted to get off the island and at least back to Florida. A man like Moreno or Scar might have the connection to help me do that. I'd cross whatever bridges I had to when they got to me.

"Jay, I get it," I agreed. "I don't plan to sell my soul or anything. It would just be nice to have a backup plan in motion."

He sighed again. "No promises. It better be a last resort."

"Thanks, Jay. I'll try to call again. Hopefully, you'll have some news for me."

We hung up, and I handed the phone back to the driver.

"Is there a post office around here?"

"*Sí.*"

Five minutes later, the driver pulled in front of a small one-story building that could have been an old garage from the outside. I didn't see any signs indicating it was a post office, or that mail had ever passed through the building.

"Is this it?"

The driver nodded.

"Wait right here, please," I said.

"*Sí.*"

Inside, there was a small counter with supplies. It felt more like the back room of a dry cleaner who didn't actually do dry cleaning. The kind of place where one could bet on a cockfight. I found a large envelope among the supplies being sold. The pages I took from Turchin's closet slid into the envelope. I addressed it to Jay with the Tilly Inn's address. I didn't want it to go directly to him. While I didn't expect the mail to be that fast, I wanted some security for Jay.

The postage cost me another 200 pesos. Luckily, the clerk didn't strike up a conversation. The surly clerk seemed miserable in his job, and there was no intention of befriending anyone who had the gall to mail something.

Back outside, I was relieved the cabbie hadn't taken my fare and left me here. He drove me another fifteen minutes to a three-story building. I ascended the steps to a terrace overlooking the harbor. At a table near the edge, Lidia sat facing the entrance. Two glasses of white wine sat at each place, and an order of steak carpaccio sat in front of her. The tiny fork in her hand picking at the meat. She offered me a soft smile.

24

"William Thompson was at the embassy," I told Wallace and Leo when I got back to the apartment.

It was late in the afternoon, and I wasn't in a rush to head back to the flat. I enjoyed being out of sight of Wallace, although it wouldn't surprise me if she'd sicced Watkins or Leo on me to keep tabs on my movements. I hadn't seen a tail, but both of them had the training to hide it.

Since I'd sprung the lunch on Wallace after both of them left, I assumed neither had time to double back and follow me. If they'd done anything, it would be to pick me up at the restaurant. If that was the case, they got to follow along as I rode with Lidia to the Hotel Inglaterra, where she and I spent the next few hours. I'd considered taking her back to the Hotel Gran Caribe, but at some point, I might push my luck.

"You said he left during the party," Wallace muttered.

"First, that was yesterday. He is entitled to come back if he wants. However, second, I said 'was.' Past tense." Nothing sounded more passive-aggressive than pedanticism.

Wallace folded her arms. Her annoyance gleaming on her face.

"He left with Mikhalov," I explained. "Lidia said he'd been at the embassy for the past week, but before the party, Mikhalov and Turchin talked about moving him to the mansion."

"Why?"

"She didn't say," I told them.

"Think she knew?" Leo asked.

I pursed my lips and shrugged. "Who knows? The lady is quick, though. And boy, does she hate Russia."

Wallace's eyes lit up. "Really."

"No, after this we leave her out of it," I demanded, realizing I'd said too much.

"Forget about it, Chase," Leo warned. "You done baited the hook."

I locked eyes with Wallace. "Don't try and recruit her," I warned.

"I can't make that promise, Lieutenant," she responded.

If anyone could handle themselves, it was Lidia. She was smart and capable. I'd like to pretend I'd manipulated her today into spilling all the beans, but the truth varied. She played along as I milked her for information, but the manner she fed it to me was meticulous. Lidia seemed to know my intentions, and while I didn't share any of that with Wallace, I wondered what that meant. Was she stringing me along with false info?

I doubted that.

No, Lidia might have been stringing me along for something, but I bet she intended to make an offer. The woman wanted out of not only her marriage but also the country. Whether that was just Cuba or Russia too was yet to be determined.

"We'll go in tonight," Wallace stated. "Gordon, you and Watkins will enter the mansion, find Thompson and the document, and get out."

"Just because Thompson is there doesn't mean the file is," I pointed out, wondering if I'd already taken care of that problem.

"Once we have Thompson, he can either point us to the file, or we can enlist Lidia Turchina to find it."

I let a long, hot breath out of my nostrils. "I told you we would not involve her."

"That isn't something you get to decide, Lieutenant."

The way she continued to use my rank derisively annoyed me. Wallace didn't understand my relationship to the service, and she prodded me with the rank as a reminder I was under her chain of command. Determined to prove to me she controlled everything, she tried reminding me how she'd pulled me back.

It didn't work like that. I respected the Corps more than I did most things. My rank wasn't a barb in my side—even in my retirement. When I spoke to General Shaw, she always referred to me as "Lieutenant." From my former commanding officer, it was a sign of respect. A title that I'd earned through years of dedication and hard work.

When Wallace attempted to use it to deflate me, she didn't understand I wasn't ashamed of it. If anything, she was reminding me of a duty I'd sworn. An oath I'd keep even if I wasn't on active duty. I suspected Danielle Wallace of attempting to subvert the thing I swore to protect.

All she was doing was reminding me that if she turned out to be manipulating me, I'd do exactly what my rank demanded of me.

For now, I waited.

"We go in tonight," I said. "What about Leo?"

"He'll cover your retreat," she informed me. "He's also going to be your eyes. Between him on the ground and me with the cameras, we'll have eyes all over the house."

"Just not inside," I pointed out.

"We got you, man," Leo suggested.

"I assume since I'm the only ranking military officer here, I'll be on point," I asked.

Wallace glared at me. If she wanted to remind me I was an officer, I'd remind her of the chain of command.

Leo smirked.

"Yes, however, I cannot stress enough that if they catch you, the United States Government will disavow you."

"Yeah, yeah, yeah," I muttered. "They can pull me back without a thought, but if I'm in a jam, it's 'fuck you, Gordon.'"

"Seems like you summed up the government perfectly," Leo remarked.

"While you stare at your shows, Leo and I are going to recon," I told her.

She waved me off, annoyed with me.

Leo trailed me out of the flat. "You trying to piss her off?" he asked as we took the stairs down to the ground floor.

"I don't trust her," I told him bluntly.

"Don't blame you," he remarked somewhat sympathetically.

"How often have you worked with her?" I asked.

"First time," he said. "She reached out to me through a guy I've done some work with."

"Thoughts?"

"I've dealt with worse," Leo explained. "At least she's something to look at. Seems to me she's only got eyes for you, though."

"She can keep them to herself," I said.

"C'mon, man. She's a hottie," Leo argued.

"True, but she's relying too much on it. She'd be just as capable though, if she'd lean into her intelligence."

"I don't know, man. The two of you are dancing around like bumblebees."

My eyebrow lifted as we reached the Volkswagen. "Bumblebees?"

Leo opened the driver's door. "Bumblebees," he repeated. "They fly around, just bumping into each other and landing on flowers until they decide to mate."

I shook my head. "Do you understand how bumblebees procreate?" I asked him.

"Pretty sure I saw a BBC documentary."

"Oh, I'm sorry," I announced. "I didn't realize that. From now on, I'll defer to your expertise."

"Everyone should," he quipped with a slight smile.

He weaved through the small Havana side streets. In twenty minutes, we parked a block over from Mikhalov's house. The neighborhood was a crass contrast from most of Havana. Opulent homes with breathtaking views over the sea. While a cliff wall lifted the mansions from beachfront to ocean view, it didn't diminish the appeal.

Leo led me up a steep hill across from the mansion. The arduous, rocky terrain prohibited construction, but it made a nice cover for Leo to watch the home. As we approached the top, a figure rose, pointing a Glock 19 directly at us.

"Slow your roll, hoss," Leo blurted out, and Watkins lowered his weapon.

"What are you two doing here?" the SEAL asked.

"Wallace wants to go into the house tonight and retrieve Thompson," Leo explained.

"Who's going in?" Watkins asked, eying me as if he already knew.

"You and Chase."

He nodded. "What time?"

"If I had my choice," I suggested, "it would be about four in the morning."

Watkins nodded. "Perfect. Everyone is nice and asleep by then."

"Yeah, and anyone on guard duty is getting bored and lax," I added.

"Is Wallace good with that?" he questioned.

"She's going to be," I told him. "We are putting our necks on the line."

The man shrugged.

I asked, "You've been watching. What are the best points of ingress?"

"That's easy," he said with a smile. "Because of the hills, they built a drainage tunnel right under the property."

His fingers pointed toward the east. "There is a drain just there. We drop through the hole and walk through the tunnel. There is a drain right next to the house."

The spot he indicated was just on the other side of the hedge from the blue water of the swimming pool. The line of bushes isolated the pool deck from the rest of the property.

"We should be able to cut across the deck and enter the house there. There are two doors leading to the pool. Easily breached."

I nodded. "What do we need?"

"The openings have metal rebar blocking them. Gotta cut through that. It's not a problem—small torch will do the job quietly. Otherwise, it's some climbing gear to get down and climb back out."

"Have you scouted them already, Aaron?" I asked.

He grinned. "Of course. It's an easy jaunt. If you don't mind the crocodiles."

I glanced at him.

"I don't think they'll be a problem," he joked.

"Total time to enter the drain and get back out?" I asked.

"Half an hour."

"Exit strategy?" I questioned.

"Same way if we're lucky," Watkins said. "If not, we can jump off the cliff."

"Let's put a pin in that one, unless you have a strategy for not hitting the rocks at the bottom."

Watkins shrugged.

"Any idea where the president's son is inside the house?"

He shook his head. "No clue. We have a schematic of the house in the flat. I know there are six bedrooms upstairs. Only one on the first level."

"We can assume he is upstairs," I pointed out.

"My thoughts exactly."

"How many guards does Mikhalov have?"

Watkins answered, "I've counted eight plus whoever is in the SUV. I'd say ten is a good round number."

"I'm sure Wallace would like us to get in and out with no casualties," I said.

"Sure," Watkins agreed in a singsong voice. "I'd like to have one of those four-hour erections, too."

Leo chuckled. "Damned squids never think shit through."

"Oh, I've thought that all the way through. I could work my way through half of Miami."

"Which half?" I asked wryly.

Leo laughed.

25

Night time in the Caribbean was magical. Even in some of the more populated areas, the stars glowed brighter than in South Florida, where the constant building and expanding created more light pollution every year. The ocean breeze after dark pushed the heat from the day away, usually bringing the smell of salt and, strangely, whatever flowers were blooming at the time. When I felt the air move across my face, flickering the strands of hair I'd let grow longer than normal, it left me longing to making an overnight crossing in *Carina*.

Tonight, I wasn't on board my sailboat, listening to the waves lap against the hull. Instead, I stood in dark combat fatigues with a coiled rope over my right shoulder. Watkins hunched over the drain, cutting the remaining bars.

He explained when he scouted the pipe, he'd trailed back half a mile to find an opening where the metal bars were already loose enough to fit his frame. Even if we'd entered that opening, he'd need to cut it open wide enough for us to fit easily. If we were going to cut anyway, we might as well save the half-mile hike through the mildewed and slimy drain.

While he cut, I scanned the sea behind Mikhalov's house. Lights from boats anchored offshore shone like stars. The array of boats varied from small fishing piroques to a couple of large yachts. The closest was easily seventy to eighty feet long. In the dark, I couldn't distinguish from this distance its actual size.

The captain had anchored only a half mile from shore. Perhaps the owners wanted to stare at the big houses or flaunt their big boat. It seemed somewhat childish. The people living up here could afford a yacht, and someone with a yacht like that could obviously afford a house like Mikhalov's. People are strange though, and I doubt I'll ever understand them.

The whoosh of the handheld torch was almost drowned out by the night breeze. When the last bar broke free, three clinks echoed out of the hole as the metal dropped into the darkness and bounced around the pipe.

Leo's voice in my ear said, "The sea is calm." His signal that there was no movement around the house.

Once he gave us the cue, Watkins signaled the "go ahead," and I uncoiled the rope from my shoulder. With a quick knot, I secured the end around the thick trunk of a palm tree. Watkins dropped three glow sticks into the hole. The loose end of the rope fell into the hole, and I slid down into the darkness. The glow rods illuminated the area at the bottom of the pipe. They cast a shadowy glow about fifteen feet in every direction.

I jerked the rope twice and stepped out of the way. Watkins descended the rope, splashing into the puddles at the bottom.

Both of us had night vision goggles on top of our heads. I lowered the lenses over my eyes, and the surrounding view glowed green. Watkins took the lead, moving down the tunnel. Each of us carried Beretta SC70s, which Watkins supplied. The small carbine machine guns were lightweight, holding thirty rounds. I wasn't sure where the SEAL found the guns, since I hadn't seen them lying around the flat. He either had a stash of equipment or an excellent source. Probably both.

It's the part of mercenary work that doesn't appeal to me. I have a satisfactory armory in South Florida, and if I added what Jay kept at his house, I could arm a small militia. However, mercs move all around the world. It requires a substantial network to get what they need. I don't have the energy to maintain that kind of inventory.

I prefer to expend my energy diving or surfing. It seems like far more work, and while the job was more than profitable, given what he told me he was making, I like a more simple life.

We moved along the drainage pipe. The only sound was the splashing of our feet in the water on the floor. When we reached our egress, we paused for Watkins to remove a coil of rope from his shoulder. On one end of the rope was a lead weight. The opening allowed a dim beam of light in the pitch-black tunnel. Watkins raised his goggles and tossed the lead weight up at the grate over us. The first throw failed, dropping the lead anchor back through the same opening. He threw it again. This time the rope fell over the bar, dropping to the bottom.

I signaled for him to go up, and he passed me his pack. Without testing the bars, we wanted the first ascent to be as light as possible. He scaled up the rope and attached a clip to two bars. He hung from what amounted to a sling from the metal grate. The whoosh of flame echoed through the dark as he ignited the torch.

As Watkins cut at the metal bars in the middle of the drain, I stepped back out of the path of falling magma. The sound of the torch ceased after three minutes. He made a clicking sound before he dropped the small tank. I caught it before it clanged against the pipe.

"Goodyear, what's the status?" I asked Leo in the throat mic.

"Weather's clear," he announced as Watkins shimmied through the opening, pulling the loose rope with him. Nearly a minute passed before the end of the rope dropped back into the hole.

I secured his pack to the rope and tugged twice. The bundle ascended slowly as he reeled the gear up. Once he'd removed the rope from his pack, the loose end of line fell through the opening again. Hand over hand, I pulled my weight up the line until my head breached the opening. While I squeezed through the gap, Watkins stood sentry over the hole.

Once in the open air, I checked the Beretta and dropped the night vision goggles. The hedge around the pool deck was thick, and we skirted along the edge until we found an overlap between two plants. The branches of each hedge entwined with the other, but since they weren't connected, we could push through slowly.

"I've lost you in the fog," Leo said in our ears. We were out of his line of sight. From here we wouldn't have his sniper rifle as back-up.

"We have our running lights," I acknowledged, signaling him we were proceeding.

In the lead, I pushed through the hedge and emerged on the other side. My night-vision visor illuminated the pool and scattered chaises in a green aura. When we studied the blueprints, we all highlighted the best locations for security cameras. From where I stood, I located the one all three of us guessed correctly. Right above the far corner. It was an obvious choice based on the wiring of the house. That camera could get the most coverage without stretching too much cable. It was typical.

Even if the budget for construction is wide open, the contractor would operate like he always did. That generally meant he was efficient or greedy. If it was the former, he'd want to keep the wiring to a minimum in order to keep costs down or reduce a loss of integrity in either power or data. The longer a stretch of cable ran, the more likely there could be a problem along the way. No one wants to rip out entire walls to find a break in the line.

On the other hand, if the contractor was greedy, then he might charge for longer runs and still cut them down during installation. The irony was that the reasons were different, but the result was the same. Either way, we were correct in our assumption.

With two fingers, I directed Watkins to the camera. He gave me a nod. I led us along the hedge on the opposite side of the camera. While it was likely we were in the frame, I wanted to use the shadows and speed to move out of view.

Security cameras were funny things. They provided the idea that one was being watched. However, like Wallace staring at the twelve angles of video feeds, it required patience. The human body wasn't always capable of that level of discipline. There was a difference between the two. Wallace was searching for something. A guard, if there was even a human body, watching the security feeds here, wasn't looking for anything. They were simply there to catch something if it were to occur.

Guess what? Nothing ever does. Weeks pass with the only movement on camera being a moth attracted to the light. At four in the morning, it was worse. Even the most diligent person drooped. They need a cup of coffee or to relieve themselves of the cup they had an hour ago. People got lax. Human nature. We were counting on it.

By the time we were under the camera and out of the view, we waited. No alarms sounded. No shouts, gunshots, or responses.

While I kept watch, Watkins tried the door. He carried a small metal diamond-tipped blade to score the glass. However, no one felt dumber than the guy who cut his way through the glass, only to find the door already unlocked.

The knob turned, and he glanced at me, bemused. Once again, the roaming guards and security cameras offered a false sense of security. I knew I possessed a jaded opinion, but then I was the one breaking into a mansion at the moment.

The house wasn't dark, but most of the lights were off. Accent lights around the downstairs illuminated enough of the rooms to maneuver around the furniture. It made sense. Most of the people in the house were visitors or guards. They needed to move about without cracking a shin on every piece of furniture.

A sound came from another room, and we ducked down, moving behind a large settee. Footsteps entered the room, and we waited. Watkins unsheathed a KBAR blade that glinted in the shadow.

Whoever entered the room chewed—rather loudly. The chomping of his jaws seemed to come from right behind us. When the snacker shifted, the distinct squeak of leather bending almost reverberated through the quiet room. It was the noise of a belt or holster being readjusted. In a blur, Watkins vaulted over the settee and tackled the man. By the time I stood, the gurgle of air bubbled through the slice Watkins made across his throat.

The tall figure collapsed backwards, grasping at his throat. Watkins supported the man's weight as he slipped down. A half-eaten Bimbo snack cake fell to the floor. The wheeze of air continued to bubble out of the wound as Watkins dragged him out of the walkway.

I came up behind him, watching the area he'd come from. If he was part of a guard rotation, there might be another one still making a sandwich in the kitchen. No one came out. As quietly as one could drag a dying man, Watkins moved him to the corner.

We moved into the kitchen where we knew a flight of stairs wound to the next level. Based on the blueprints, this was the second set of steps. The first went up from the foyer by the front door. However, those stairs were built directly over the master bedroom, where we assumed Mikhalov would be sleeping. Any creak of wood might echo in his room.

We took the kitchen stairs slowly. At the second level, I stopped. The hallway was something out of a nineties home. Shag carpet and colorful wallpaper highlighted this corridor. I glanced at Watkins, who made a face of disgust.

I pointed at the first door. The most efficient way to find Thompson was a room-by-room search. Unfortunately, it meant only a twenty percent chance we'd find him behind the first door. The odds were greater that we'd stumble on a sleeping guard.

When he pushed the door open, we realized our odds weren't even that good.

Two men stared at us from a card table where they were playing chess.

The shorter of the two shouted something in Russian, and the other reached for his side. The Beretta in Watkins's hand fired twice.

And the entire house woke up.

26

The bullets that Watkins fired were on target, striking each man in the chest. The shots weren't fast enough to prevent the taller man from firing off his pistol. While the man never had the opportunity to aim, the three gunshots were enough to stir everyone awake.

Behind me, the door across the hall jerked open, revealing a man wearing nothing but a pair of white briefs. He raised a nine-millimeter, firing as it came up. I shoved Watkins forward into the room as the bullet hit the door frame.

"Guess the fun started," Watkins hissed, spinning around and raising the Beretta.

I dropped to the floor and rolled around, facing out the door. My trigger finger squeezed, sending a burst of gunfire out, driving Tighty-Whitey back into his room.

"Go!" I urged Watkins, who moved out into the hall. He fired a burst of four shots at the door as I scrambled to my feet.

Watkins kicked the door open and fired into the room. I moved behind him to see Tighty-Whitey sprawled back on the floor. It wasn't a manner I'd like to be found, spread eagle on the floor in only my underwear. I'd almost find it preferable to be completely naked.

"I'm seeing lightning in the distance," Leo said. There was visible activity in the house from his viewpoint.

The door behind me opened before I could respond. I spun around as a mass of flesh struck me. The man barreling into me weighed about 350 pounds, most of which was muscle. He slammed me into the wall, and the entire hall vibrated. The man's body pressed the barrel of the Beretta down, and he pinned both of my arms against the wall. He punched me in the gut as he smothered me. I gasped for a breath, but he hit me again.

"Hey asshole," I heard Watkins shout.

The weight of the man eased as he twisted me around. The first shot from Watkins's gun whizzed past my ear, snapping the man's head back. I pulled away from him. My side ached from the blows to my stomach. I straightened up and pointed toward the room where the giant emerged. The SEAL held up his Beretta as I moved to the door.

"Clear," I stated. To Leo, I replied, "Acknowledged."

There were two more rooms down the hall. Neither door opened, but if anyone was in them, it was a given the occupants were awake. At the next door, Watkins pushed it open. In the corner, a figure squatted, shaking with fear. I flipped the light switch to see William Thompson. The president's only son quivered.

"Please!" he begged.

"Mr. Thompson," I announced. "We will not hurt you."

"Who are you?" he blubbered.

"We are here to get you home," I told him.

"Americans?" he asked, sucking in the sobs.

"Yes," I assured him. "But we need to go now."

William Thompson rose to his feet. He was wearing pajama pants and a Yale Rowing t-shirt.

"Mr. Thompson, Valeri Mikhalov has a document you signed about the Danube Delta. Do you know where it is?"

"The what?" he asked, confused.

"About drilling for oil in the Danube Delta," I clarified.

He shook his head again.

"No time for that," Watkins told me.

"Get some shoes," I told Thompson. To Watkins, I asked, "Can we get out the back?"

"Might as well try. I've counted five down."

"That leaves five, doesn't it?"

"Unless our numbers were wrong," Watkins suggested.

Somehow, I didn't think we'd be that lucky. I grabbed Thompson's arm after he'd slipped into a pair of loafers. They weren't ideal for running, but bare feet would be worse.

"I don't understand," he mumbled as I pulled him along.

"Just stay with us, sir. We'll get you out of here."

The three of us moved toward the back steps when two figures came up behind us on the main stairs. One of them shouted in Russian as the other fired at us. I twisted around and fired a spray of gunfire.

When a bullet hits flesh, it has a distinct sound, like slapping raw meat. Even in the din of gunfire, I heard a few shots hit one man. The other took cover, but not before firing wildly down the hall.

"Argh!" Thompson wailed as I dragged him into the stairwell.

"He get you?" Watkins asked.

"My shoulder," he whined.

Watkins turned to return fire as I checked Thompson. One round hit him high on the back, just below his right shoulder. The bone probably stopped the bullet, but he'd end up needing some surgery.

"It's not too bad," I told him. "It won't end your rowing days, I'm sure."

"What the fuck is going on?" he moaned.

Ignoring him, I said, "We'll get you bandaged up once we are out of here."

"We need to go," Watkins urged.

"Come on," I ordered Thompson. "We'll be out of here soon."

The president's son still looked bewildered. It had been less than five minutes since the first gunshots erupted to now. Thompson found himself jerked from his sleep to be dragged through a gunfight. To him, the event might feel like a surreal movie, and he hadn't gotten the chance to let reality dawn on him.

Unfortunately, there wasn't time. Careful not to put pressure on his shoulder, I pulled his opposite arm to move him down the stairs.

"Wait here," I demanded as I stuck my head into the kitchen where Watkins and I came up the stairs.

The kitchen was empty.

"Goodyear, how's the weather?" I asked Leo.

"Cloudy," he replied—he couldn't tell.

I signaled for Watkins to move forward. At least Leo hadn't indicated the opened drains had been discovered. If we could make it to the opening, it was a straight run out. Once we were in the pipe, we could double-time our way to the other end. It would take time for anyone following us to find the entrance we made.

As we came out into the first room where Watkins cut the first guard's throat, I swept the barrel of the Beretta across the room.

A voice shouted in Russian, and I twisted to see Mikhalov stumble out of his room. In his right hand, the rotund Russian waved a pistol. Watkins fired a shot, and the oligarch's head exploded, spewing blood and brains against the wall. His body slumped against the wall and slid to the floor slowly as if his legs were the last body part to get the notice to cease operations. Two more men ran from the hallway, and I pushed Thompson behind me as Watkins shot them both.

"Move," I ordered Thompson.

"You shot him," he muttered, still staring at Mikhalov's body.

"Move," I repeated, pushing him out the door.

Once we reached the pool deck, I pressed Thompson against the wall. Cameras weren't the concern now. I wanted to keep the man out of any stray gunfire.

Watkins fired another burst into the house.

"That way," I urged Thompson toward the break in the hedge where we'd come through.

The president's son jumped through the opening, and I turned back to Watkins.

The SEAL swung the butt of his Beretta into my face. Instinctively, I raised my arm to block it, but the blow was fast. Pain shot through my temple as the end cracked against my skull. My arm raised the Beretta in my hands to fire, but I couldn't get it up before he hit me again with the side of the gun.

My calves struck a chaise lounge, and I tumbled back over the chair, smacking the concrete with the back of my skull.

The lights around the pool seemed to flicker for a second, before I could blink myself back into the present.

Rolling off my back, I got my arms underneath me. Inside my stomach, everything seemed to roll around as a wave of nausea slapped me.

Focus. That voice in my head was screaming at me.

A copper taste tinged my lips. Blood was dripping down my face. I resisted the urge to touch the gash on my head, but the sea breeze stung as it blew across me.

The Beretta in my hand came up, and I charged through the hedge. I started to call out to Leo when I stopped.

Everything happened quickly, and I needed a second. I'd suspected the entire operation was a setup.

Dumbass, the voice reprimanded.

I should have seen something coming. Now Watkins had Thompson. To what end?

They didn't get the documents. If the president's son was killed, the media would be in more of an uproar about that. The Russians could release all the documents they wanted, but if the blame pointed at them, no one would care. The public was a fickle beast.

My head still spun around, but I stumbled back to the drain. If I was going to save Thompson, I needed to get to Wallace. Find out what she had planned.

When my feet splashed into the bottom of the drainpipe, I leaned against the side and threw up. When I finished, I straightened up. The lightheadedness was still there. I guessed I had a concussion. There just wasn't any time to dwell on that.

The nausea passed mostly, and I sprinted down the pipe. When I saw the hole we'd come through ahead, I slowed down. If I wanted to kill a rat, I'd sit outside his nest, waiting for him to stick his head out.

I crept by the opening, staying out of the light beaming through the gap. When I'd cleared the opening and reached the far side, I picked up my pace. Eventually, I was running again down the drain.

After several minutes, I paused to dry heave again. My brain warned me by forcing my stomach to revolt. When I regained my composure, I continued.

The diameter of the pipe narrowed as I proceeded away from the sea. Half a mile later, I reached another drain. This one was the one Watkins claimed was rusted through. I worried that when I got there I would find he'd lied about it. Luckily, it was where he told me, and it was within reach if I jumped.

My right hand caught one of the remaining bars, and I prayed the metal held while I hoisted myself up. The surface of the rebar flaked off layers of rust under the palm of my hand. When I pulled myself up enough, I reached my left hand through the opening and gripped the lip.

A minute later, I rolled on my back, catching my breath under the early morning sky.

27

I stared at the sky for a few minutes, hoping the swirling pain in my head would subside. There seemed to be no end to it anytime soon, and I pushed to my feet. I was further up the hill I noticed. I should have been just under the ridge where Leo hid in his sniper nest. He would be about a mile the other way.

My hand reflexively touched the radio earpiece. The plastic end fell out of my ear, and I realized the wire was dangling loose. When Watkins struck me with the Beretta, the impact must have shattered the radio. Maybe that's the only reason Leo didn't call out.

Or he was in on it, too.

But where Watkins ambushed me was out of his line of sight. He wouldn't have seen it happen. If Watkins got out of the hedge and warned Leo that I'd attacked him, there would be no refuting it.

A nagging thought pressed against my subconscious—why didn't he shoot me?

Watkins had the upper hand. Why not kill me? He had to know I'd come after him. The safest course was elimination. But he didn't.

That fact bothered me. I climbed along the ridge toward the Volkswagen. When I saw it, it surprised me Watkins hadn't taken it. That meant he had a different exit strategy.

The cliff.

I didn't see Thompson being able to make the climb down in the best of conditions, but with a bullet in his shoulder blade, it would be an impossible task.

Unless he had help.

Leo.

Before I got to the car, I stopped again as my stomach continued to answer to the warning calls of my brain. Bent over a pile of rocks, my stomach convulsed, hoping to empty its contents. Unfortunately, that had already happened.

The Beretta hung from my shoulder. I didn't want to go unarmed, but it would be daylight soon. Prudence suggested I ditch it. I climbed up the hill about seventy feet. After wiping it clean, I covered it with rocks. I didn't bury it completely, but it wouldn't be easy to see until someone was right on top of it.

After catching my breath, I got into the Volkswagen and started it.

The path I took was circuitous. I doubted anyone was following me since Watkins and Thompson took a different route. The SEAL had no intention of returning to the flat. If he'd killed me, that might have been an option.

I parked several blocks over. It was almost six in the morning, and the sky to the east began lightening as the sun prepared to rise. Havana was waking up. Shopkeepers prepared to open. People trekked along the sidewalks.

When I saw the building, I stopped in a doorway, watching from a block away. No one seemed to watch the building from the street. I scanned the building across from it. The roof appeared clear, but it would be easy to put a spotter in one of the darkened windows. There'd be no way to see them.

Finally, I gave in, making a cautious approach. An elderly woman came out of the front door as I reached the steps. She didn't seem to pay me much attention, and I slipped into the building. When I reached the flat, I paused.

The door to the flat was ajar. I studied the door frame where the latch splintered from a sudden kick. They had constructed nothing in this building to provide a lot of security. Each door only had a single lock—not even a deadbolt.

I pushed it open, wishing I'd held onto the Beretta now. Before I stepped across the threshold, I sensed it. My brain would say it recognized the smell of death. I don't know, though. It might be something like an acute sensation.

When I stepped inside, though, I saw her.

Wallace leaned back in front of the screens limply, as if she was a jacket tossed haphazardly on the chair. A small .22 caliber pistol lay on the floor. Whoever came through the door startled her, but not so quick she didn't pull her gun.

Still, the bullet struck in the face, marring the pretty girl image she relied on. The wound was fresh within the last hour. About the time we were coming out of Mikhalov's back door, I guessed. I couldn't be certain. Even a pathologist could only estimate that, but it was logical.

How fast could Leo get from the house to the apartment? The radios could carry a distance, and Leo might have been talking to us while he crossed the city.

Every question and doubt I had before suddenly ballooned to enormous proportion. For the second time in the last few days, I was standing over a dead woman. The first was staged, I was sure, right down to the police banging on the door. This was a cleanup. Whatever plan Watkins ran with, he had an accomplice.

I grabbed the twenty-two off the floor and moved to the case where Wallace pulled out the wads of pesos yesterday. There was an envelope filled with bills, and I grabbed them, stuffed the money in my pocket, and headed straight for the door.

The corridor was empty, and I pulled the door closed so the broken door jamb wasn't obvious. I ran down the steps and onto the sidewalk.

My head still pounded, but as I ducked into an alley, I tried to piece together what my next move was. Someone was pulling Watkins's strings. He didn't do something like this unless he was getting paid. I had to assume Leo was the same. But I'd focused my suspicions on Wallace for too long, and somehow missed whoever was behind it.

Wallace had immediately rubbed me the wrong way. We hadn't worked together long enough to build up a rapport. I don't think it ever would have happened—I didn't trust her.

Our first meeting, she knew about the murdered girl. Somehow she was involved. Or was she just a pawn?

Another thought occurred to me. The Russians. Yura Turchin might have gotten wise to Wallace. They could have found the bugs—somehow traced them back to the flat.

I needed a place to hide and regroup. It took me a few extra minutes to get back to the Volkswagen, and I headed south. Half an hour later, I saw the Vista Hotel, and while it didn't actually seem like much of a vista, it was off the beaten track enough. After parking several blocks over, I hiked back to the hotel.

The man behind the counter didn't speak any English. He was in his fifties with a thick black mustache and a Denver Broncos t-shirt. It seemed like an odd shirt to find in Cuba. He took cash for a room without too much conversation. However, he looked at my forehead, no doubt wondering who clocked me. I didn't like being remembered, but after I regrouped, I planned to leave anyway. Ideally before noon.

"*Catorce*," Bronco told me.

I blinked, trying to recall my numbers, and the man touched the key he handed to me with "14" imprinted on it. The only gratitude I offered was a smile. He nodded, and I followed the hallway around until I found number fourteen.

The Bronco t-shirt started my wheels spinning as soon as I closed the door. He'd probably found it at a thrift store, or maybe there was a local equivalent of Walmart that sold American items.

Thompson was wearing a Yale rowing shirt. I hadn't even given it much thought. It made perfect sense. William Thompson likely came from an Ivy League background. I even assumed he'd been on the rowing team, commenting on it when I checked his wound.

He packed those items. It seemed more unlikely that Mikhalov would have a Yale shirt, let alone a rowing one. I got an annoying inkling as things clicked into place.

What if Thompson hadn't been kidnapped?

He could have been doing some perfectly legitimate work with Mikhalov. But the CIA told me the Russians were holding him, and I believed that.

I had seen him at the embassy. And Lidia was quick to tell me he'd moved to Mikhalov's house, but she didn't tell me why.

Now, I had another sick realization that seemed to tie with the nausea. I helped kidnap the president's son.

The room had a small sink next to a window about six inches wide and two feet tall. In case anyone tried to slip in or out of the slit, iron bars ran horizontally over the glass. I took the towel from the bar and washed my face and head. The gash on my head wasn't too bad—two inches long. Luckily, my skull wasn't showing through, but the scalp still peeled back like a small flap.

After I left here, I would need to find something to bandage the wound. After traipsing around a drainpipe, even a terrible doctor would advise to clean it.

Once I had the blood cleaned off, I turned the television on. Everything was in Spanish, which shouldn't have been a shock. Somehow, I was still disappointed.

I fell back on the bed and closed my eyes. With a concussion, it's common knowledge one should not sleep. I knew that, but I didn't care. After a few minutes of listening to a man drone on about a soccer match in Spanish, I drifted to sleep.

When I woke up, I felt better. The mental timer in my head told me I'd only been asleep for a little over an hour. It was enough to ease the pain in my head, and luckily, I wasn't in a coma.

Straining to sit up, I still heard the monotone Spanish on the television. I needed to get moving. If I stayed here too long, it might give the desk clerk time to wonder about my head wound. Better to move on now.

I straightened up as the scene on the television switched to security footage. I froze as an image flashed across the screen.

The television showed a clear image of me ushering William Thompson across the pool deck of Mikhalov's house. The Beretta in my hand added an ominous touch. Across the bottom of the screen, a banner reading *"Secuestran al hijo del Presidente de Estados Unidos"* scrolled past.

28

"Shit!" I exclaimed, staring at the screen.

I didn't need to understand Spanish to get the gist of what was being said. I was being blamed for what happened at the mansion.

Everything kicked into gear. Now, I didn't have the luxury to wait here. Once the clerk saw the television, he'd remember the American with the bleeding head. Without a plan, I hurried out the door. Right now, I had to count on the fact he hadn't seen the news.

As I passed through the lobby, I breathed a sigh of relief. There was no television behind the counter. As I avoided eye contact, I stepped outside.

It wouldn't be long before my image got passed around. If it made it to the news, it was a given the police had it now. Any hotel in Havana would be too dangerous.

How did they get it out so quickly?

Even if the police were called, how did they have time to release the video?

It was still part of the set-up. Not only had I helped kidnap the president's son, but now the media spread the irrefutable proof to the public. Someone leaked that video. Watkins? Leo? It didn't seem like their style. Besides, Watkins was as much on tape as I was.

In fact, as I replayed the raid through my head, I realized he did most of the killing. I dropped one guard upstairs after we found Thompson. He killed the first guard downstairs, the two men in the room playing chess, Tighty-Whitey, and Mikhalov.

Dammit.

How did they set me up like this? If it was Wallace, why did they kill her?

I reached the Volkswagen and slid into the driver's seat. If they had the video from the house, wouldn't they have the make of the car too?

"Ugh," I groaned, getting back out of the car.

Don't look back.

Immediately, I started south again. More touristy areas might be safer to hide out in, but they'd also be where the police would concentrate. The airport would be out, not that it mattered. I didn't have a passport.

There was the American Embassy. I could surrender myself there.

It was a ludicrous notion. If I showed up and surrendered myself, I'd never get a chance to talk to anyone. Hell, I was already almost to Gitmo. They'd ship me over there until they got the answers they wanted. Unfortunately, those were the same answers I wanted.

Go to ground. That was my only choice.

If I could find a phone, I could call Jay again. That might be stupid, too. If the video reached the U.S., I'd be a wanted man there too. The FBI would set up on Jay as soon as they got my identity.

I stayed on the smaller streets, winding my way south. When I passed what looked like a combination thrift store and junk shop, I ducked inside. It didn't take me two minutes to find what I needed, an old cap with a faded Tampa Bay Buccaneers logo. I imagined at some time, this hat washed up on shore. Time turned the once rigid bill flaccid, and the yellowed material faded to a near white. Despite its condition, the damned thing still cost me seventy pesos, but it hid the gash on my head.

A tiny woman in her sixties, who I assumed was the shop owner, barely glanced up from her constant tidying to take my money. That was all right with me.

As I paid her, I noticed a stack of shirts she'd been sorting. I found a double extra-large, a size that was a bit too big for me. It cost me a hundred pesos, but when I hit the street again, I shed the black flak jacket I'd been wearing that morning. The tropical styled shirt made me look like a tourist, but at least the black attire the television showed me wearing didn't single me out.

With the hat pulled down on my head, I hastened along the alleys. I'd only use the major streets to cross to a less trafficked road.

Finally, I reached the only destination I had. I rounded the corner and read the sign, "*Comida China.*"

When I came through the door, Mai's mother glanced up at me. I smiled, and she shouted something I didn't understand. A second later, Mai came through the swinging door.

"Chase?" she questioned. "What are you doing here?"

"I'm in a bit of trouble," I told her.

Mai's mother blurted out something in Vietnamese. Her daughter responded, and while I didn't understand a single word, the tone sounded like a daughter putting her mother in her place.

"I'm sorry," she said to me. "My mother said you were on the TV."

I nodded. "Yes, but it's not exactly what it looks like."

Mai cocked her head. "They say you kidnapped the son of the American president."

My head shook, a movement I regretted as the pain in my head spiked. "It was supposed to be a rescue mission."

"I thought you were going to the American Embassy?" Mai questioned.

"Everything got more complicated after I left you."

"The Brotherhood of Pain hasn't been around," she explained. "Did you do that?"

"I don't know," I admitted, thinking about the war zone in Kotov's warehouse. "At best, it's disrupted. They'll regroup and be back. People like that never go away completely."

She sighed. "Why do they think you kidnapped that man?"

"Someone wants to blame me for it," I told her. "I just need a little help, Mai. Once I get that situated, I'll get out of your way. The last thing I want to do is bring you more trouble."

"Of course. What do you need?"

"If I give you some money, can you find me a phone?" I asked. "Something not traceable. We have prepaid phones in the States."

She nodded. "Why don't you come back to the kitchen?" she asked. I didn't blame her. She wanted to get me out of the public view. I was probably ranking as the most wanted man in Cuba right now.

As we passed through the swinging door, she spoke to her mother about something in Vietnamese.

"I told her you were innocent," she explained. "She's worried you might bring more trouble."

"She's probably right," I admitted.

Mai shrugged. "She also said you helped us earlier. Although she thinks it was stupid of you."

I smiled, for the first time since I went into the drainpipe with Watkins.

"There's a store a few blocks over that sells electronics. They'll have a phone, I think."

"Thank you, Mai," I said. "Can I do anything to help while I wait?"

She shook her head. Her hand came up and lifted the hat off my head.

"Chase, that's a terrible cut!" she exclaimed. "Sit down."

Mai ushered me to a chair. "We have some medicine for burns and cuts back here."

The girl shuffled around a small cabinet until she pulled out a tube shaped like toothpaste. The words were in Vietnamese, and I trusted she knew what she was doing. Gently, Mai applied the gooey salve to the cut. Once she thought the salve covered it enough, she placed a large adhesive bandage over it.

"This won't stay because of your hair," she explained. "With the hat on, it should help protect it though."

"Thank you," I replied.

She took a thousand pesos from me, promising to hurry back.

Once she was gone, Mai's mother came back into the kitchen, likely to check on me. Each time the scowl on her face tried to singe at my soul. I offered her a smile, hoping to alleviate her worries. It didn't seem to have the effect I hoped it would, but she wasn't chasing me out of the restaurant either.

The woman toiled at a wok, frying up rice and vegetables. As she tossed the contents around, she squeezed a stream of soy sauce into the mixture. The wok sizzled each time she shot the liquid into the pot.

After about five minutes, she ladled the rice into a bowl. When she placed the bowl in front of me, the act seemed to be done begrudgingly. I nodded my appreciation with a congenial smile, and the woman strode out of the kitchen with her own bowl, leaving me to eat my lunch in solitude.

I hadn't eaten since last night, and the fried rice was delicious. While I ate, I continued to replay the last few days in my head. Nothing made sense to me still. Well, not nothing. I understood that almost everything had been a ruse designed to put me in that house, helping to kidnap William Thompson.

If the goal all along had been to grab Thompson, why bother bringing me in at all?

I started working backwards. The only pieces fitting together made little sense. Why me? There could be a million reasons to snatch the president's son, and setting up the entire thing like a rescue even made sense, especially if Wallace was also a dupe in this affair. Could she have been naïve enough for someone to manipulate her, too?

Watkins mentioned working with her before. Perhaps he or whoever dangled his strings brought her in, so Watkins had a reason to be involved.

To what end?

Why not just send Watkins and Leo in on their own? Even bringing in a third guy to make the grab made more sense than kidnapping me and setting the last few days in motion.

It was too many things that might go sideways.

I remembered Kotov again. He said, "No one wants you." It was the kind of statement one makes after a deal falls through—like he tried to trade me to someone.

Who did I piss off enough to drag me into this?

With any luck, I could reach Jay before the FBI clamped down on him. I'd talked to him before everything turned sour today. He knew what I knew about Thompson. At least, he'd give that information to the Feds. Whether they accepted what he said was another issue altogether. The evidence was stacked against me right now, and even if the FBI didn't believe it, the PNR in Cuba might. With enough dead Russians on Cuban soil, they'd be searching for me. This wasn't the same feint as the dead girl in the tub. I was on national television, and the cops couldn't afford to ignore it.

The back door of the kitchen opened, and Mai appeared, holding a paper bag.

"I have it," she announced with a smile.

As I stood up, the door she'd just entered swung open again, and Leo stepped through raising an M45.

I sprang to my feet, pulling Wallace's twenty-two out. Mai screamed, dropping the paper bag and covering her head.

Leo stared at me over the scared girl, his gun's barrel stretching past her shoulder.

29

"Mai, get down," I ordered.

The swinging door to the dining room flew open as Mai's mother stormed in. A gush of Vietnamese poured out of her. Since she was behind me, I wasn't able to see the pissed-off glare I assumed she sent our direction.

"Mai, down," I repeated.

The girl crouched down and sprawled on the floor. She said something to her mother. The response sounded like a plea of some sort.

"Leave them out of this," I insisted, staring down the barrel at the other Marine.

"I'm not going to hurt them," he declared. "Put your gun down, Chase."

"You shouldn't have left it when you killed Wallace," I pointed out.

"Damn, boy," he whistled. "I didn't kill her."

I studied him. "How did you find me?"

"I picked you up outside the flat this morning," he explained.

"No one was following me," I said incredulously.

He offered a half-shrug without letting the forty-five waver.

"I didn't kill her," I added in defense.

"No, you probably didn't," he replied. "You'd just left the building in quite a hurry. She'd been dead long enough that I realized you hadn't killed her. Besides, why would you kick the door in? Wallace would expect you to come in."

"How do I know it wasn't you?" I asked. "Are you in this with Watkins?"

Leo shook his head. "I didn't know what happened until I heard the news report. Even then, I wasn't sure."

We stared at each other for a few more seconds.

He continued, "I watched you come out without Watkins or Thompson. Even from where I was, it was obvious you were staggering. Honestly, I thought you had caught a bullet. No one was answering the comms. But you didn't come out."

"Not where we started," I responded.

"After I waited for another hour, I headed back to the flat. You were scoping it out when I got there. It was obvious you were being careful. So, I held back. Once you came back out, I found Wallace."

"You didn't follow me," I replied. It was a statement, not a question.

"What happened inside the house?" he asked, ignoring me.

"Let them go," I insisted again.

Leo's mouth widened in a big shit-eating grin. "I'm not keeping them here," he said.

My eyes flicked to the girl on the ground. "Mai, get your mother and get out of here."

The girl's head turned up to me. "Chase?"

"Just go, please. I don't want you hurt."

She scrambled to her feet, and her head swiveled between the two guns Leo and I pointed at each other. Her mother grabbed her hand and pulled her out of the kitchen. When I heard the front door open and close, I knew we were alone.

"Will she call the police?" he asked me.

"Can't say I blame them if they do," I replied. "How did you get this job?"

"Guy I know who worked with Wallace before couldn't do it. He reached out to me."

I wondered if I could trust him. It made sense that he might think the same thing.

"Watkins attacked me after we got out of the house. Right before we exited through the hedge."

"Where the camera wouldn't see?" he asked.

"Shit, yeah," I replied. "Stupid, I didn't think of that."

"When Wallace sent me after you the other day, one of the reports she got was you had an altercation with a couple of Cubans trying to extort a restaurant owner. If your story was truthful, you didn't have a lot of places to go in this city. I just took a chance."

I lifted an eyebrow.

Leo continued, "I followed the girl to the store, where she bought a cheap cell phone. Figured that was the move you'd make."

I sighed. It was logical, and if I was wearing his shoes, I might come to the same conclusion.

"Okay, how about we try to trust each other?" I suggested.

Leo nodded. "On three?"

I lowered the barrel of the twenty-two. If he was going to shoot me, he could put the bullet between my eyes. I'd never hear the gunshot. Instead, he let the forty-five drop for a second before lowering it completely.

"I don't think we can stay here," he suggested. "Like you said, the ladies would be in their right mind to call the cops."

"Where do we go?"

"I have a room," he explained.

Again, I lifted an eyebrow with curiosity.

"I never worked with Wallace or Watkins," he explained. "I arranged for another room before I got here. In my opinion, it's better to have an exit strategy in place."

Before I followed him out, I grabbed a pen and paper, jotting "Thank you, Mai. CG." She deserved proper gratitude, but a note seemed the best option without drawing her into more trouble than I'd already done. I picked up the paper bag and stuffed it under my arm.

Leo holstered his M45, and I followed suit before trailing him out of the kitchen. He had the little Toyota he stole from Kotov's warehouse parked three blocks over.

"Extra car too?" I asked.

"I figured the previous owners weren't using it," he remarked.

When I climbed into the front seat, I said, "We need to find Watkins."

"I have an idea about that," Leo suggested.

When I didn't respond, he said, "He had to go to the sea. I never saw him or Thompson, and the only angle he had was that way."

"We'll never get near the house to see," I told him. "I'd have to think the police are all over the scene by now."

"If they jumped through all the hoops to get Thompson, Watkins is going to deliver him off the island, right?" Leo suggested.

"A boat," I acknowledged.

"From my point, I had a clear view of all the boats on the water yesterday. Of course, someone could slip in without being seen, but they'd need to run dark. Follow me?"

I nodded.

"There was one nice big sumbitch that dropped anchor yesterday. I couldn't help but notice it. Sucker was huge. Over a hundred feet easily."

"Surely there were plenty of other boats out there?" I suggested.

"Probably, but this one was out of place. Everything else was mostly fishing vessels."

"Those probably fit under the radar, though," I pointed out.

"I considered that, but Watkins wasn't the type to run a fishing boat ninety miles to Key West. Besides, would they take Thompson back to the States?"

I didn't have an answer for that. Without knowing who was behind this, I couldn't guess. If I were the FBI, I'd put Key West on high alert. Make sure the Coast Guard was sweeping the coast for someone coming north.

"That big sucker, though," Leo suggested, "could motor anywhere in the world."

"I don't suppose you got a name off the hull?"

He shook his head. "Yeah, I kick myself now, but I don't think I could have seen it from the angle they sat."

"Let's see if it's still there," I said.

As he drove, I pulled the phone out of the bag. It was a simple flip phone, something that was right up my alley. The instructions were in Spanish, which meant it took me a lot longer to get it working. Mai thought to buy a calling card so I could add minutes to the phone. Luckily, it included international calling.

Once I had it up and going, I dialed Jay's number.

"Hello," my friend answered.

"It's me."

"Ain't you in a world of shit right now," he stated. It wasn't a question.

"Tell me about it," I said.

"Well, I have what I thought was some good news, although after a Special Agent Gardner showed up here asking about you, I'm not sure it actually is good news."

"What?" I asked.

"According to General Shaw, there is no order recalling you into active service."

"Great," I remarked with a heavy dose of sarcasm.

"Yeah, I thought you might see it that way now," he replied. "At least if you were following orders, you might have a defense."

"They played me?"

"Wallace?" he asked. "She's an actual agent, although from what I've determined, her aspirations outweigh her authority."

"She said it was 'off-book,'" I replied.

"Taylor has an exemplary record. Looks like he would give me a run for my money on the range. Watkins, on the other hand, is listed as KIA."

"KIA?" I questioned.

"They redacted everything. Although, it looks like he was working on some side projects, and the Navy just covered it up."

"He has William Thompson," I told him. "He clocked me on the way out."

"Leaving you to take the fall," Jay acknowledged. "And Taylor."

I glanced over at Leo. "He's with me."

"Can you trust him?" Jay asked.

"That is to be determined."

"I can't do much else for you," Jay said. "If the Feds aren't listening in yet, they will be."

"I sent something to you," I told him. "Check with Missy."

"Your friend in Miami gave me a number," Jay said, rattling off a number. I committed it to memory.

"Thanks, Jay," I replied.

"Do me a favor and get out of this," he told me. "I don't want to find a new bartender."

I hung up with him.

"Your buddy check up on me?" Leo asked.

"He said you might be better than him at the range."

"Oh, there's no doubt there," Leo quipped. "I bet I do better with the ladies, too."

"I don't know," I joked. "He's got three ex-wives."

Leo laughed. "I'm definitely smarter than him there."

He pulled off along the road. We were looking at the harbor from a different angle than the house, but the only thing we saw was a yacht about eight to ten miles out. Too far to make out much other than it was big enough to be the boat we were looking for.

"We need to find a radio," I told him.

"Why?"

"There's a cruiser community here," I explained. "They notice things like big boats. Someone will have gotten the name."

Leo pointed toward a marina down in the harbor. "We might find one there."

It took ten minutes to weave around the winding road to get to the marina. Obviously, I waited in the car while Leo went inside. It helped he was almost fluent in Spanish too. While he was gone, I sank down in the passenger seat. I didn't want anyone passing by the car and recognizing me.

It took him five minutes to return.

"Didn't need a radio," he told me. "First guy I ran into was a Brit. He said the yacht was an Oceanfast 48."

I sat up in the chair.

"An Oceanfast?" I questioned. "Really?"

"Yeah," Leo answered.

"Did he know the name?"

"Said it was Italian. *Bella Notte*."

Suddenly, I realized who might be behind Thompson's kidnapping. He'd hate me too.

The only problem was he was dead.

30

"We need to get to that boat!" I exclaimed.

"What do you suggest?" Leo asked. "We could steal a boat."

The thought occurred to me, but we'd need something fast enough to catch up to the *Bella Notte*. If Watkins and Thompson were on the boat we saw on the horizon, they were ten miles out. If I remembered correctly, the Oceanfast couldn't run fast, but she would do about twelve knots. That wouldn't matter, because the farther she got from us, the harder it would be to track the vessel.

"You figure out what's going on?" Leo asked, staring at me.

"Not quite, but something."

"It looks like you saw a ghost," he remarked.

"Not yet, but close," I said. "Can you run back in and see if they have nautical charts? Even a map would do."

Leo stared at me for a second. "Want to fill me in first?" he asked. "I don't mind charging off, but I'd like to get a gist of what windmills I'm tilting toward."

"Ever hear of a man named Joe Loggins?"

Leo shook his head.

"Few people have," I explained. "That's what made him so successful. He was a political fixer."

I continued, "When he fixed something, it didn't matter how he did it. Usually it involved extreme measures."

"Including kidnapping?" Leo asked.

"Yes, and William Thompson might make the perfect target."

"You deal with him before?" Leo asked.

"I killed him."

Leo stared at me. "But you think he's behind this?"

I shook my head. "I am positive the man I killed is dead. But *Bella Notte* was his boat. It seems like too much of a coincidence."

"If he's dead, someone else probably owns the boat."

My eyes stared out across the marina. "I don't like coincidences."

He nodded. "What's his endgame?"

"That was above my pay grade," I admitted. "But the boat was owned by a shell company. The FBI investigated the company, but after he died, it might have gone nowhere."

"This is a stretch to believe a man you killed is back from the dead."

"He's not," I declared. "He is definitely dead."

In the back of my mind, I wondered if I'd been wrong. The man I killed was the man I knew as Joe Loggins. What if he wasn't? Or it was some Dread Pirate Roberts gimmick?

"Just a minute," Leo said, leaving the Toyota and venturing back into the marina. In five minutes, he returned with a chart book.

"This one do?"

I opened it up to show the larger image of Cuba. My finger traced the imaginary line from *Bella Notte's* anchorage toward the direction she appeared to be going.

"This isn't an exact science," I announced. "I'd like a better heading. However, look here."

The page thumped as I tapped the chart. "They'll head somewhere they can stash him. It's about ninety miles to Key West,

250 or so to the Bahamas, and three to four hundred to Mexico. They'll want to get out of Cuban water as quickly as possible, so I don't think they'll circle around the island to the Caymans or Jamaica."

"Seems they might not want to go to Mexico for the same reason," Leo suggested, dragging his finger along the northwest coast of Cuba from Havana to the western point.

"True," I agreed.

"Would they go to Key West?" he asked.

I shrugged. "There are still a couple of things. The Oceanfast has the resources to cross the ocean, so it can stay out at sea for a long time. They could cross the Gulf and park it in New Orleans if they wanted. That's why we have to catch them soon."

"I'm open to ideas," he said.

After a second, I pulled my phone out and dialed the number Jay got from Scar. The other end rang three times before someone answered.

"*Hola,*" a voice said.

In English, I replied, "Julio Moreno gave me this number."

"You are American?"

"Yes," I told him.

"The one who killed all the Russians?" he asked.

"Uh..."

"Esteban told me you might call," the voice assured me. "He asked me to help you."

"Thank you," I said. "We are in a bit of a hurry."

"What do you need?"

"A fast boat full of gas."

"That will take some time," he replied.

"We don't have that," I insisted. "There is a boat leaving Havana now with the president's son on board."

"The news says you kidnapped the president's son."

I sighed. "Don't believe everything you see on television."

The man on the other end of the line chuckled. "You want to catch this boat?"

"Yes," I answered.

He laughed again. "Esteban said you were trouble."

"Listen, friend, I appreciate the help, but if you can't help me, I need to come up with a new plan."

"Where are you?"

I paused for a second. Was it safe to trust my location to a man associated with Scar? Surely there would be a reward if he turned me in.

The little voice in my head continued to warn me. However, I had an unusual relationship with Scar. If he told me something, he'd do it. On the other hand, if I got in his way, the man had no qualms about killing me and feeding me to the sharks.

The voice relented. "I'm five minutes from the Marina Tarara."

"Twenty minutes," he replied.

"It would help if the boat had radar and AIS."

"Americans," the man muttered. "Always want more. I'll call you in twenty."

He disconnected, and I glanced at Leo. "He said twenty minutes. Do you have more guns?"

Leo grinned. "Trunk's got a couple of SIG Copperheads."

I blinked without a word.

"They came with the car."

"The Russians had new Copperhead machine guns?"

He shrugged as if that was the only explanation I needed.

"However," he added, "I only have sixty rounds. So thirty each."

"I'll take it," I replied.

"Have you eaten?" he asked.

"Yeah."

"Well, I haven't," he told me. "There were some sandwiches in the marina store."

"A water, please," I suggested with a nod.

"We might need a couple," he suggested as he got out of the car.

When he was gone, I tried to call Jay back. The phone didn't ring, sending me instead straight to voicemail, which, of course, he had never set up.

Instead, I sent a text. "WT on board the *Bella Notte*. Joe Loggins's boat. Left Havana heading northeast an hour ago. Alert Coasties."

That was the best I could do right now. I tried to remember what the boat looked like. If I recalled, it had a swim platform on the rear, but that was the only place we'd be able to board the vessel. If it was traveling at full speed, we'd be jumping from one boat to another at about fifteen knots.

That also meant Scar's friend needed to come up with a boat fast enough to catch them.

My eyes scanned across the chart. There were a couple of small islands between Cuba and Andros Island in the Bahamas. The small grouping of cays was just inside Bahamian water, but they weren't much more than raised sandbars. I'd spent a little time snorkeling around the area, and the whole time I was there, I didn't see a single soul. Being so far from the bulk of the Bahamas, there was little chance of a patrol passing through.

Using my fingers as a ruler, I guessed the islands were 120 miles away. It would take them nearly twelve hours to get there, but it might make a nice stopping point for the night. It was also just out of the way enough to hide a high value target.

At least, I hoped the plan they had only involved hiding him. I couldn't imagine a scenario where killing William Thompson made sense. Of course, from what I remembered of Loggins and his machinations, they were far more complex than I would develop.

No matter what the endgame was, eventually Thompson would have no more value to them. Loggins wasn't the kind to expose himself, and releasing Thompson would do that. Whoever was now manipulating the strings Loggins held wasn't likely to fall into that trap, either.

Thompson's time was running out. But how long did he have?

My phone buzzed, and I answered it.

"Slip E-7," Scar's friend told me. "Key's in the bilge."

"It might not come back," I warned him.

"Not my boat," he admitted. "Esteban told me if you needed it, to take care of it."

"Thank you," I said. "I'll thank Esteban when I see him."

He chuckled, and I worried what that might entail. "Esteban told me you helped him, and this was just payback."

"Is Esteban a friend or associate?"

Instead of an answer, I heard a click.

I spotted Leo coming up the walkway from the docks. He carried a small paper sack in one hand. His other hand was holding half a sandwich that kept moving towards his mouth. When he was closer, I got out and waved at him.

"I have a boat," I told him.

"Where is it?" he asked.

"Dock E," I said.

He turned and scanned the docks. The marina spread out along the shore with about ten piers that connected to land. As he pointed to each pier, he recited the alphabet until he got to the letter E. I squinted in the sun to make out the sign denoting it as E dock.

"Chase." Leo's voice reverberated with warning.

I turned toward him, and his eyes shifted to the car pulling into the marina's parking lot. The word "*policía*" written across the side door.

Swiftly, I turned away from the cops as they parked. The two men climbed out of the car leisurely. I let out a sigh. They weren't looking for me—at least not here.

"You need to get out of sight," Leo said as the driver turned his head in our direction.

"Too late," I muttered as the officer's brain took a full second to recognize two Americans. Another second passed as he thought he recognized me. Finally, two and a half seconds after seeing me, the officer said something to us in Spanish.

Leo answered him, also in Spanish.

"What did he say?" I whispered.

"Basically stay there," he told me.

The two cops were a hundred feet from us. The driver should have gotten closer before announcing himself. From here, I could hit him with the twenty-two. It might not kill him, but he'd go down for sure.

"Tell them we are just tourists about to leave," I said.

"I don't think it will work," Leo advised.

"We can't kill them," I muttered. These two officers were only doing their job. My morality, though sometimes verging into the gray zone, prevented me from killing innocent people just because they got in my way.

"I agree," Leo replied, and I let out a sigh of relief. I had hoped he had the same thought process as I did.

The driver shouted an order at the other cop as he pulled his weapon and moved toward us. I lifted my hands, but only to the level of my chest. From the corner of my eye, I watched Leo do the same thing.

"Do you understand me?" I asked the cop.

His face registered nothing. Instead, he blurted another directive in Spanish.

"He said get on the ground," Leo mumbled.

"Too bad I don't understand him," I replied.

While I would not obey the man's command, I wanted him to think it was because I didn't understand him. He moved closer, and obviously he believed that. His hand motioned for me to get down. I forced my face to appear confused.

"What do you want?" I asked, imitating the motion with my right hand as if I was asking him.

He repeated the same phrase, which Leo translated as "get on the ground."

The other officer was on the radio.

"He's calling for back-up," Leo pointed out.

I turned around, putting my back to the cop. My hands lifted a few inches but stayed just level with my shoulder.

"We need him to come over here too," I said to Leo.

"This might not work," he replied. "If that one doesn't get closer, we might have to at least hurt them."

"Nothing permanent," I demanded, following it up with, "Please."

Leo rolled his eyes.

The driver called to his partner.

"He wants him to get over here," Leo murmured. "If they cuff you, it won't be easy."

I blinked twice. The driver's hand caught my right wrist. Unfortunately, the second policeman hadn't gotten halfway to us. With no choice, I rotated right, twisting my right hand to catch the cop's arm just below a cheap wristwatch. The sudden jerk startled him, but I'd pulled him off balance. The gun fired, but in the mayhem, I'd twisted out of its path. My left hand chopped the officer in the throat.

He gasped, instinctively reaching for his throat as my left fist slammed down on his gun hand. The revolver clattered to the ground, and I kicked it to Leo, who scooped it up and fired at the other policeman. Nothing hit the other man, but the barrage of bullets sent him clambering behind his vehicle for cover.

I slammed the officer next to me into the car hard enough to stun him. Leo popped the trunk and pulled a duffel bag out of the back.

When he was clear, I rolled the officer into the back and slammed the lid. Leo fired two more shots at the cowering officer. The man peeked over the back of his car, and Leo waved the keys at the man before hurling them across the parking lot.

We both broke into a run for E dock. There was only one way out now.

31

Behind us, the one policeman fired wildly at our backs. Both of us ran in quick, sporadic S-patterns; the officer wasn't even getting close to us. The only worry was when we hit the walkway for the pier, we'd be running perpendicular. If the man was any kind of marksman, it would be a lot easier to hit us. As our feet hit the wooden planks on the pier, Leo raised the driver's gun and fired at the car again. The other cop's head dropped like a mole, avoiding the whack.

Slip E-7 held a thirty-nine-foot Cigarette GTS 390. It was nearly brand new—less than two years old. On the stern of the vessel hung three 450-horsepower Mercury Racing Outboard motors. Unlike many of the older, go-fast rumrunner-style boats I'd seen, this one had an open bow with nearly immaculate vinyl seats. The merely decorative hardtop over the helm was little more than an arch which would protect about eight inches of a person from the sun—assuming the sun was behind a cloud.

"Damn!" Leo whistled. "How fast will this bitch go?"

"We're about to find out," I announced as I jumped onto the boat. "Better cover us."

My eyes tracked to the officer running toward E Dock. In the distance, I heard a wailing siren.

"Yeah, we got company," he admitted.

Leo reached into the small duffel he'd pulled out of the trunk. A Copperhead machine gun came out in his hand.

"Where'd you get that?" I questioned.

"I'm always prepared," he grinned.

The weapons were pretty new on the scene. SIG Sauer developed them several years ago for the Army, and now they were available for the public, but they weren't cheap. It wasn't the easiest thing to find a couple in Cuba. I respected the way Leo thought. He hadn't trusted the situation either, and he intended to have an exit strategy in place. He was probably carrying at least two different passports.

No, I bet there are three. He appreciated redundancies.

He dropped the bag off his shoulder, letting it land on the passenger seat. "Better get that thing running," he stated.

While Leo moved into position to keep the cops from coming on the pier, I ducked below and lifted the access panel to the bilge. Taped to the underside of the panel was a silver key attached to a floating ball with the logo for Cigarette Boats emblazoned on it.

When I got back to the helm, I started the engines. All three rumbled, and I pointed toward the lines on the bow. Leo rushed forward to untie us, as I checked the gauges. The fuel tank was full, although I had to guess how much that was—anywhere between forty and a hundred gallons. The water tank was almost empty. Again, there was no indicator about how much was supposed to be in there, but the less weight we carried, the faster we'd go.

Leo fired a single shot. I didn't bother to see what was going on. In a battle, a man had to rely on his team. Everyone had a job. The rule was always do your job and trust your brother to do his.

Once I felt comfortable, I pulled the throttle back, reversing the engines quickly. A lot of people grow nervous at the idea of leaving and entering a dock. This Cigarette was only a little shorter than *Carina*, but it didn't have the nearly sixty-foot mast to deal with. Taking everything slowly is the best way to go. Don't overreact, because driving a boat isn't like a car. There are no brakes. If you overcompensate, it's tough to stop and start over like in a car. Add some wind or waves, and maneuvering grows trickier. Even experienced sailors and boaters eventually find themselves in a pickle. Like most things, it's best to remain calm.

Of course, the luxury of taking things slowly wasn't available to us.

The vessel moved back quickly. We were lucky in this harbor. A jut of land protected the harbor, leaving still waters to back through.

"All aboard!" I shouted.

Leo fired another single shot before running down the slip and jumping into the open bow as it cleared the slip. I spun the wheel and cut the throttle, stopping the motor's backward propulsion. Just like I wanted it to do, the bow of the boat swung around toward the sea. The inertia was driving us too far around, though. Before I drifted too far, I pushed the throttle forward. The three Mercury motors howled as we shot forward in the channel.

"Say goodbye to Cuba," I told him.

Leo grabbed the back of the passenger's seat, trying to steady himself as I turned sharply at the end of the channel. Boats on either side of the canal bounced as the wake I threw rocked the still water. As a boat owner and marina resident, I hated throwing such a large wake, but with the police onto us, we needed to be out in the open water before they closed a net around us.

Whoever built this marina dredged a thin channel from the sea and created a small pond. The depth meter varied between two and a half and three meters—roughly nine feet. It was deep enough to handle almost any pleasure craft, but there were some restrictions. An extremely low tide might pucker the butt cheeks of a few captains, but that would be it.

The canal wound a quarter of a mile from the marina to the sea. Once I hit the channel, I pressed the throttle down a bit more. The three motors ripped through the water, and I winced as we tore past a small center console fishing boat. The driver screamed at us—rightfully so. I was being a royal asshole, and the man had no idea why I was trying to get out of there so fast.

It was an unforgivable act—the kind even priests couldn't properly absolve me of.

When we hit the open water, I sighed with relief. My hand pushed the throttle the rest of the way down, and the sound of the engines crept up a few more decibels.

In front of me, a blue screen with a small triangle showed our progress. The chartplotter indicated the depth outside of the dredged channel was around five feet. Good enough for the Cigarette, and I turned northeast.

The speedometer read 111 kilometers per hour. I hated doing the math, but that was somewhere north of sixty-five. We should be far outpacing the Oceanfast. With any luck, we'd get close enough to pick them up on the radar, if not the AIS. AIS was short for Automatic Identification System. If another boat had AIS, its name would show up on the screen. Instead of a random dot like on the radar, I'd see the name of the vessel and its location. The only issue with it was this boat had one too, meaning the Cubans could send out a welcoming party.

"Take the wheel," I ordered Leo. Holding the windshield, he shifted around to grab the helm as I slipped out from under him. I ducked below the dash, searching for the wire from the AIS. If I could trace it back to the source, I could disconnect the transponder without detaching the receiver. In which case, I'd be able to see the other vessels without being identified myself.

We crested a wave, and my body lifted off the floor before slamming down again. A groan came out of my mouth when

I hit, but I continued to follow the black-and-white cable until it went below deck. As I scrambled to my knees, we hit another wave, and my head slammed into the underside of the helm. The blow sent a sharp pain through my head, starting at the opened gash.

"Sorry," Leo shouted.

I pushed out from under him, waving it off. I'd prefer he keep up the speed rather than slow down for me to work.

"Keep going," I urged as I climbed below into the cabin.

The seas were rough, and at the speed we were going, most waves felt like a car racing over a series of speed bumps. The hull echoed with the tat-tat-tat across the top. My hands switched from one handhold to another as I moved to the electronic cluster mounted under the driver. The black-and-white wire fed into a group of wires tightly bound with a black zip-tie.

My fingernail dug beneath the black plastic tie and tugged. After several tries, the bind snapped, and the wires fell loose. My fingers grabbed the black-and-white wire I'd identified above and slid over it to the two components fed off it after it split. Luckily, the manufacturer of this boat labeled everything in English. It was likely the more common tongue among boat owners. The white wire trailed into the small black box that read "Transponder." There were other words, too, but that was the only one I cared about.

I yanked the white wire out, and the curled copper end came free of the transponder.

"Chase!" I heard Leo shout.

Another wave dislodged me as I tried to climb out of the hole. With some care, I climbed back on deck.

"We have company," Leo cried, pointing behind us.

Half a mile behind us, a black cutter raced after us.

"Shit!" I exclaimed. "Think it's the Cubans?"

"I doubt they're delivering pizza," he remarked. "You want to take over? I'm betting you are better at the driving side."

We rotated positions again, and I checked the gauges. The Cigarette skimmed over the wave at around seventy knots. If we weren't catching air on every wave, we might gain another five to ten knots.

"Are they gaining on us?" I asked.

He shook his head, shouting, "No, but we aren't losing them either."

"They'll be on top of us as soon as we catch up to the *Bella Notte*," I pointed out.

"I don't think they'll be in the mood to help us stop the yacht either," Leo suggested.

"Hang on," I warned. "We are going to come about. I hope you can hit a moving target."

Leo grinned, slid into the passenger seat, and pulled the straps around his chest. I followed suit, and once we were both properly restrained, I pulled the throttle into neutral.

Boats don't have brakes. In fact, one of the most dangerous things in boating is inertia. If I just spun the wheel, the rudder would turn us. Our forward motion would continue driving us in that direction even if the bow was now pointing on a different tack. That kind of move can easily result in a boat rolling across the surface at sixty knots—a prospect I'd seen occur and wanted no part of.

Since I cut out forward momentum, we continued forward but slowed rapidly. I cut the wheel when we dropped to about twenty knots. The hull of the Cigarette bounced into the waves, sending a gush of salt water over the gunwale and dousing both of us. Immediately, my hand thrust the lever forward, jerking the boat forward at a dash.

The cutter gained on us while we slowed, but they weren't about to turn at their speed either. Leo released his safety strap and bounded to his feet. He had the SIG Sauer Copperhead in his hand as we zipped on the starboard side of the cutter.

The machine gun fired three times, but the din of the engines drowned out any sound. I focused my attention on taking us as close to the cutter as I could without hitting them. As soon as we passed them with their gunwale only five feet off of ours, the Cigarette bounced over the Cuban wake.

In the cutter, three Cuban officers stared dumbfounded as we flew by them. The Cigarette shot about five hundred feet past the cutter when I cut the throttle again. As soon as we were coasting about twenty knots again, I spun the wheel and gunned the engine.

"Damn!" Leo cursed as another wave of seawater poured over the gunwale. "Don't you want to keep some ocean out of the boat?"

"Did you hit them?" I asked.

"I hit both motors," he acknowledged. "That didn't seem to slow them down."

"You get one more shot," I warned as I saw the Cuban patrol vessel coming around toward us.

"Roger that."

This time, the two Cuban passengers raised their sidearms and fired at us as we charged toward them. Both of us cowered below the dash. With my head down, steering the speedboat became more difficult. I peered over the windshield as my port side scraped against the cutter. We were moving at fifty knots, and the glancing blow barely moved us off course. The Cubans, however, careened away from us, jolted by the larger vessel's impact.

Leo raised up and fired three more shots. I eyed him in the rearview mirror. He exercised delicate precision, ensuring the ship's crew didn't get hit.

"That should do it," he announced, and I twisted around to see a small plume of smoke coming from the cutter's starboard motor. "Even if they don't stop now, it can't go too long."

Silently, I agreed as I pressed the throttle all the way down. We'd lost a little time, but our speed should compensate for that.

"They'll call in reinforcements," he pointed out. "If they put a bird in the air, it's gonna be harder to shoot them down without injuring anyone."

"Let's hope by the time they get one airborne we are too difficult to find."

Every minute we raced away from the Cuban shoreline, the larger the area anyone would need to search for us. Unfortunately, that held true for the *Bella Notte* too.

As we continued along the same heading we thought the yacht left port. I studied the radar and AIS for any pings. Several small vessels lighted up the radar screen, but most appeared to be small fishing crafts.

Then the radar pinged. A second later, the AIS flashed a new ship on the edge of the scope.

The name *"Bella Notte"* flashed on the screen.

32

The yacht clipped along about twelve knots. I slowed us down to thirty, hoping to catch up to her.

"We need some line," I told Leo. "Look through the compartments."

He nodded before digging under all the spaces, under the seats and cushions. He raised his hands triumphantly. In each, he held a coil of brand-new dock line. The packages both said thirty meters—plenty to do what I wanted.

"Take the wheel," I ordered, jumping out of the captain's chair and taking the rope.

"Keep it steady for a minute," I told him as I moved into the open bow.

On either side of the bow, a cleat sat on the gunwale. Normally, this is where the dock lines loop to keep the boat tied to the pier. Now, I created a harness, connecting both cleats to the opposite end of the line. The rope stretched into a V shape. The rest of the line wound back up into a coil.

When I returned to Leo, he asked, "What do you have in mind?"

"Ideally, we are going to need a way off the yacht, and their dinghy won't make it to Florida."

"Is that your next stop?" he asked.

I shrugged. "Only if we get William Thompson off that boat alive. Otherwise, I'm going to be looking for a nice place where extradition is really difficult."

"Sudan is nice," he remarked.

Groaning, I countered, "It isn't. I've been there."

"We better get him off then," he suggested.

"Close the gap," I told him. "We need to run almost onto their ass to make this work."

Leo sped up. The stern of the *Bella Notte* grew larger as we drove down the middle of her wake.

"Get me close enough to jump," I explained.

The Cigarette continued to overtake the yacht.

"They are going to see us coming, Chase," he pointed out.

I grabbed the other Copperhead and pulled the sling over my head. "Once I jump, you'll need to hold the speed long enough for me to attach the painter."

"What next?" he asked. "I cut the power and take a running jump?"

My eyes didn't blink. "Not exactly," I explained, holding up the other rope.

"Damn," he muttered. "Guess if I'm going to die, it might as well be today."

"I promise to pull you in," I assured him as I tied the end of the second line to him.

The Oceanfast 48 came with a swim platform on the stern so that its crew had easy access to the water. It wasn't likely the boat would stop for us. That meant we had to board it at speed. Ideally, we'd have a larger team with a driver who could stay back once the unit disembarked. Since we didn't have that, I intended to treat the Cigarette just like the dinghy I towed behind *Carina*.

Perched on the bow, I slid my arms through both coils and waited. Leo pushed the boat closer, and I measured the distance in my head. The jump itself shouldn't be difficult—three to five feet was a piece of cake. No, the problem came in landing and maintaining balance.

Much like the challenge of turning at sixty knots, inertia again proved to be a problem. This time, I had to make the jump from a faster vessel to land on one going slower. A physicist could run the numbers on a chalkboard, but I still wouldn't know if it would work. This all relied on speed and reaction.

I took off some slack from the coil of line with the bridle attached to the bow. I didn't want to jump with too short a length and let the boat yank me back like a Yo-Yo.

The distance between the two vessels shrank, and I pulled back, took a deep breath, and jumped to the other boat. The momentum of the Cigarette boat stalled as soon as I jumped. I hit the swim platform in a running stumble forward.

Leo dropped the throttle back, and despite the Cigarette's momentum, the rumrunner lagged back, suddenly dragging the line wrapped around my shoulder. Unfortunately, I was going with it. My feet came out from under me, and I landed hard on the fiberglass platform. My fingers caught an eyelet before I fell off the back.

The Cigarette sped up as Leo realized his mistake. The bow lunged forward, and I rolled back as the hull scraped up over the platform.

My arm slugged the line off my shoulder and into my hand as I searched for the end. Leo dropped back some, but he compensated quickly, keeping the boat closer to the Oceanfast. I made a quick hitch knot around a cleat. Once I secured it, I moved to the other side of the stern and repeated the process with the line attached to Leo.

I glanced back as he pointed above my head. The din resonating from all the motors still muffled the gunshot, but the fiberglass at my feet exploded with tiny shrapnel. A figure leaned over the upper deck, but the angle he was firing at didn't give him a clean shot.

The Cigarette fell back. Leo must have dropped it in neutral. He raised up and fired the Copperhead at the man above me. He gave me a quick thumbs-up just before he threw himself over the gunwale.

I got back into position, grabbing the line and heaving it in. Life at sea offered me lots of opportunities to reel in big fish, but I'd snagged nothing like a 225-pound Marine. The effort to pull him against the drag he was creating was exhausting. After I hauled about ten feet in, I wrapped it around a cleat so we wouldn't lose it all and have to start over.

With a quick breath, I shifted my gaze back to see Leo surface and catch a breath before the tug of the rope dragged him back under. He was trying to conserve his strength, but eventually, he wouldn't be able to get the gulp of air. Or worse, seawater would gush down him like a high-powered fire hose.

I made another loop, and as I reached for the line, a figure jumped from above, landing on me. My elbow shot behind me, catching the bulky figure, and he pulled away. I rolled away from him, throwing my right foot back in a kick that barely connected.

My hand wiped the water away from my face, and I saw the man get to his feet. He charged at me, and I scampered away, trying to swing the Copperhead around from where it hung off my shoulder. He barreled into me, and I twisted around, using his own momentum. The move threw me against the transom, but he stumbled off the platform.

The deck popped as someone above fired at me. To minimize myself as a target, I pressed against the hull. Without coming down, they couldn't get their sights on me. However, it wouldn't take long to figure out they had a clean shot at the man being dragged behind the yacht.

Without being pummeled, I found it much easier to pull the SIG machine gun around my body. I aimed it up over my head, directing the barrel blindly toward the people above me. The gun fired smoothly when I pulled the trigger. Six shots spat out fast, and hoping the shooter ducked, I took the chance to turn and get a better aim. I squeezed ten shots off before I charged for the steps leading up from the platform.

I couldn't risk the glance to check on Leo. If I didn't get the gunmen out of the picture, it wouldn't matter. He'd be dead before he hauled himself out of the water.

They fired down at me, but I stayed behind the cover of the stairs. When I reached the top, I dove through the opening, firing to the left where two men stood with guns drawn. My shots were low, but the rounds ripped along the deck and into all four ankles. Their shots went wild, or at least they didn't seem to strike anything around me. I hurried out of the opening to shield myself behind an outdoor galley.

Despite the injury to their legs, they peppered the back of the terra-cotta bar. After a second, they learned—each taking turns to fire suppressing rounds. They'd be able to hold me down long enough to move into position and get a kill shot.

My back pressed against the cabinet where a propane tank fed into the flat-top griddle. Quickly, I unscrewed the tank and pulled it free. It was a traditional one holding about fifteen gallons of propane. And it was full.

The Copperhead raised over my head and spat out four shots. While I prayed the two gunmen ducked for cover, I threw the tank up in the air, arcing it over the flat-top.

When the clatter of metal slamming into the deck sounded, I raised up, firing at the two men and the tank. There was a ringing ping when the round struck metal.

Nothing is like the movies. When someone shoots a gas tank, it rarely explodes. Any fuel needs a spark, and unless the shot is lucky enough, the only spark is from the gun. What it does is punch a hole in a pressurized container, sending streams of gas out like a rocket. The tank flies about like a balloon when the gas is rushing out. Here, it bounced around the deck between the walls like a pinball, bowling the two gunmen over.

I came around the corner, firing at the two dazed men. The first dropped with a kill shot to the head. Unfortunately, despite taking a round to the chest, the other one squeezed off a shot—in a small area where a propane tank spewed its contents. The subsequent flash blew me back. It wasn't enough to cause a gigantic explosion. Most of the gas was dissipating quickly, but enough ignited to create a rather large flash bang.

My face tingled from the heat that flared out and licked my skin as it shoved me back. I might have lost an eyebrow hair or two, but that was the only injury incurred.

Back on my feet, I ran toward the steps when the distinctive "chunk-clunk" of a shotgun caught my attention. Instinct caused me to dive toward the two bodies of the dead gunmen as what sounded like a twelve-gauge exploded. The handrail leading to the swim platform exploded in chunks as the blast ripped a hole where I'd been standing.

"Chunk-clunk," the shotgun shouted again. Its wielder was one deck up, and if I came up at all, he'd have my head.

My neck strained back, trying to get a look at the shooter. I didn't risk coming up. He wouldn't risk coming down either. Once he rounded the corner to get a shot, I'd kill him. Probably not before he pulled the trigger, leaving me with a gaping hole in my body.

I grabbed the now empty propane tank, which was much lighter after spewing its contents, and tested his vigilance, tossing it forward. The shotgun exploded, and the round, white tank flew off the deck. I watched it disappear, likely ending up in the water.

"Chunk-clunk."

A "tat-tat-tat-tat-tat," barely audible over the drone of the Oceanfast's engines, interrupted the warning cry of the shotgun. A clatter of metal falling to the deck sounded like a large gun falling from the deck above. I raised up slowly to see a man's limp hand hanging awkwardly over the railing above before the rhythmic motion of the boat caused him to slide out of view.

Turning around, I found a gasping Leo Taylor, drenched and holding his Copperhead up in the firing position.

33

"You said you'd pull me in," he muttered when he took up position beside me.

Leo's chest still heaved as he tried to catch his breath. The man was nothing but muscle from years of training, but crawling hand over hand up a line while fighting the drag of the ocean was no easy feat. He needed a few seconds to catch his breath.

He gagged again, spitting out more saltwater he'd inhaled.

"Sorry, we had a barbecue while we were waiting for you," I joked.

The man glanced at the singed gunmen on deck. "Too rare for me," he replied. "I'm good, let's go."

I stood guard while he took his breather. Now he got to his feet and followed me.

The last time I'd seen this vessel, it was at a dock at Bahia Mar in Fort Lauderdale. The private security prevented me from getting aboard, so I didn't know the exact layout. However, after several years around boats, I understood how the designers laid them out. From where we stood, there was another deck five steps up, where the man with the shotgun had been. That deck would lead through a sliding glass door into the larger living area. My guess was a salon connected to the galley.

It would also be the one easily covered by gunmen. Anyone inside would have a clear view of us crossing the deck while we'd get the reflection from the sun and sea. The setup might not be as easy as shooting fish in a barrel, but the advantage wouldn't be ours.

"How many men do you think we have here?" Leo asked.

"It could easily accommodate twenty," I suggested. "But we're four down now."

"Don't forget Watkins," Leo reminded me. "Those four were amateurs compared to him."

"He's a fucking squid," I snipped.

"Oorah," he grunted behind me. The Marine battle cry.

"Let's flank them," I said. "You take the starboard side. I'll go port. There'll be a forward door. Expect it to be covered, though."

"I'd be disappointed if it wasn't," he replied with a wry smile before crossing to the other side of the deck.

He scaled along the edge of the deck. I stepped over onto the opposite side. In order to maneuver forward along the edge, we'd both pass expansive windows. Much like the sliding glass door, the bright Caribbean day turned those ports into two-way mirrors. Unfortunately for us, we were the ones staring at our reflections while the occupants would see us clearly.

I lowered myself below the bottom edge of the glass. It wouldn't help if someone moved right up to it, but it was the best I could do under the circumstances.

"Gordon, damn you are persistent," a voice called over the wind—Watkins.

The SIG Copperhead in my hand came up as I searched for the SEAL. Somewhere on the fore deck, the man hid, probably waiting for a clean shot.

"Aaron, I have a big fucking headache thanks to you," I shouted. "Why don't you come on out and let me pay you back for it?"

He fired at me with four successive shots. I cowered down and searched for him. The shots came from the flybridge. Made sense. He'd want a bird's-eye view for a direct line of sight.

"Argg!" I screamed, twisting around with the Copperhead firing wildly at the upper helm. The nine-millimeter rounds ripped into the railing and the hardtop covering.

I scrambled forward, trying to find cover before Watkins recovered enough to fire again. My reprieve was short-lived as he came over the railing, firing down on me. I dove forward, sliding under the lifeline and rolling over the gunwale.

My left arm wrapped around the stanchion as my feet dangled twelve feet above the water's surface. Lifting the Copperhead, I squeezed the trigger, driving the SEAL back from the edge. The slide locked back when I burned through the last round. As I tossed the Copperhead up on deck, I heaved myself up under the lifeline and crawled forward.

I pulled the twenty-two out. The little automatic only held twelve rounds, and the stopping power of such a small caliber could be ineffective. Not that a twenty-two wasn't deadly, but in order to be so, it required accuracy. I wasn't as efficient as Jay or Leo, but I was proficient enough.

I rolled back and fired three shots into the forward windows. The small rounds punched through tempered glass. The impact didn't break the window, but sent spider-webbed cracks across the front. Charging forward, I threw myself through the glass with my back and shoulders driving through. Shards scattered upon impact, and I crashed onto a queen-sized bed before rolling onto the floor.

"Aaah!" someone screamed.

I jumped up with the pistol raised. William Thompson shrank into the corner. He burrowed his head between his knees.

The cabin door opened, and I fired into the opening crack. There was only a brief glimpse of a face before the .22 caliber bullet hit it.

I jumped over the bed and jerked the door open as another man wearing a white polo shirt came down the corridor. I fired again as Polo lifted a Glock 17 toward me. My shot struck him in the throat. He stumbled forward before face-planting in front of me. I bent over and scooped up the Glock before stepping back into the cabin.

"Mr. Thompson?" I asked.

The man lifted his head to stare at me.

"Why do you keep doing this?" he questioned.

"I'm sorry, sir. This time I'm actually rescuing you."

"You said that last time," he muttered. "I wasn't even in danger."

The cabin door jerked as someone fired at me. I raised the Glock, squeezing the trigger twice. Whoever fired at me remained around the corner. I shoved the door closed, locking it.

"I was told last night we were rescuing you," I explained. "That was a lie."

"No shit," the man snapped.

"If you want out of here, we need to go now."

The door shook, and it wouldn't take much force to splinter the wood and break through.

I fired two nine-millimeter rounds into the wood. The bullets tore through the thin wooden partition as if it were paper.

A grunt sounded from the other side—I'd hit him, at least.

"Go out the window," I ordered Thompson.

The whimpering man crawled to his feet and climbed out the window as someone slammed into the door. The frame splintered as the door flew open. I fired three times into the man on the other side. He crumpled to the floor as more shouting echoed down the corridor. I jumped back over the bed and dove out the shattered remnants of the window.

It occurred to me they gave Thompson a delightful view, at least for a prison.

Gunfire erupted from a deck above us, and I grabbed Thompson, pulling him back. Another spat of gunfire sounded. But he deck around us remained calm.

"Clear!" I heard Leo shout from above.

I stepped back to see the sniper give me a two-finger salute.

"I got the man," I shouted. "Let's get the hell out of here."

Leo jerked suddenly before pitching over the railing. He slammed into the deck, and the Glock in my hand came up as a figure appeared on the deck.

A woman.

She was Asian, but I thought I knew her. She held an H&K forty-five. The Glock bucked as I fired it at her, and she vanished from sight.

The hotel.

I remembered her face now. She was the woman in the room I'd woken up in. The one who'd answered the door when I went back to look around.

"Check him," I ordered Thompson as I stepped back, searching for more combatants.

"He's alive," Thompson claimed. "The bullet hit him in the shoulder."

Leo was lucky. If the woman hit him closer to center, the forty-five would tear through him like the nine-millimeter did to the cabin door. Instead, it knocked him forward. The fall might have done as much damage.

"Thompson, can he move?"

"How do I know?" Thompson cried. "I'm not a damned doctor. We need to leave him."

My head swiveled toward the son of the Commander-in-Chief. "That will not happen," I shouted. "Get him to his feet. We have to get to the back of the boat."

"He's unconscious," Thompson shouted.

"Then carry his ass," I ordered. "Unless you want to keep everyone from shooting us."

Resigned, Thompson scooped Leo up under the arm. I hoped he had the sense to get him from the uninjured side, but at the moment, I didn't have time to worry about it.

Leo let out a groan.

"You with me, man?" I asked him.

He grunted incoherently.

"Stay with me," I demanded.

Thompson nodded.

A shot came from Thompson's cabin, and I jerked around to fire at a silhouette in the doorway. He shrank back, and I waved Thompson to hurry.

There was no easy way to get Leo to the aft of the *Bella Notte*. The expansive windows were still between us and the swim platform. By now, any remaining goons should be taking up a position in the rear. They knew we needed to get there, and they'd set themselves as a literal roadblock.

The silhouette I'd fired at now took form as he clambered out the window. I shot the Glock over Thompson's shoulder, hitting the man in the chest.

"You have to jump," I urged.

"What the fuck?" he blurted out.

"We can't make it to the back like this," I explained. "You take Leo and jump. The yacht will leave you behind. I'll get to the back and bring our getaway back to pick you up."

"What happens if you don't make it?" Thompson asked.

"The same thing that happens if you stay. We all die."

"That's bullshit," he muttered.

"I have a better chance of getting past them," I told him. "With Leo, we're sitting ducks."

"We leave him then," Thompson snapped.

"I plan to leave you before I leave him," I growled, locking my eyes on him.

"You know who I am, don't you?" he asked.

"Do you know who he is?"

He shook his head.

"He's a fucking Marine!" I shouted. "He goes with me."

Thompson nodded meekly.

"Now, your best bet is to jump."

He nodded again.

"Keep him above water," I ordered. "If I get back to you and he's gone, I'm leaving your ass in the water. Understand me?"

Leo groaned again. "I'll keep him alive," he mumbled, coming around.

I almost laughed at the absurdity. "Damned straight Marine. Now, go, Thompson."

No one had taken a shot at us in several seconds. I doubted we'd cleared all the crew yet. Watkins and the Asian woman were still out there. It made sense they were all stationed to keep us from reaching the stern.

Thompson hoisted Leo up higher with his shoulder under the sniper's arm. He dragged the Marine to the edge, and before jumping, he glanced back, hoping I came up with a new plan. I gave him a nod, and the president's son leapt off the gunwale, dragging Leo Taylor with him into the sea.

I waited several seconds until I saw the two heads emerge just inside the Oceanfast's wake. Now, I moved forward to the foredeck. No one was standing at the next level, and I ran up the sloping outer wall of the cabin. The slick surface made it difficult to find any traction, but with a running start, I reached the bottom of the rail with my left hand.

For the second time, I pulled myself up onto the next level. Two corpses lay on the deck—neither was the Asian woman nor Watkins. On my belly, I wiggled toward the edge.

My suspicions proved correct. Five men stood near the grill where I'd taken cover earlier.

When I pulled back from the edge, I checked my ammo. There were seven rounds left, including the one in the chamber. In one motion, I launched myself to my feet and fired down on the men. With only half a second between shots, I shifted the sights from one to the next, starting on the port side and working starboard.

In a moment like that, any delay can kill. I didn't wait to see if I'd hit my target before moving to the next. That also meant I was counting on hitting them. After the fifth shot, I vaulted over the railing, landing on the sun deck just below where I'd been standing, and a level higher than my five targets. As I dropped, I saw all five men had gone down. Without pausing, I ran as soon as the soles of my feet connected. With a broad jump, I leapt up and pushed my right foot off the next railing to jump over the small galley.

My estimation was off. I don't know by how much, but when I pushed off the railing, my foot slipped. Instead of another graceful leap over the heads of the fallen men, I tumbled sideways and fell.

Crashing down, I slammed into the edge of the terra-cotta grill station where I'd found cover earlier. The impact on my back knocked the air from my lungs, and I rolled off the grill, hitting the deck.

"Damn," Watkins mocked. "That was a spectacular fail."

I turned my head up to see the disgraced Navy SEAL staring down at me over his M45. The woman who shot Leo stepped up beside him.

34

I rolled to my side. The Glock wasn't in my hand, and at least for the moment, I remained stunned, unable to react quickly. Mentally, I scanned my body. Everything hurt, but I'd been lucky. If one could call some cracked ribs and enough contusions to cover my body lucky.

"I have to admit," the woman remarked. "I thought you were just a lucky son of a bitch."

With my head, I offered her a gesture as if to point out the inaccuracy of that statement.

She laughed. It wasn't a pretty sound either. There was something alien about the laughter—it didn't match the face. She was attractive, even gorgeous, but in the way a cobra was beautiful.

One wanted to stroke the shiny scales despite the danger.

She exuded that. In fact, compared to Watkins, this woman scared me a great deal more than the SEAL.

"I'm afraid you have me at a disadvantage," I said, trying not to wheeze the words out, but portray an air of superiority.

"It seems I have you at several."

I shrugged again. "Who are you? Joe Loggins's wife? Not his daughter. A girlfriend?"

A scoff uttered from her lips.

I smiled. "Not even that, huh?"

"What does that mean?" she asked.

"Were you his Girl Friday?" I questioned. "He disappears and you take the reins. Seems apropos, doesn't it? Although, maybe instead of coming after me, you should thank me."

Her arms folded. I was irritating her, but I figured I had little to lose.

"After all," I added, "you'd still be fetching coffee if Joe was still around."

Watkins stepped in, punching me in the face. My head snapped back, cracking against the tile.

"Keep it up, asshole," I growled.

"Or what?" he snapped.

I turned back to the woman. "All of this was about revenge?" I asked.

"Don't be ridiculous," she scoffed. "That was an added benefit. You seemed to pop up in my business enough, it seemed like a good time to—what's the military term?—neutralize you."

"I've never met you," I spouted. "How am I in your way? After all, I killed Loggins. Now you get his nice boat and probably a fancy office somewhere."

"This has been fun," she remarked. "You've certainly outperformed anything I thought you might have done. In retrospect, Watkins should have just killed you at the mansion."

"That would have been smarter," I said.

"I can remedy it," Watkins retorted, pulling the same K-Bar knife he'd used to slice the guard's throat at Mikhalov's house. He twisted it so the sun reflected off the blade.

"Just kill him," she ordered. "Then toss him over. I need to find Thompson and the other one."

"They left," I blurted out.

"What do you mean?" she asked, turning her head to me. The dark brown eyes almost appeared to glow red when she scowled into my face.

"I mean, they aren't on the boat anymore," I stated, smirking as I pushed myself up a little more.

The woman straightened up and instinctively turned toward the Cigarette still dragging behind us. Watkins couldn't help himself—he mimicked her. As he looked aft, I kicked my right foot out, connecting with his left kneecap. The blow buckled his leg, and as he fell, I roused to my feet, moving away from the two.

Watkins recovered, charging after me. Anger boiled through his veins, and his face reddened as he swiped the K-Bar toward me. I leapt back as the flash of silver whipped past my torso.

The SEAL had the advantage over me. I was still reeling from the fall I'd just taken. Every muscle hurt, but a new flush of adrenaline coursed through me.

Watkins knew he had the advantage. He grinned wickedly as he rocked back and forth on his feet, taunting me with the threat of another strike. Over his shoulder, I watched the woman raise a Glock—my Glock. Technically, it belonged to the man I'd killed earlier, but semantics didn't seem to matter. She'd retrieved it from the deck after I dropped it.

There seemed to be little I could do. If I bested Watkins, she'd shoot me before I had the time to savor the victory. If I didn't beat Watkins, he'd kill me before she ever got the chance to fire.

"Aaron, I don't get this. How much is she paying you?"

"Plenty," he snarled.

My eyes shifted to her. "Why didn't you ever try to buy me?" I asked.

She grinned. "You flew three thousand miles and hiked up a mountain in a blizzard just to kill Loggins. Why? Because he was going to kill a girl you just met? I don't think scruples like that are for sale."

Watkins lunged, and I jumped back, parrying down with my left forearm. His hand dipped, and my right fist balled up and fired into his face. The punch was quick and stunned him. Before he could get the knife back up, my right hand caught his wrist and jerked him forward.

The blade dug into my thigh as I slammed my forehead into his nose. Stunned, he released the grip on the handle, and I wrenched him around, wrapping my left forearm around his throat.

For a split second, I locked eyes with the woman. For a split second, she froze. My right hand caught the side of Watkins's head, and with a quick twist, I snapped the man's neck. Even my teeth ground with the crunch as the vertebrae in the SEAL's neck split. I pulled his body up as the woman started firing.

She only had two rounds in the Glock, and I let the impact into Watkins push me backward. My back pressed against the railing, and I rolled back over the side. My body struck the water, and I sank below the surface.

There was no time to waste, and I kicked into the wake of the Oceanfast. The blade in my thigh burned like a red-hot poker as it continued to cut through the flesh with every movement.

No time to focus on it.

I surface as the Cigarette barreled over me. My hands pushed against the hull, shoving me deeper.

Under the water, I made out the shape of the propellers cutting through the water. My hands caught the skeg of the port motor. I got both hands around it and pulled myself forward. As soon as I could, I wrapped my left arm around the lower unit. Thankfully, Leo cut the engines before he got off because the propeller pressed against my chest. If someone started the engine now, I'd end up looking like a lemon after being juiced.

My head strained above the water to catch a breath. Unfortunately, rumrunners like the Cigarette weren't expected to be used as swim platforms like so many boats in the Caribbean Sea. They had one purpose—to get from point A to point B fast. Very fast.

The speedster didn't have a swim platform. Hell, it didn't have a ladder. What it had was a one-foot clearance between the port outboard and the edge of the transom, which was made up like a small shelf to hold the outboards.

As if someone considered the possibility of needing to get from the water into the boat, a small eight-inch handhold hung on the port side gunwale just above the transom. It would require thirty-inch arms to reach from the water, and from where I was being dragged, I would need almost three and a half feet between my shoulder and hand to get to it.

My right hand stretched up the shaft of the outboard until it reached the lip where the motor cover attached to the midsection. My fingertips dug into the crack and pulled myself up. I worked to keep my left arm looped around the shaft as I struggled to get up out of the water. I'd never be able to hold myself by the fingertips, and when I lost it, I didn't want to lose all my progress. Or worse, my grip on the boat.

When I had the chance, I relaxed my fingers and reached higher on the powerhead. Now I lifted my knee onto the triangular whale tail attached above the propeller. The metal piece prevented the propeller from creating a tunnel of air and cavitating, which happens when the propeller suddenly has no water to push. The intent is to keep the boat's momentum from stuttering when cavitation occurs.

For now, the whale tail gave me a platform from which I could reach the handhold. When I finally rolled into the boat, I flopped on the floor like a fish. My eyes watched the blue sky overhead for about six seconds before I pulled myself up.

Ahead, the *Bella Notte* trudged along. The woman seemed to be the only one left on board. At first she hadn't noticed me, assuming I'd gone under and hopefully gotten run over by her yacht. When she finally realized I was on the Cigarette, she bent over and picked up a gun. Her shots, wild and inaccurate, seemed to be harmless, but I ducked as I ran to the bow, knowing either her luck or mine could turn at random.

My right hand reached down, grabbing the handle of the
K-Bar still jutting from my thigh. I gritted my teeth as I pulled
it out.

Blood dripped off the blade, but it had hit nothing too vital.
I'd need to staunch the bleeding, but it would have to wait a few
minutes.

She fired again. This time, a round struck the hull below me.
I waved at her, and she stopped shooting. With one finger raised
on my left hand, I sliced the blade down with my right, severing
the taut line connecting the Cigarette to the Oceanfast.

Immediately, the boat slowed, and I moved to the driver's
seat, where I started all three motors. The sound of the engines
screamed across the surface of the water. The helm spun in my
hand, and I pressed the throttle down.

All boats leave a trail, and a large one like the Oceanfast might
leave one for miles before it dissipates. I sped along the line left
behind. The internal timer in my head told me fourteen minutes
passed from the time Thompson and Leo went overboard until
now. I wasn't sure how fast the yacht was traveling, but in my
head, I estimated ten knots. If my math was any good, they were
about two and a half miles back.

In the distance, I could make out the faint line that was
Cuba just above the surface of the water. While I wanted to
get back quickly, if I went too fast I might pass them without
seeing them. I just hoped Thompson was smart enough to make
himself seen. I should have warned him how hard it might be to
spot him when I came back. At the time, I was more worried
about getting him to commit to jumping. No point in adding
to any fear and anxiety he might be experiencing.

I watched the trail I was leaving on the chartplotter. When I
neared two miles from where I'd turned about, I slowed down.
With my hand on top of the helm, I raised up to my feet. Blood
still poured down my leg, and I realized I needed to tend to
my own wound. I was still losing blood steadily, even though it

wasn't a massive bleeder. However, I could be searching for the two men for a while, and if I passed out because of blood loss eventually, it would mean all three of us die out here.

The first aid kit was located exactly where it was supposed to be—under the helm. With the K-Bar's blade, I cut the pants away, exposing the cut. With some gauze, I stuffed the cut closed before wrapping a cotton bandage around my thigh. Within five minutes, I thought I'd stopped the bleeding.

Now, I motored slowly. Every few minutes, I glanced back, halfway expecting the *Bella Notte* to turn around. Surely, whoever that woman was, she wasn't dumb enough to expect to catch me.

My brain continued to count off seconds as I slowed to a putter. Except for the faint outline of Cuba, blue water was all I around me. Trailing toward the horizon, the faint impression of the Oceanfast's wake remained visible, but within the next few minutes, it would be gone too. My eyes fixed on the distant shape, trying to keep some sort of landmark as a heading. By watching the progress on the chartplotter, I could hold the boat on a somewhat straight trajectory.

After thirty minutes, worry crept in. Had I missed them? Did they drift too far away? I'd been searching off to either side with no luck. The Cigarette's motors idled, barely pushing me in a straight line.

Using a trick I'd learned from an old sergeant, I unfocused my eyes as I searched across the waves.

After several passes, I stopped. Something struck me as unnatural.

That's how it can be on the sea. Everything is chaotic. Waves always look different, and I'm often taking another look because I thought I spotted a dolphin or something. Usually, it's just a trick of the eye. When a dolphin surfaces, there's no mistaking it. I might need to wait for it to resurface, but the sight was always definitive.

Which was exactly what I knew. Something definitely bobbed in the waves. It might have been trash, but it was there. When the waves lifted it up, I got another look. A figure waving frantically toward me.

My shoulders sagged as I let out a sigh of relief before motoring toward the bobbing shape.

35

The United States Navy met us when we were ten miles out from Key West. The USS Key West came alongside.

Leo, who had regained consciousness while bobbing around the Caribbean Sea, was lifted out. His injuries weren't life-threatening, but the ship's doctor intended to make sure he would recover. Once they got him aboard, they would come back for me.

For the moment, two Master-at-Arms stood guard over me.

"I'll talk to my father," Thompson assured me before I called over the radio to surrender myself.

I shrugged. "It was my own fault," I admitted.

He shook his head. In the last few hours, I'd gotten to appreciate him a little more. He had been out of his depth, having been kidnapped—twice effectively. But it turned out he'd been working to ensure the Danube Delta wasn't harmed during the extraction of natural gas. He'd been negotiating with Mikhalov and Turchin. Of course, now that might be for naught.

Before the Navy took Thompson off the boat, he swore again, "I'll get you out of this."

The Naval doctor was kind enough to stitch up the knife wound in my leg. The gash on my head required some extra care as he shaved the hair around it and rebandaged it. I'd lost Mai's handiwork somewhere after we made our escape from the marina. Once the doctor seemed assured I would not have any more issues, the Master at Arms dragged me to the brig.

During my time in the Corps, I'd never ended up in the brig. I've seen plenty of jail cells in my time, and the brig on a frigate is about the smallest confined space one can legally throw someone. The space wasn't much bigger than a pantry. In fact, I had to fold the bunk up against the wall if I wanted to use the head, which also folded out of the bulkhead.

It didn't matter. Once I dropped onto the thin mattress, I fell asleep. The drugs the doctor gave me might have hastened the slumber, but I knew it was really the exhaustion that overwhelmed me.

When I awoke, the timer in my head told me I'd been asleep for ten hours. I stretched and sat up, placing my feet on the cold metal floor. The Navy didn't even pretend to offer any comfort in the holding cell.

An ensign appeared an hour later, carrying a metal plate with eggs and sausage. A piece of toast with a single pat of butter hung off the edge.

"You want coffee?" the ensign asked in a squeaky voice.

"Please. Black."

He opened a small door and passed the plate through the opening. Then he disappeared. Three minutes later, he returned with what amounted to the smallest cup of coffee I'd ever seen.

"I don't suppose I get any refills?" I asked.

The ensign stared at me incredulously. "No, sir."

"Next time I'll just get some water."

"There's water in your basin," the kid told me, pointing at the small sink at the back of the cell.

"Can I keep the cup, then?" I asked.

He shrugged. I hoped he displayed a little more initiative and respect around the other sailors. Maybe I'm just some civilian who tried to kidnap the president's son.

I folded the toast in half, filling it with sausage and eggs. Within seconds, I devoured the sausage-egg toast I created. Once I finished it, I scooped the rest of the eggs from the plate into my mouth.

With a clank, the metal plate bounced against the deck, and I leaned back on the bed, savoring the smallest and apparently the weakest coffee in Key West.

Given that the frigate wasn't moving, I guessed by now we'd docked at the base. We would have made it back to land within an hour of the time they picked us up. By now, I expected William Thompson to be back in D.C.

I wondered what happened to Leo. His injuries weren't too bad, but I wondered if they dropped him in the same bucket with me. I didn't hear anyone else in any of the other cells, but he might be under guard in sick bay still. As far as I knew, none of the news outlets showed him, so maybe he was being considered an innocent in the whole affair.

That was unlikely. He was a former Marine too. How likely would it be that the Navy rescued two Marines with the president's son? He'd be guilty until proven innocent.

Anytime I want to stretch out an affair, like drinking the only coffee I'd had in two days, it seemed like an arduous process. There wasn't enough coffee in the cup to keep it warm, which meant I needed to consume it with some consistency. But coffee, even weak-ass Navy coffee, was something that needs to be enjoyed.

Nonetheless, I found myself soon with an empty cup—and some sadness. I set the cup down before I rolled over on the bed and closed my eyes.

I wasn't tired, but I let myself drift into a realm between awake and asleep. At this point, most people might be worried about what was next. I didn't concern myself with it right now.

What coursed through my brain was anger mixed with curiosity. Who was the Asian woman? I thought my guess about her being his assistant was close. That remark pissed her off enough to be true.

Why would she come after me, though? What I told her about thanking me should be true. If I hadn't killed Joe Loggins in his cabin in Canada, she'd still be fetching coffee.

No, it was more than that. She said I'd interfered in other things.

Interfering tended to be my superpower, but I don't know what it could have been.

The only thing I really knew was she was still on that boat, and I pissed her off. I worked very hard to leave women with a favorable opinion of me. This woman hated me though, and that worried me more than whatever the United States government might throw at me.

Before long, I drifted back to sleep. Even though I already rested, I'd learned in the Corps to sleep when the opportunity availed me. It wasn't deep, but I dozed for several hours.

"Gordon, upenatem," a voice jerked me out of my doze.

I bounced onto my feet, forgetting for a split second I wasn't in the military anymore. On the other side of the door, a Master at Arms stood.

"Come on," he ordered, unlocking the cage.

I waited as he swung the gate open, expecting him to cuff me again. He didn't.

"They are waiting for you," he announced, ushering me out.

Our footsteps echoed inside the metal hull as the Master at Arms escorted me up two decks. When he opened the door, the more comfortable side of command became clear. A situation room with a long table and carpeted floors showed the distinct difference between where the officers worked and the enlisted.

I froze in place when I saw the face at the other end of the table. Jacob Thompson, the president of the United States of America, stared at me from the opposite side of the room.

"Lieutenant Gordon," he greeted me. "Please come in."

After he spoke, I realized six officers already occupied the table. To my right, I saw the face of General Judith Shaw. She wore her dress blues, and the sparkle of the gold buttons glinted under the fluorescent lighting. She offered me a nearly imperceptible reassuring nod.

"Mr. President, how are you?" I stammered.

"Have a seat, please," he ordered.

I obeyed, sitting at the end of the table.

"I've talked with my son," he assured me.

There was no question, and I'd long ago learned when a commanding officer spoke to me like that the dumbest thing I could do was answer.

"He swears you rescued him from his kidnappers," he stated.

I resisted the urge to nod. The president was leading up to something, and the best option seemed to let him get there on his own time.

"However, the video footage released to the media indicates you were involved in his kidnapping."

Waiting, I inhaled slightly.

"Well, Lieutenant Gordon, which is it? Did you kidnap my son or did you rescue him?"

Obviously, he knew exactly what happened because I'd explained it to William Thompson once I dragged him aboard the Cigarette.

"Both, Mr. President," I stated.

The Commander-in-Chief folded his hands in front of him. His eyes narrowed as he stared down the table at me. They demanded more explanation.

"Sir, a woman claiming to be a CIA agent named Danielle Wallace approached me. She insisted I help her, claiming to have used US Code 688 to recall me into active duty. According to the orders she gave me, I was to answer to her for this one operation."

"What was the operation?" a man two seats to the right of the president asked.

"Rescue William Thompson, who was being held by a Russian oligarch named Valeri Mikhalov. We were also to obtain documents proving that William Thompson was working with the Russians to exploit an area off the Black Sea called the Danube Delta."

The president's right index finger tapped slowly against the back of his left hand as he listened.

"In truth, I didn't trust Wallace. My presence in Cuba at the time was—you might say unplanned. I assumed she had been behind this."

The same man asked, "You claim someone kidnapped and left you in a hotel room in Havana?"

"I'm sorry, sir. I don't know who you are."

He contorted his face, appalled I didn't recognize him. "James Lacher. Director of the Central Intelligence Agency."

"Again, I'm sorry, sir. I don't watch the news much," I told Lacher. "But to answer your question, Mr. Lacher. Yes, I woke up in a hotel room with a dead body."

"And you think Agent Wallace was behind that?"

I shook my head. "I thought she was, but now I suspect this woman on the boat orchestrated the whole thing. She had Wallace killed, which at least cemented in my mind that Wallace wasn't the brains behind it."

The president flashed a wry grin. "Why did you try to rescue my son after you realized what was going on?"

I shrugged. "It was my job to rescue him, and it seemed like I needed to do that."

"Commendable," he remarked.

"Not completely," I admitted. "It seemed prudent to find your son if I wanted to prove I didn't actually kidnap him."

"Prudent, huh?" the president asked, and I noticed Shaw suppress a grin.

I shrugged.

"What do you do for a living now?" Thompson asked.

"I'm a bartender," I replied.

"Who lives on a boat?"

"Yes. It's in Puerto Rico right now," I told him.

"James, do you want to make your proposal?" the president asked.

My eyes shifted to the CIA director. Lacher cleared his throat. "The president thinks you might make an excellent asset. We've spoken with your former commanding officer, General Shaw, and she confirms you would be the right person."

I glanced at Shaw curiously. If I remembered her opinion of the agency, a recommendation like that seemed out of character. Of course, she now worked in the Pentagon. Certain relationships required a delicate balance.

"The right person for what?" I asked.

"We'd like you to take an occasional assignment—off-book—for us."

My lips pursed as I shook my head. "I'm fairly happy not working for the government right now."

"We'd like to help you find this woman who kidnapped William," Thompson offered.

"She worked for Joe Loggins," I said. "Track down his employee records."

"Loggins didn't technically have employees," Lacher stated. "However, we are looking into it now."

"What about Wallace?" I asked. "Was she working for you?"

Lacher glanced at the president before nodding. "Danielle Wallace was very ambitious. It's another thing we are looking into. Based on our investigations, someone she thought was her superior contacted her about this operation."

"You have a leak?"

"No," Lacher denied. "We had a hack. Someone very skilled got into our system and created a fake email for Wallace's superior."

"She just followed orders in an email?" I questioned.

"They arranged a meet with a contact in the Russian Embassy."

"A woman?" I asked.

Lacher nodded. "It appears so."

I sighed. "She thought she was doing her job," I remarked. "This lady fed her all the wrong information, and she ate it up thinking this was her big mission. Off-book, but the chance to save the president's son. That would go a long way to cementing a career."

"That's what we surmise so far."

"What happens if I say 'No?'" I asked. "Back to the brig?"

Thompson shook his head. "No, Lieutenant, when we finish here, you will be free to go."

"Then I'll have to politely decline," I told them. "I don't like the idea that someone played me. Somehow, I imagine Wallace experienced the same thought right before someone shot her. If I found out I had to kill someone simply because you wanted to swing an election or something, I doubt I'd take too kindly to that."

"It won't be anything like that," Lacher explained.

"Director, I've been around the block a few times," I countered.

"It's an opportunity to help your country," he implored.

"I did that already," I said.

"Lieutenant Gordon," Thompson interrupted. "I would consider it a favor if you took some time to think about the offer. You strike me as a guy that wants to do the right thing, and this might be that opportunity for you."

Nothing like having the leader of the free world ask for a favor.

"I'll think about it," I agreed.

The president smiled.

I turned my attention toward Shaw for a second. "What about Leo? How is he?"

Shaw responded, "He's recovering nicely. I think he's already heading back to Memphis."

"Sorry I missed him," I acknowledged.

"Lieutenant, it was a pleasure to meet you," Jacob Thompson stated. "I'm sure someone will be in touch."

As the president rose from his seat, everyone at the table followed suit. I waited as he passed by. The man extended his hand. "Thank you," he said graciously before exiting the situation room.

Lacher paused in front of me. "We'll have someone reach out to you," he told me.

"I never agreed," I explained.

He nodded and followed Thompson. After a moment, the only two people left in the room was me and Shaw.

"It's good to see you, General," I told her.

"You too, Lieutenant. Big day, huh?"

"I suppose," I admitted. "I don't get to see you often enough."

She grinned. "Always the charmer."

"I do what I can," I offered.

Her eyes shifted to the door as if checking that we were alone. "You should only take the jobs that are right to you," she told me.

"Right now, I just want to get back to Puerto Rico."

"Do you know why this woman wanted to kidnap you?" she asked.

I shook my head. "No, but I suspect she and I are going to meet again. Whether or not I like the idea."

"Watch your six," she warned.

"Always, sir."

"Let's get you off this boat," she told me, ushering me out the door.

"General, I don't suppose you have a few bucks you could float me?" I asked. "I left my wallet in Puerto Rico."

Epilogue

TWO WEEKS LATER

"Thanks for letting me have a room," I told Missy.

"Oh, it's nice having you right here in the hotel," Missy purred as she rested her head on my chest. I stroked her bare back while staring up at the ceiling.

"Yes, it was," I admitted.

"But you're ready to return to *Carina*?" she asked with no jealousy.

"I didn't exactly plan to leave her for almost a month," I replied.

Initially, I tried to catch the first flight back to Puerto Rico, but I was stymied by a shortage of funds and, even more importantly, a lack of identification. I was more disappointed when I called the marina in an attempt to reach Gabriella. I missed her by a day. She'd sailed out on a small charter sailboat as their diving guide. The impression I got was she assumed I'd skipped out on her, and there wasn't much point in waiting around.

Despite the current events, I was a little brokenhearted. It wasn't that Gabriella and I had developed past the initial infatuation, but it was the potential that excited me.

"Whatever. I know what you really want," she teased, as if reading my mind. "Although it's going to be a busy weekend. I need a good bartender."

"You have Hunter," I pointed out.

Missy lifted her head. "Hunter doesn't have quite the same skills as you," she quipped.

I raised an eyebrow.

"When do you fly out?" she asked.

"Jay's dropping me at the airport tomorrow afternoon. The flight leaves at six."

"I can't believe Jay's leaving me too," she moaned.

My fingers stroked her hair. "I'm sure he'll be back to visit," I promised.

"Oh, speaking of Jay," she announced, sitting up suddenly.

Missy slid off the bed, and I watched her naked figure as she padded over to her purse. She pulled a familiar manila envelope from the bag.

"I think this is actually yours," she said, tossing me the pouch.

The addressee was Jay Delp, however, the handwriting was mine. A postmark from over two weeks ago read, "*Republica de Cuba.*"

"Guess they don't worry about speed," I remarked. "I could have sent it via pigeon and saved thirteen days."

She grinned, plopping down across from me on the bed. I enjoyed being naked with her. Something about the intimacy of that level of comfortability. There was no rush to cover up. Not that Missy was shy normally, but at least with me, it felt natural to be like this.

"Does your phone have the translation app?" I asked.

She crossed the room again, retrieving her phone as I ripped open the envelope.

"You just have to take a picture of the document," she told me.

"Here." I handed her the first few pages with William Thompson's signature.

Missy spread the sheets of paper on the bed so she could get a clear picture. After nearly two minutes, she had them all uploaded.

"It'll take a second," she explained.

"How accurate is it?" I asked.

"I don't think if you were trying to sound natural that it's that useful, but I use it for business documents all the time. Even emails if I'm sending to people overseas. It's perfect for that."

The phone dinged as the app completed the translation. She passed it to me, and I scanned through the pages. Some were transferring property to Thompson, almost like a bill of sale. However, I didn't find a price on it.

I continued to read.

Then, I stopped. It took three times rereading the wording.

"What is it?" Missy asked. "Your face changed."

"He lied to me," I stated.

"About what?"

"Everything," I said. "He wasn't trying to protect the environment. He was being bribed."

"Son of a bitch," Missy uttered. "What are you going to do about it?"

I considered it for several seconds. No matter what his initial intention was, he couldn't go through with the deal. Everything became too public when all the news outlets covered his kidnapping. He'd even come out in interviews since then, claiming the same thing he told me. Who was left to argue with him? Mikhalov was dead, and Turchin would avoid the spotlight it might shine on Russia. That meant, for now, the Danube Delta remained protected.

"Can you put this somewhere secure?" I asked.

"You aren't going to do anything with it?"

I nodded. "I am. It's going to be insurance."

"Insurance?" she questioned.

"Yeah. If something happens, you'll be able to drop this bomb."

"Chase?"

I smiled. "Don't worry. Nothing will happen. It's like any coverage. We'll never use it."

Leaning in, I kissed her lips before returning the papers to the envelope.

"Now, I do have to leave tomorrow," I pointed out. "Should I pick up a shift in the bar tonight?"

Missy shook her head, shaking the shoulder-length brown hair. "No, it's covered," she assured me. "You can stay right here in bed."